Christmas Secrets at Villa Limoncello

Christmas Secrets at Villa Limoncello

DAISY JAMES

First published in the United Kingdom in 2019 by Canelo

This edition published in the United Kingdom in 2020 by

Canelo Digital Publishing Limited
31 Helen Road
Oxford OX2 0DF
United Kingdom

A CIP catalogue record for this book is available from the British Library.

Print ISBN 978 1 78863 974 3
Ebook ISBN 978 1 78863 345 1

Look for more great books at www.canelo.co

Printed and bound in Great Britain by Clays Ltd, Elcograf S.p.A.

To my amazing family for all their help and support, and for taste-testing the Christmas recipes – I know it was hard work but someone had to do it!

To my sister Hazel, and my friends Elaine, Gill and Sue for listening to my story ideas and providing such fabulous, unstinting encouragement.

Chapter One

A tiny attic flat in Clapham

Colour: Psychedelic blue

'Is that the smoke alarm, again?' asked Izzie, reaching for a mistletoe-bedecked tea towel to flap at the safety device that had squawked at her with increasing regularity all afternoon.

'No, it's the doorbell this time!' Meghan giggled. 'Don't worry, I'll get it. Jonti mentioned that he might pop over after work to bestow us with his gastronomic wisdom.'

'Great. Just when I thought the day couldn't possibly get any more stressful, Mr Parisian Patisserie himself decides to grace us with his presence!'

While Meghan ditched her apron and skipped off to answer the door, Izzie cast an eye around the kitchen, surprised that she, the supposed Queen of Control and Neatness, had presided over such culinary clutter. The place looked like a scene from the Great Christmas Cake Explosion!

Cooking utensils and baking ingredients littered every available surface, from whisks to wooden spoons, from sultanas, raisins and cherries to oranges with their zest removed and miniature bottles of brandy that she'd bought to add flavour to the home-made mincemeat but which had ended up in their coffees as the stark reality of what she had agreed to hit home. Not only had that day's variations on the humble mince pie been a disaster, but yesterday's attempt at making gingerbread snowmen had looked more like a brigade of zombies in the middle of a world apocalypse, and Wednesday's stab at a luxury twist on an English trifle had tasted like toxic washing-up liquid. Wherever her talents lay, they were not at the end of the artistic spectrum labelled 'culinary'.

She turned her back on the mess and slumped down onto her over-stuffed leather sofa and sighed. *Last Christmas* blared from the radio Meghan had insisted should accompany their Christmas bake-athon when she'd arrived to injection a dose of much-needed optimism into Izzie's festive cake-baking fiasco. She hoped that now Jonti was here he would offer his advice on how to produce at least one batch of mouth-watering Christmas goodies before she left for Villa Limoncello the following day, where she'd promised to partner Luca on the Snowflakes & Christmas Cakes course.

Ah, Luca.

Her stomach performed a delicious somersault of pleasure as a snapshot of his smiling face floated across her vision and she relived a few delicious moments of her summer sojourn in the terracotta-roofed villa in Tuscany. It was exactly that image that had caused her to jump at the chance to go back, to take her place at his side as he demonstrated the intricacies of Christmas-themed Italian patisserie – whilst she tried to do justice to the British version – for a group of avid foodies.

Except, judging from her efforts so far, she feared disaster. She glanced down at her hands, covered in plasters where she had scraped her fingers on the grater or whilst slicing a lemon. Who would have thought that baking a few festive treats could be so dangerous! Give her a square of fabric, a pair of pinking shears and a glue gun any day! Why couldn't she have suggested that Luca handle the patisserie part and she demonstrate the intricacies of handmade Christmas decorations? That way she could have slipped into her comfort zone of all things fabric- and sequin-related, and spent her days guiding their discerning guests in the art of wreath-making, table decorations, home-made advent calendars, glass bauble painting. But she couldn't renege on her promise now, because this might be the very last course Villa Limoncello was going to offer.

'Darling!' exclaimed Jonti, leaning forward to hug Izzie and place two regulation air-kisses on her cheeks. 'Oh my God! What's happened to your hair? Am I missing something? Is extreme bouffant the new Christmas craze? I'm sorry, Izzie, don't take this the wrong way, but you look like a copper-headed Medusa on speed!'

Then, before he had chance to draw another breath, his bleached blonde eyebrows shot up his forehead and he wrinkled his nose in disgust.

'What's that awful smell?'

'That, Jonti, is the fragrance of Christmas – cinnamon, nutmeg, cloves, orange zest…'

'No, I think you'll find *that* is the aroma of a kitchen catastrophe. Mmm, caramelised pastry with a side order of seared sultanas…'

'Oh my God! The mince pies!'

Izzie rushed into the kitchen, grabbed the oven gloves and yanked open the door to the oven – her previously pristine, still-packed-with-polystyrene oven that hadn't been sullied with any kind of food preparation in the eighteen months she had lived there until that week. A baptism of fire, you might say! She still had to get to grips with the controls which looked more like the dashboard of the Starship *Enterprise* than a cooker – with an instruction manual it would take a professor in engineering to understand.

She pulled out a tray of burnt-to-a-crisp mince pies and dropped the whole chargrilled mess onto the wire cooling rack, sending a cascade of dried cranberries to the floor. How could she have so seriously underestimated her skills as a pastry chef?

'Grab a seat, Jonti, I'll make us some coffee.' Meghan smirked, reaching for the kettle as though Izzie couldn't be trusted to even boil water.

'What festive treats were you aiming for here?' asked Jonti, peering over the top of his multi-coloured glasses at the mince pies as though they were lumps of smouldering dynamite.

'Today is the Marvellous Mince Pie Marathon,' said Meghan, spooning coffee into three mugs. 'They're Izzie's St Clement's Sizzlers, with orange and lemon zest in the pastry.'

'And these?'

'Mince pies with a custard and crumble topping.'

'Mmm,' said Jonti sarcastically, prodding the blackened tartlets. 'I'm not sure what Luca was expecting from a woman who lived on toast and coffee for two years! And what, may I ask, is in this bowl? It looks like something those guys from *Avatar* would eat for breakfast.'

'It's frosting. I was going to use it to decorate the gingerbread stars I made yesterday, but I think I might have used too much blue food colouring. I thought it said four *table*spoons.'

'How many Great British Christmas bakes have you said you'd showcase?'

'Five – one for each day of the course.'

Izzie stretched her lips into a smile and surreptitiously crossed her fingers behind her back as Jonti took a sip from the skinny latte Meghan handed to him, then ran the tip of his tongue along his bottom lip as he contemplated the enormity of the task ahead. Despite his quirky sartorial appearance – faux snakeskin trousers, orange winkle-pickers and the craziest Christmas jumper Izzie had ever seen – she noticed that his immaculately styled, bleached-blonde quiff was wilting, and there were smudges of tiredness encircling his piercing blue eyes.

Guilt nipped at her heart – working in the most famous cathedral of consumerism in London during the festive period would take its toll on even the most energetic of personalities. It was Friday night and there was nothing Jonti liked better than to relax with a Dirty Martini and have a good old gossip with Meghan about the shenanigans of their various Harrods colleagues. It was testament to their friendship that he'd sacrificed his night out on the tiles in return for one of her famous limoncello cocktails and a slice of overcooked pizza.

'And this… this concoction of loveliness?'

Izzie giggled. Nigella she was not!

'Erm, that's supposed to be a traditional trifle with a Christmas twist,' she said, crouching down so that the ornate glass bowl was at eye level. 'This is a layer of orange jelly with fresh cranberries and crumbled gingerbread – *which* I made myself – then there's a layer of custard infused with cardamom and vanilla, and it's finished off with whipped Chantilly cream and a generous scattering of these lovely holly leaf sprinkles. I think the cream might have been off, though, or else it could have been the splash of lemon juice I added, I'm not sure?'

'O… kay,' muttered Jonti, upending his lips as he exchanged a glance with Meghan. 'So that's three recipes? What are the other two?'

'A yule log with lemon drizzle sponge and limoncello curd, covered in thick white chocolate buttercream, then dusted with this gorgeous silver-coloured edible glitter. And look! I've bought these cute sugar-paste penguins and igloos to go on the top.'

'So you've at least perfected a passable Swiss roll?'

'Erm, no, not exactly…'

'But Izzie, you're flying out to Florence tomorrow!'

'I thought I'd practise it when I got to the villa – the kitchen is so much bigger than mine. All the patisserie sessions are scheduled in the mornings so the five participants can take what they bake to their choir practice in the studio in the vineyard afterwards. That means I'll have every afternoon free to run through the next day's recipes. Did Meghan tell you our guests are part of a community choir from York who are rehearsing for their Christmas concert?'

'A community choir of five?'

'Oh, no, there's fifteen of them. Five are booked on our Snowflakes & Christmas Cakes course, five are doing an art gallery and museums tour, and another group are going skiing in their free time.'

'Skiing? In Tuscany?'

'That's what I said when Gianni told me to bring my snowsuit when I fly over next weekend,' said Meghan, flicking her raspberry-tipped hair from her eyes as she licked the icing from a gingerbread snowman, turning her lips an electric shade of blue. 'Apparently, there's already a covering of snow on the hills, and he's promised to take me snowboarding, then to spend some time relaxing at the thermal baths afterwards. Heaven knows I'll need all the pampering I can get after the awkward, baring-of-the-soul dinner I've got coming up with my parents on Wednesday night!'

Meghan gave a humourless laugh before quickly changing the subject.

'Do you think you'll have time to enjoy the snow, Izzie?'

'I think I should concentrate all my spare time and energy on making sure this course is a success, don't you? Especially after what happened with the Wine & Words course in September.'

'But that had nothing to do with you, or with Luca, or Villa Limoncello!' declared Meghan loyally.

'I know, I know, but I still feel guilty that the course didn't go ahead. Luca lost a lot of money – although not as much as he would have done if he'd had to pay cancellation fees to a professional wine connoisseur and a creative writing tutor. Thank God for Gianni and Riccardo!'

Izzie saw Meghan's eyes sparkle at the mention of Villa Limoncello's vineyard manager, who had ridden into her world on the back of his rust-blistered quad bike and turned her life upside down. Since then, every spare weekend she got, she'd hopped onto a plane to spend time with the man who made her heart skip a beat after years of unsuccessful Internet dating.

'Gianni was gutted he didn't get to impart his knowledge of Tuscany's world-famous Chianti and Brunello di Montalcino, but still, there was one good thing to come out of the whole debacle.' Meghan smiled, reaching for a second gingerbread zombie to dip into her coffee. 'At least he and Riccardo are no longer mortal enemies – Riccardo was equally devastated that his debut as a creative writing tutor didn't come to fruition.'

'Did I tell you that Isla, the woman who booked the Wine & Words course, sent me and Carlotta a gorgeous bouquet of sunflowers and yellow roses as an apology for all the trouble their group had caused?'

'Did you find out any more details about what happened?'

'Not much, but she did say their book group had folded, and that Sue's husband had started divorce proceedings citing Phil as a co-respondent.'

'It's great material, though, isn't it?' Jonti smirked; he had been transfixed by the unfolding story of adultery and skulduggery when the gossip had materialised. 'A clandestine affair played out under the noses of fellow book group members, blasted into the open by careless whispers, the battle lines drawn as each member takes sides – who knew, who didn't, who provided the alibis. I still think they should have sucked it up and followed through with the Wine & Words course – there's a fantastic story there if romantic suspense is your genre.'

'I think Isla was worried that, mixed with copious amounts of the local wine, there was a serious risk it would have turned into a murder mystery!'

Izzie experienced a kaleidoscope of emotions as she thought back to the shambles of the previous Villa Limoncello course. She'd hoped so much that it would be a success and that there would be an avalanche of subsequent bookings which would allow her to stay on in Tuscany, a place that had been instrumental in healing her heart after the vicious grenade that life had thrown into her path.

Renovating the careworn villa had reignited her passion for interior design. She had jettisoned the mantle of gloom that had smothered her creativity, and her artistic sprites now danced with exuberance as she created projects filled with colour and sparkle, things that had been in short supply after the loss of her twin sister to a brain aneurism. Her frozen emotions had thawed under the Tuscan sun and she yearned to return and spend more time with the man who had ushered her along the path to hope. When she had agreed to stand alongside him for the Snowflakes & Christmas Cakes course, he had been delighted, and the pleasure in his voice had sent her spirits sky-high – except now there was something else clouding the horizon.

'So, what did Luca say when you told him about Harry's offer?' asked Jonti, tossing back his last mouthful of coffee before noticing the daggers Meghan was sending his way. 'Oops, sorry, have I said something I shouldn't have?'

'It's okay, Jonti. Yes, I've told him.'

'And did he demand that you reject the project instantly, high-tail it back to San Vivaldo so he could swear his undying love for you, and then ask you to not only be his 'Partner in Patisserie' but in life and love and all things limoncello? You know, I've already got my wedding outfit picked out – Jules from the menswear department has earmarked this absolutely gorgeous mulberry velvet suit with drainpipe trousers and—'

'Jonti...' interrupted Meghan, frantically trying to signal restraint.

'And Grant in the footwear department has suggested these amazing crocodile—'

'Jonti!'

'Sorry, darling, sorry, got a little carried away there, but you know how much I adore weddings.'

'Actually, Luca said Harry's proposal was too good an opportunity to turn down and I should take my time to carefully weigh up the pros and cons...'

'And we all know there's no one better at doing that than our very own Isabella Jenkins, lover of lists!' Jonti smiled, clearly keen to make amends for assuming Izzie would ditch her life in the UK without a second thought to run off into the Italian sunset with the handsome chef and villa owner with eyes the colour of espresso and a penchant for citrussy cologne. 'And Luca's right; Harry's proposal *is* the chance of a lifetime, *career-wise*. I mean, creative director of Hambleton Homes *does* have a fabulous ring to it, not to mention the financial security that shares in the company will give you, and the fact that the project is in St Ives, your childhood home, is the icing on the fruit cake, wouldn't you say?'

Jonti's eyes scorched deep into Izzie's soul as he waited for her confirmation or her denial, and a squirm of discomfort coiled through her abdomen. Like Jonti, when she'd rung Luca to tell him about the offer, she'd hoped his reaction would give her an indication of how he felt about her, whether he still experienced that intense swoop of desire, that pulse of passion they had kindled when she'd stayed at the villa in the summer. Instead, he had urged her to follow her dreams, just like *he'd* done when he'd ditched his lucrative job in the banking industry and invested in Antonio's Trattoria and a dilapidated villa in his hometown in the Tuscan countryside. She knew it was sensible advice from a man who was thoughtful, generous and kind, but his encouragement had saddened her, not uplifted her.

Did his enthusiasm mean he wanted her to stay in the UK? Had their dalliance in the sun come to a natural conclusion – just another holiday romance that had run its course and this was a convenient way out without the pain of rejection?

'I really don't know what to do, Jonti. I mean, I love Tuscany, but it hasn't been plain sailing, has it? In fact, Luca describes it as a catalogue of catastrophes, and we're still far from certain that it's going to be financially viable, which means there's a very real possibility that Luca will have to sell the place because Antonio's can't keep bailing the villa out.'

'It's not all about the villa, though, is it?' interjected Jonti. 'That's *not* what kept you in San Vivaldo for four months or why Meghan spends every penny she earns on airfare!'

'Oh, I don't know...'

But Jonti was right. Since arriving back in London, Luca had never left her thoughts. Not a day had gone by when she hadn't contacted him in some way to relay a snippet of news, ask for his opinion on a pasta dish, or a new Italian wine she'd come across. So it had come as a shock when he'd waxed lyrical about how Harry's project to upgrade four farm cottages would be a fabulous opportunity to showcase her rejuvenated talent for creating cutting-edge interiors and that if she wanted to withdraw from the Snowflakes & Christmas Cakes course, then he would understand.

She had refused his offer, desperate to see Villa Limoncello again, even if it was just to say goodbye and to thank all the people she had met in Tuscany for their friendship, their love, and their support in setting her firmly back on the road towards a life in which her grief no longer defined her. She had loved Anna with every fibre of her being, but she had also grown to understand that her sister would not have wanted her to cloak herself in misery for the rest of her days, but to embrace every single moment and live her life to the full for the both of them.

'Hey, cheer up, Izzie, you look like Eeyore's little sister! Look, you don't have to make any decisions just yet. Fly over to Tuscany, spend a delicious week with Luca by your side and when the guests have left to sing their merry hearts out at their Christmas concert, you can relax in that gorgeous *limonaia* you're always going on about, and talk it over with Luca face-to-face, read his body language, see from the look in his eyes how he truly feels. And, I actually wanted this to be a surprise but you know me, can't keep a secret if my life depended on it. Guess what? Your week in snowy Tuscany just got even better because...'

Jonti paused for dramatic effect, his eyes wide, his smile bright.

'What? Come on, Jonti! What?'

'Brace yourselves, darlings! I've decided to pack up my Gucci holdall and join Meghan on that plane next Saturday to indulge in my own little slice of Tuscan paradise and to inspect those Italian stallions who've stolen the hearts of my two best friends in the whole wide world.'

'That isn't the reason you gave me when you asked me which flight I was booked on!' Meghan smirked.

'Well, I *might* have an ulterior motive.'

'Which is?' asked Izzie.

'That I'm desperate to make the acquaintance of the celebrated Carlotta and to ask her if she could sprinkle a little bit of her matchmaking magic on yours truly! Now that *would* be a Christmas present made in heaven. What do you say?'

'Oh, Jonti, I'd love that!'

Izzie pulled Jonti into a tight hug, her heart blossoming with love and gratitude for the staunch support of her friends and, despite the fact that the previous two courses at Villa Limoncello had been fraught with challenges, from severed electricity cables to allegations of food poisoning and the repercussions of clandestine affairs between the guests, it was surely third time lucky, wasn't it?

Chapter Two

Villa Limoncello, San Vivaldo, Tuscany

Colour: Sugar pink

Izzie grabbed her wheelie suitcase from the carousel and made her way towards customs. She had already decided to hire a car, one of those cute little Cinquecentos in a gorgeous sunshine yellow colour, instead of taking a taxi. She felt a warm glow of affection when she thought of her usual choice of transport when she was in Italy – the sugar-pink Vespa, currently slumbering amongst the gardening paraphernalia in one of the outbuildings at the back of the villa. She smiled – it was a shame Jonti wouldn't get a chance to ride it when he arrived. She knew he would adore the nippy little scooter even though it was more like something Barbie would use for a day out chasing rainbows.

However, when the plane had started its descent into Florence Airport, she'd been surprised to see a light dusting of snow which made the whole of the medieval city look as if it had been topped with a generous layer of royal icing. It was picturesque, certainly, but not the kind of weather she wanted to travel around on a Vespa in.

As she emerged into the arrivals hall, she glanced down at her chosen outfit and groaned. Why hadn't she listened to Luca and chosen more suitable attire for the dash from the car hire desk to the car park? Of course, she knew it would inevitably be a trek and she resigned herself to turning up at Villa Limoncello with hair like a bird's nest rather than Sunday best – though that was nothing new.

She shrugged. No matter how much time she devoted to her appearance, with a profusion of curls like hers there was no way she could hope to achieve the polished elegance of the travellers milling around her, greeting family and friends with hugs and kisses, sporting sharply cut designer overcoats, soft leather loafers and looking as though they'd just stepped from a catwalk or the beauty salon – the women *and* the men. Even those who were clearly students possessed a certain panache that spoke of the effortless style Italians seemed to exude in abundance.

Izzie looked around the brightly lit concourse; something was strange, but she couldn't put her finger on it. Then it came to her. Despite Christmas Day being less than three weeks away, there were no over-the-top decorations – no oversized fir trees laden with baubles and wrapped in yards of tinsel, no fake snow sprayed on the glass partitions, and no tinny Christmas music being pumped through the loudspeakers – in complete contrast to the extravagance she had seen in the avenues of Heathrow, which she suspected had been displaying its gifts and garlands since the first week of November, if not before!

At last she spotted the familiar yellow and black logo of the car hire company and, once through the metal barrier, she swung off to her right, her heels click-clacking on the marble flooring. She'd taken only a few paces when she halted, her heart crashing against her ribcage in disbelief and delight.

'Luca! Oh my God, what are you doing here?'

Luca laughed at her surprise, his dark brown eyes crinkling attractively at the corners, those cute dimples she loved so much bracketing his lips like commas as he ran his palm over his stubbled chin in a familiar gesture.

'What do you think I'm doing here, *Is… a… bella*?'

Oh, that accent! thought Izzie. The way her name rolled from his tongue, coated in that sexy Italian cadence that caused ripples of desire to travel the length of her spine and fizzle out to her fingertips.

It had been two months since she'd said *arrivederci* to him – to fulfil a contract to renovate a friend's house in Knightsbridge that would allow her to pay the rent on her flat until the end of the year – and if it were possible, Luca looked even more handsome than she remembered in his buttock-hugging black jeans and pale lemon sweater with sleeves pushed halfway up his forearms to reveal a smattering of dark hairs. But it wasn't his appearance that caused her to lower her lashes and inhale a long lingering breath – that particular pleasure was caused by the faint whiff of citrussy cologne that would forever remind her of the long summer days she had spent at Villa Limoncello, strolling around the grounds, soaking up the sunshine and kissing Luca underneath the magnolia tree.

She smiled, taking a step forward to receive the customary greeting, and when his lips lingered briefly at her earlobes, she shivered with delight. When Luca held her gaze for a few moments longer than necessary, Izzie's heart bloomed, overjoyed at seeing him again, grateful that he'd taken time out of his busy day at the trattoria to collect her from the airport. Then her eyes snagged on something he was holding in his left hand.

'Oh, yes, these are for you.'

Luca handed her a bouquet of smiling yellow sunflowers, artfully arranged with glossy foliage and wrapped in cellophane, which she immediately recognised as her friend Francesca's work.

'Thank you, they're gorgeous.'

She smiled again, still unable to believe Luca was standing there in front of her, his eyes boring into hers, sparks of electricity snapping through the space between them. All she wanted to do was melt into his arms and kiss him until she was breathless – irrespective of their audience of travellers and tourists. She hoped that Luca felt the same way, but just as she took a tentative step forward, Luca reached out to grab the handle of her suitcase, spun on his heels, and headed for the door.

Disappointment and confusion whooshed through her body, but she followed in his wake, happy to save their real reunion for the journey back to the villa, but when they arrived at the exit she stopped in her tracks.

'Oh my God! It's freezing!'

Luca looked at her and she saw the familiar flash of amusement in his eyes.

'I knew you'd say that! Everyone thinks Tuscany is blessed with wall-to-wall sunshine all year round. It's December, Izzie. We get snow, but you'll be pleased to know that I've come prepared, even if you haven't.'

Izzie wrinkled her nose, looking from left to right to see if that meant he'd parked his scarlet Alfa Romeo Spider nearby, but instead Luca unzipped the rucksack he was carrying, withdrew a bulky package, and handed it to her.

'What is it?'

Luca smirked. 'Open it.'

She hesitated as she accepted the soft, squashy gift, then ran her finger under the join. She chanced a quick glance at him again and saw a spark of mischief dash across his expression.

'Luca?'

But he simply shook his head and waited.

Izzie removed the wrapping paper and pulled out a pair of grey hand-knitted mittens and a matching hat.

'Oh, these are lovely. Thank you.'

Luca simply raised his eyebrows, still watching her closely but saying nothing.

'What?'

She looked back down at the hat-and-gloves combo, slotted her hands into the mittens and unfolded the hat, then burst into laughter.

'What's it supposed to be?'

She stuffed her hands into the hat and held it out in front of her for closer inspection. Two long pink-and-grey ears flopped from the top of the hat.

'*È un asino!*'

Luca watched her reaction carefully and suddenly she realised the significance of the gifts he had given her – the sunflowers, the woolly hat topped with a pair of donkey ears – and without further hesitation she flung her arms around him, unconcerned about what people thought as they pushed past them, anxious to be on their way home.

'Remember?'

'Of course I do!' she giggled.

'I'll never forget the way we met, or how you looked when you realised it was me who ran you off the road and sent you scooting into the field, interrupting that poor donkey's lunch of sunflowers and artichokes.'

'Neither will I!' laughed Izzie, pulling the hat over her curls and striking a pose. 'What do you think?'

'Attractive!'

With her arm linked through Luca's, Izzie followed him to the car park, grateful that their previous awkwardness had dissipated. Meeting Luca had been the best thing that had happened to her since losing Anna and even if it had meant she'd had to endure the indignity of communing with the local mule, then it had been worth every moment. Whilst an ember of pain still simmered whenever she thought of her beloved sister, she had learned to stitch her sadness into the fabric of her life and move forward, and the person she had to thank for steering her in the right direction was sitting next to her, revving the engine of his Alfa Romeo like Lewis Hamilton's younger brother.

Whilst Luca navigated the serpentine roads of the Tuscan countryside with the calm nonchalance of a seasoned local, Izzie settled back in her seat to enjoy the picturesque scenery that flashed by her window. She exhaled a long, contented breath – she was happy to be back. Luca flicked on the radio and instead of the cheesy Christmas songs that were played back-to-back at home, the car was filled with a classical aria that soothed her traveller's nerves.

'How did your baking practice go?' asked Luca, glancing sideways at her, a smile playing at his lips.

'The honest version?'

'Sure.'

'Not so good. I think I've got three of the recipes sorted, but I'm struggling with the last two.'

'Then you will be pleased to know that I have the perfect solution.'

'You do?'

'I had a phone call this morning from Nick Morgan, the choir's leader and also the guy who booked the Snowflakes & Christmas Cakes course. Apparently, one of our guests stumbled across the fact that Isabella Jenkins is an *award-winning* interior designer and has asked if you'd mind running a couple of Christmas craft workshops.'

'Really?'

Izzie's spirits shot up a notch – give her a paint brush or a staple gun over a whisk and a wooden spoon any day!

'I told him I'd float the idea by you. What do you think?'

'I think it's a fantastic idea. Oh, I could do a glass bauble-painting tutorial, or a Christmas wreath-making session, or we could make home-made advent calendars, or candles infused with dried flowers and winter spices, or…'

'They all sound fabulous. I thought we'd do three days of baking and two of crafting?'

Izzie beamed, and the nugget of dread that had festered since her Swiss roll practice sessions hadn't turned out as she had hoped was replaced by a tickle of excitement.

'Great. I'll amend the itinerary and order the supplies this afternoon before I laminate the instruction cards and finalise everyone's folders. Have you made any changes to the Italian patisserie recipes?'

'Would I dare? You worked so hard to get everything sorted and order in all the organic, free-range and locally produced ingredients. The files look very professional, by the way. I'm sure our guests will be relieved to see their photographs on the front of them – just in case they forget what they look like!'

'Well, after what happened during the Painting & Pasta course, I really want everything to run as smoothly as possible and that means preparation, preparation, preparation!'

'Everything *will* run smoothly! This time our guests will be focusing on their choir rehearsals – which Nick was at pains to make sure I understood. I thought *you* were obsessed with timetabling and schedules, but it looks like you might have met your match! The other guests might think they're here to relax and have fun, and create a few delicious desserts for their fellow choir members, but Nick has got every single one of their singing sessions over in the old barn planned out with military precision. He kept stressing over and over again that he would not tolerate our cookery classes extending even one minute beyond the one o'clock deadline. I assured him that with Isabella Jenkins in charge, nothing could possibly go wrong.'

Izzie thought it was probably prudent not to list the potential pitfalls waiting for them so soon after she'd arrived, so she decided to change the subject.

'How are Gianni and Carlotta?'

'Gianni talks of nothing but his wine – which is apparently going to be the best Chianti Tuscany has ever produced – as well as the snowboarding trips and spa treatments he's organised for when Meghan arrives. Carlotta and Vincenzo have just got back from visiting his grandson who's at university in Milan, and you won't be surprised to learn that whilst they were there, Carlotta struck up a conversation with a waitress in a cafe next to the theatre, introduced Matteo, and as they say, the rest is history. How does she do it?'

'Well, she'll have another assignment on her hands at the end of the week!' And she went on the fill Luca in on Jonti's imminent arrival and his hopes for a sprinkle of Carlotta's matchmaking magic.

Izzie felt the Alfa Romeo's engine change its tone as they negotiated the steep incline that led up to Villa Limoncello and within moments the wide wrought-iron gates hove into view. An intense feeling of homecoming suffused her body as Luca swung the steering wheel to his left and they crunched down the pebbled driveway lined with a parade of cypress trees pointing proudly into the clear azure sky. When her gaze fell on the house, a plethora of emotions welled up inside her. Until that moment she hadn't realised how much she had missed the place, how much a part of her life the careworn building with its terracotta roof tiles, its honeyed façade and its green, paint-blistered shutters, had become.

She loved it there; the wisteria-covered pergola where she took her early morning coffee, the whitewashed gazebo where she had held her painting classes, even the dilapidated tennis court that she and Luca hadn't yet got around to renovating despite their good intentions. But the part she loved the most was the *limonaia*, the large glasshouse on the south gable wall that had given the house its name – Villa dei Limoni. Whenever she strolled through the gardens, inhaling the sweet smell of rosemary and lavender, a feeling of complete serenity descended. Time didn't seem to knock so ferociously here as it did in London, and that had provided her with the space to deal with the numerous poison-tipped arrows life had fired in her direction.

She jumped out of the passenger seat, leaving Luca to wrestle her wheelie suitcase from the back seat of his Spider. He followed her to the terrace where they paused, side by side, to take in the view. The sun had climbed higher in the sky, warming the air and washing the whole vista with a golden hue, highlighting the higgledy-piggledy rooftops of San Vivaldo and bestowing the vineyards and olive groves with an almost Tolkienesque quality, and the final vestiges of Izzie's anxiety melted from her bones.

'Ah, I've missed all this. It's an oasis of calm in a world of chaos and confusion!'

Izzie turned to smile at Luca, but instead of returning her gesture, she saw him stuff his hands into the front pockets of his jeans, his jaw taut, a pensive expression on his face.

'And it's the perfect place to contemplate what the future might hold,' he said, his accent thicker and more pronounced than usual. 'When did you say Harry needed an answer by?'

'The end of the week, but Luca, I…'

'Okay, then, I'd better let you get settled in before the guests arrive. Carlotta's made up the sunflower suite for you and she'll be over at seven thirty tomorrow morning to help you with breakfast. I'll see you at nine thirty for the first patisserie course. *Ciao!*'

Izzie stared at his retreating back, taken by surprise at the sudden turn in the conversation. She had hoped to share a coffee with him, maybe even that he would stay to help her check in the guests who weren't scheduled to arrive until later that evening. By the time she had recovered her senses and rushed in his wake, the Spider was zooming away down the drive, scattering pebbles like confetti at a wedding.

Chapter Three

The kitchen, Villa Limoncello

Colour: Crumbled biscuit

'Okay, everyone, hello and welcome to the first session of the Snowflakes & Christmas Cakes course here at Villa Limoncello. As you'll see from the itinerary in the personalised folders I've prepared for each of you, every morning this week either Luca or I will be presenting a tutorial themed around Christmas, starting with the most amazing festive bakes, from both Italy and the UK, which you can then take over to the studio you'll be using for your choir rehearsals to share with the rest of your group.'

'We'll need *something* to sustain us during the musical marathon Nick's got planned for us,' muttered Sofia, who, at twenty-two, was the youngest of the group and had arrived for the baking class sporting a trendy denim jacket and a thunderous expression. She tossed her glossy hair over her shoulder in a practised gesture and fixed her amber eyes on Izzie.

'So,' continued Luca, taking up the presentation baton, and looking extremely handsome in his chef's whites and jaunty black-and-white neckerchief. 'This morning we'll be making crumble and custard mince pies and *panforte* tartlets with fresh figs and a lemon liqueur cream topping. And for those of you who've signed up for Izzie's Christmas crafting sessions on Tuesday and Thursday, you'll be creating hand-painted baubles using glass from Colle di Val d'Elsa, a local town that produces fifteen per cent of the world's crystal, and then Christmas wreaths, assisted by San Vivaldo's floral genius, Francesca Accardi.'

'It's really kind of you to add the crafting sessions at the last minute, Izzie.' Jennie smiled, patting the chunky, multi-coloured necklace at her throat before leaning forward to flick through the folder with her photograph on the front. 'I'm really looking forward to learning about how the Italians decorate their homes at Christmas and I've promised to do a talk for the ladies at my gym and the golf club when I get back home so I'll be taking extra notes. Oh, no, can you hang on a minute – I've forgotten my glasses!'

'Oh, God, Jennie, hurry up, will you?' snapped Nick, running his fingers through his lion's mane of dark bouffant curls, irritation stalking across his face. 'This is exactly the sort of thing I wanted to avoid! If we start on time, we'll finish on time, and I want us to meet the others at the studio at two o'clock prompt. There's not a moment to waste if we want to be note-perfect for the concert.'

Izzie saw Sofia exchange a smirk with Phoebe and Dylan, the other two members in the group – clearly this wasn't the first time Jennie had held up the proceedings because she'd forgotten something.

'Don't worry, I'm sure we'll finish on schedule,' said Luca in his most conciliatory tone. 'Okay, so while we wait for Jennie, can I ask you all to wash your hands, put on your Villa Limoncello aprons, and take your places at the table in front of a set of ingredients.'

Izzie watched the four guests jostle for position at the sink, then exclaim with delight over the aprons that had been hand-embroidered with their names and the motif of a lemon, before selecting a spot at the table. As the group had arrived later than expected the previous evening, after she'd shown them to their suites all they'd wanted to do was take a shower and fall into bed. They hadn't even taken advantage of the home-made limoncello cocktails she and Carlotta had prepared, although she did notice the look of wistful regret on Phoebe's face before following the others upstairs.

Izzie had wondered why Phoebe had chosen to travel all the way from York to Tuscany in a sharply cut business suit, complete with crisp white blouse and four-inch stilettos, but she was even more surprised to see that she had stuck with her sartorial preferences for that morning's cookery course, wearing another smart outfit: a jacket in a gorgeous cerise tweed fabric with three-quarter-length sleeves and braided cuffs, twinned with a beige silk vest top and matching pumps. Her pale blonde hair was salon-fresh and twisted into an elegant updo, her make-up flawless, and she wore a slender silver watch which Izzie suspected cost more than her monthly rent. She wondered if Phoebe was in the fashion business, a thought that caused a ripple of fear to shoot the length of her spine after what had happened at their Painting & Pasta course in July.

But no matter what she thought of Phoebe's choice of attire and accessories, they were run-of-the-mill compared to what Dylan had arrived in the kitchen with strung around his neck like an oversized medallion. Thankfully his guitar was now slumbering like a favoured pet in the chair next to the back door, basking in the sunshine whilst its master worked on his baking skills. She had warmed to Dylan straight away – he seemed the most laid-back of their five guests with his artistically torn jeans, crumpled grey T-shirt and Converse trainers. He was also the only one who hadn't flashed worried glances in Nick's direction every time he opened his mouth to speak.

'Sorry, sorry,' gasped Jennie, scooting back into the kitchen, her bejewelled glasses bouncing from a thick gold chain at her chest as she took the last remaining space next to Nick.

'So, do you think we could get started now?' snapped Nick, tapping his watch with a conductor's baton he'd produced from the inside pocket of his paisley waistcoat as if he were a sergeant major rallying his wayward troops. Izzie suppressed a giggle. With his exuberant wardrobe choices and loud booming voice, he looked, and sounded, like Brian Blessed's zany younger cousin.

'Okay, let's begin with the *panforte* tartlets, shall we?'

There was a murmur of consensus and all eyes turned to Luca.

'So, first of all I want you to scatter a selection of nuts onto your baking trays. We have almonds, hazelnuts, pistachios, cashews and walnuts, so choose those you like the best, then we'll roast them in the oven whilst we get on with making our sweet shortcrust pastry.'

As Izzie had expected, Jennie was the most accomplished baker, whipping up a batch of pastry within minutes, wrapping it in clingfilm and leaving it to rest. With her choppy chestnut hair flicked up at the sides to reveal neat pearl earrings and an oversized canvas bag that seemed to house everything a Girl Guide could ask for – including a fully stocked first aid kit that came in useful when Sofia managed to burn her finger removing her nuts from the oven – she was clearly the maternal glue that held the choir together.

'Have you finished already?' sighed Phoebe, her hands covered in a gloopy mixture that resembled porridge rather than pastry. Rosy red dots had appeared on her cheeks, and wayward strands of hair sprouted from her formerly elegant chignon which she swept away with her forearm.

'Having raised two ravenous boys, I can rustle up a batch of pastry with my eyes closed,' laughed Jennie, moving over to help Phoebe so that Luca could continue to talk a panicking Dylan down from a flour-infused ledge. Izzie would have giggled at the expression on his face if he hadn't looked so absolutely petrified.

'My aunt Rosa says Doctor Harmer's surgery is run with military efficiency since you took over as their receptionist, Jennie,' said Sofia, getting aggressive with her pestle and mortar to crush her roasted nuts.

'That's very kind of her, Sofia. I always say that organisation is the key to a happier life. I think I might have met my match, though – these folders are fabulous, Izzie. I might photocopy your instruction cards and hand them out at our next WI meeting, if you don't mind.'

'No problem.' Izzie smiled, watching Jennie deftly roll out her pastry, cut it into perfect circles and line each of the twelve wells in her baking tray.

'Right, next we make the filling,' said Luca, picking up a small silver pan to demonstrate which ingredients went into the mixture. 'First, we melt the butter, sugar, honey and chocolate over a low heat, then we add the beaten egg, orange zest, chopped fresh figs and the spices. Again, you choose which you prefer – we have cinnamon, nutmeg, cloves, ginger and cardamom. Finally, we add our nuts to the pan and stir well.'

As the students got busy with the next stage, the kitchen filled with the very essence of Christmas, and when everyone's *panforte* tartlets were in the oven, sending out wafts of aromatic spices, Izzie could feel her taste buds tingling. It was the perfect recipe with which to begin the week's course.

'While we wait for our little pies to bake and then cool, let's whip up the topping!'

There followed a hilarious ten minutes as splatters of mascarpone, fresh cream and limoncello landed everywhere as the group beat the mixture by hand before piping onto the top of their bakes and adorning the finishing product with curls of lemon zest.

'Oh, my God, these smell amazing!' declared Sofia, reaching out to taste one before having her hand slapped away by Nick. If looks could kill, Nick would have been pushing up the daisies.

'There's no time! We need to move on to Izzie's crumble and custard mince pies.'

Suddenly, all Izzie's previous anxiety about her ability to produce a batch of non-caramelised mince pies disappeared, and a surge of confidence whooshed through her veins. She had practised her own twist on the humble Christmas staple several times, and as long as she remembered to take them out of the oven on time, she should be okay.

Using the carefully drafted notes in her trusty purple arch-lever file that went everywhere with her, she led the group steadily through her recipe until, with only ten minutes to spare, everyone was standing at the table with two pyramids of pies in front of them. Izzie glanced around at the fruits of that morning's labour, grateful that this was not *Bake Off* and she didn't have to rate their students' offerings, because the breadth of culinary talent ranged from proficient (Jennie and Nick) to what she could at best call idiosyncratic (Dylan and Phoebe). Sofia's attempt was passable, but that was only because Jennie had taken her under her wing!

'So, I hope you've all enjoyed your first Snowflakes & Christmas Cakes session?' asked Luca, grinning when he was met by a chorus of yeses. '*Grazie, grazie mille!* Okay, so if you'll excuse me, I'm needed to help with the lunch service at Antonio's. As you know, the itinerary has been amended so you'll have a crafting session led by Izzie tomorrow, so I'll see you all on Wednesday morning at ten a.m. *Ciao a tutti!*'

'*Ciao!*' sang the choristers as Luca nodded to Izzie and dashed out of the door.

A sharp spasm of disappointment sliced through Izzie's chest that, once again, Luca had managed to avoid spending time alone with her. But she shoved her growing concerns as to the reasons behind his behaviour into the crevices of her mind to concentrate on sorting out lunch.

'Okay, why don't we adjourn to the dining room and I'll bring—' But before Izzie could continue, Nick had taken charge of proceedings.

'I've got a few calls to make so I'll skip lunch, Izzie. But I want to see everyone on the terrace at one fifty sharp for our walk over to the rehearsal studio. No lingering over the antipasti and absolutely no alcohol – no exceptions!'

Nick strode from the kitchen, his back ramrod straight, his baton slotted behind his ear. The four remaining choir members lingered at the kitchen table until he was out of earshot, then, in unison, reached for a mince pie or a *panforte* tartlet and burst into giggles.

'Sorry, Izzie, you must think us very disloyal, rude even,' said Jennie, dotting the side of her lips with a serviette whilst Dylan, Phoebe and Sofia gathered any escaping crumbs with the tips of their tongues, rolling their eyes in dramatic ecstasy. 'Nick's obsessed with making sure this Christmas concert is up to professional standard. But we're a community choir; there're fifteen of us and we're all amateurs. We're doing this for all sorts of reasons, but mainly just to enjoy ourselves and give something back to our community, but Nick's a perfectionist and it's going to be really difficult to keep to the programme he's organised for us.'

'And we want to have some fun whilst we're in Tuscany,' added Sofia, twisting her finger into the tangle of silver chains around her neck, a waft of patchouli oil drifting into the air. 'That's why we wanted to stay here at the villa instead of with the others at the hotel in the village, so we could relax and learn something new without Nick breathing down our necks every second. None of us had any idea that Nick would choose to join us!'

'Should have known he would want to keep tabs on us, though!' Dylan grinned, reaching for his beloved guitar and settling it around his neck, strumming a few chords as though it was some kind of stress-reliever.

'Either that or he thought we were the ones in most need of his supervision?' laughed Phoebe. 'Although, I can't say he's wrong. More often than not, it's us four who end up in the pub after Wednesday night's choir practice. He probably thought we'd spend the whole week in some Italian cafe indulging in endless bottles of the local Chianti. This way he can make sure we focus on the singing.'

'Need any help with lunch, Izzie?' asked Jennie, removing her glittery glasses that looked like something

Dame Edna Everage would wear, not the local doctor's receptionist.

'No thanks, it's all done, but you could grab the tray over there with the coffee?'

Izzie removed the two heavily laden wooden boards showcasing the best in Italian antipasti from the fridge and ushered the group towards the dining room where she'd set the table with Villa Limoncello's signature linen that morning, grateful for Jennie's help. She might be forgetful, but she certainly made up for it in the housekeeping stakes.

'So, you've got a Christmas concert organised then?'

'Not just one but several! It's the most important time of the year for the Somersby Singers and, as you've probably gathered, Nick insists we have to be note-perfect. He treats it like we've been asked to sing at the Royal Albert Hall in front of the queen!'

'We've been rehearsing our repertoire since September,' added Sofia, scrunching up her nose as she slid into a chair and started to pile her plate with a mountain of food. 'My flatmate says I've been singing in my sleep! I thought we were on track, that we'd crushed it, but three weeks ago Nick announced we were *sub-par* and that we had to work harder. Mmm, Izzie, this cheese is amazing, what is it?'

'It's pecorino, from a village just to the south of here. So, is that why you're here?'

'Yes, Nick arranged everything,' said Phoebe, helping herself to a couple of sprigs of radicchio, a few tomatoes and a large tumbler of home-made lemonade. 'I don't suppose there's any chance of a shot of the famous limoncello in this, is there, Izzie?'

Jennie rolled her eyes and ignored her. 'I wasn't sure whether I could come at first. I was worried about leaving the surgery's reception desk to the whims and fancies of Darcie – who's lovely but struggles with our new computerised appointments system – but also because of the cost. I mean, two boys at university isn't cheap and Tim's not particularly generous with their financial support since the divorce and his remarriage…'

Izzie saw Jennie swallow quickly. Clearly, she was still coming to terms with her ex-husband's new relationship. She wondered if that was why Jennie was so busy – with her job, with her children, with the all the societies and clubs she seemed to be a member of. No wonder she was always forgetting things! With all that going on, even the most avid of list-makers was bound to drop a ball occasionally.

'Anyway, when Nick said he was subsidising the trip so we could all come, well, it really was a chance of a lifetime! He's told us that he wants us to use it as an opportunity to bond with each other, and to concentrate on our own singing; that way, if we don't work hard, we'll be letting our fellow choir members down. He's always like this before a big concert, but I have to admit that this year he's even more paranoid than usual!'

'You can say that again,' muttered Sofia, her jaw tightening in irritation. 'It's like every little mistake and he comes down on you like a ton of bricks!'

Heat spread across Sofia's cheeks and Jennie gave her arm a comforting squeeze.

'You've just got to learn to ignore him, Sofia, dear. His bark is harsher than his bite.'

'It doesn't feel like that when he's shouting at you in front of thirteen other people.'

'They're just happy it's not them! Don't take it personally, you're a very talented soprano and Nick knows it.'

'Yes, but some people flourish with encouragement and compliments,' said Dylan, his face darkening. 'No one likes being shamed into improving, do they? Or threatened!'

'Threatened? What do you mean?' shot Phoebe, her eyes narrowing at Dylan, who looked quickly away to help himself to another portion of couscous and mozzarella salad which he drizzled with balsamic vinaigrette.

'Oh, nothing, I just—'

'Hey! What are you playing at?' came a booming voice from the kitchen door. 'It's one thirty-five! I want everyone ready – which includes wearing the polo shirts I had specially commissioned for this trip – in fifteen minutes! No excuses, no exceptions! If we don't get through every song on our schedule this afternoon, then the trip to San Gimignano on Thursday night will be cancelled!'

With groans reminiscent of a bunch of toddlers being told their finger-painting session was over, Jennie, Phoebe, Sofia and Dylan trooped from the room and up the stairs to their rooms, leaving Izzie staring in their wake. The whole purpose of running courses at Villa Limoncello was to provide a relaxing atmosphere in which to learn a new skill, but it looked like this time their classes were going to be more a bootcamp than tranquil wellness retreat.

Chapter Four

The front step, Villa Limoncello

Colour: Smashed terracotta

Izzie lingered on the front steps of the villa, clutching her purple folder like a shield, unsure whether to wait or go off in search of the choir party. She checked her watch again – one forty-eight. Okay, technically no one was late yet, but Nick had been very clear about sticking to the schedule and, not wanting to be the target of his blustering, she had made sure she was standing on the front steps of the villa with time to spare.

When she had suggested upgrading the huge abandoned outbuilding on the other side of Gianni's vineyard to hire out for parties, weddings, village *feste*, Luca hadn't been too keen, especially the financial investment side of the venture. But with a little cajoling from Gianni, who intended to use the studio for his fledgling wine-tasting sessions, he had relented. Handling the interior design had been her dream project. The cavernous space was structurally sound and she had spent many happy hours pouring every ounce of her rejuvenated creativity into its renovation, making sure she took nothing away from its rustic charm and Tuscan grandeur.

When the renovations were complete, they installed a polished mahogany bar, four long trestle tables, and had spent a very enjoyable day out visiting the company that supplied most of Italy's crystal to source the various glasses needed for the tastings. Of course, the Wine & Words course had been cancelled at the last moment and Gianni had been devastated, but he wasn't deterred and planned to offer more courses in the New Year. In the meantime, the barn had been pressed into service for the celebration of a successful *vendemmia*, the first since Maria Rossetti, the villa's former owner, had passed away, as well as a couple of birthday parties, but this was the first time it would be hosting paying guests.

She checked her watch again. One fifty. She was about to go off in search of everyone when she saw Nick making his way across the terrace towards her, his chestnut curls floating in the breeze like a curly halo.

'Oh my God! Is it too much to ask for them to be on time!' he spluttered as he joined Izzie on the wide front doorstep, currently devoid of the luscious lemon trees that usually flanked the entrance to the villa, which had been moved into the *limonaia* for the winter.

'It's just after one fifty, Nick. It'll only take us five minutes to walk over to the studio and everything is set up as per your instructions, so you'll be able to start your rehearsal straight away.'

'Well, it's just not good enough!' blustered Nick, spinning on his heels to head back to the house to rally the reluctant troops with his own brand of persuasion.

Izzie had taken only a couple of steps to delay his mission when she caught a movement on the periphery of her vision. She glanced upwards, just in time to see a dark object racing towards them.

'Argh! Look out!' screamed Izzie, rushing after Nick, who had hunched his shoulders and covered his head with his hands. 'Nick! Are you okay?'

'I'm fine, I think,' he muttered, carefully unfolding his six-foot-two frame, his face wreathed in confusion as he brushed off specks of soil from the shoulders of his burgundy velvet jacket, before turning his attention to the smashed flowerpot at his feet. 'What just happened?'

Together, Izzie and Nick turned their gaze upwards to the long narrow window above the front door whose windowsill held a collection of terracotta plant pots containing an array of colourful geraniums that Izzie had thought gave the front of the villa a welcoming feel. Except now there was one missing, the remnants of which lay on the flagstones at Nick's feet, having missed him by inches. If he hadn't decided in that moment to march off in search of his fellow choir members, then, well, she didn't dare to think of the consequences.

'Oh my God, Nick. I'm so sorry. I…'

Izzie's breath caught in her throat and she was unable to formulate the right words to verbalise what had occurred.

'Did... did one of those pots just fall from that windowsill?' spluttered Nick, running his fingers through his hair as he realised what a close shave he'd just had.

'Erm, yes, it looks like...'

'Hey, is everything okay? I thought I heard someone scream!' exclaimed Phoebe, appearing on the terrace with Dylan only metres behind her. 'What's... Oh my God!'

Phoebe's hand flew to her mouth, her eyes flicking from Nick to the windowsill above the front doorsteps, and finally the broken plant pot, where evidence of what had happened was clear for all to see.

'Nick? Izzie, are you okay?' asked Dylan, dropping his guitar case on the table beneath the pergola and rushing forward to take hold of Izzie's arm.

'I'm fine, it was Nick that...'

But Izzie couldn't go on; her stomach was churning so aggressively that nausea was starting to travel upwards as the full force of what could have been hit her like a rampaging juggernaut. She was grateful when Dylan took her arm and guided her to a chair, Nick and Phoebe following in a mute daze.

'Oh, hi, everyone! Sorry I'm a few minutes late, I was just... What's going on? Why is Izzie looking like she's seen a ghost?' Sofia's eyes widened with anxiety, her young face splashed with distress.

'It's okay, Sofia, just a bit of an accident. Everyone's okay.'

'Accident?' cried Jennie, rushing towards the pergola, already reaching inside her cavernous canvas bag for her first aid kit. 'Who's had an accident? Is anyone hurt?'

'No, everyone's fine,' Dylan reassured her. 'But it looks like Nick just had a bit of a near miss.' He pointed to the debris on the front step.

'Oh, no, Nick, are you…'

'I'm perfectly fine,' replied Nick, brushing off their concern, 'but perhaps someone could fetch Izzie a glass of water?'

'Of course!' Jennie dashed back to the kitchen to do as bid, returning with a bottle of water.

'Thanks, Jennie. Nick, I have no idea how that could have happened. As far as I know those pots have been there for years.'

'Perhaps a sudden gust of wind…' began Sofia, as everyone looked on, waiting for direction from Nick, but it was Jennie who came to the rescue, clearly anxious to soothe ragged nerves.

'Dylan, darling, would you and Sofia mind fetching the dustpan and brush from the kitchen and cleaning up the debris. Phoebe, can you call Alan to tell him we'll need to cancel this afternoon's rehearsal and…'

'Cancel?' blurted Nick, his face the epitome of shock at the very suggestion. 'We're not cancelling the rehearsal – it's what we came all the way here for. No way, Jennie. Look, it was an accident, no harm done. We just need to get on with the itinerary. You know how important—'

'But Nick, Izzie doesn't look too…' began Dylan, rubbing his hands down the front of his jeans and then clapping them together to remove the last remnants of dirt while Sofia trotted back to the kitchen to get rid of the shards of terracotta in the dustbin.

'It's okay, I'm fine, completely fine. Nick's right, no harm done. It was just a bit of shock, that's all.'

Izzie grabbed every ounce of her energy and leapt from her chair, pushing the memory of the descending pot from her mind. If she'd been just a few seconds quicker…

She glanced up at the windowsill once again, the green shutters folded back against the wall, the windows wide open to let the warm afternoon sunshine into the hallway and staircase. Could a gust of wind be responsible for blowing a heavy pot from its resting place? Her first thought was to ring Luca, to tell him what had happened, to ask for his sage advice, but she knew he would still be busy with lunch and the preparations for that evening's service at Antonio's.

'See, everyone's fine. Drama averted. Now let's get back to our schedule. We've got a lot to get through.'

Nick grabbed the battered leather satchel that he'd dropped when he cowered from the raining flowers and stalked across the terrace, pausing on the stone steps that led down to the garden, turning his head over his shoulder to look at the five people staring after him, exchanging worried glances with each other.

'Come on!'

Dylan smiled at Izzie as he collected his guitar case. 'We can find our own way to the studio, you know.'

She smiled back at him, grateful for his concern, but she grabbed her folder, clutching it in her arms like a much-loved soft toy.

'No, I'm fine. Okay, if you'll follow me, please?'

Izzie led the group through the manicured gardens, past the whitewashed gazebo that had welcomed its first wedding ceremony in the summer, to the far end of Villa Limoncello's estate where the partly renovated barn was situated.

'Here we are, Villa Limoncello's very own rehearsal studio! Okay, so I'll leave you to your choir practice. I hope you'll find everything you need inside, but if not, just give me a call and I'll be straight over.'

'Thanks, Izzie.' Jennie smiled, patting her on the arm before following the rest of the gang into the studio. 'Oh, here's everyone else! Yoohoo, Kate, Suzie! What's your hotel in San Vivaldo like? Wait until I show you what we made at the Snowflakes & Christmas Cakes course this morning! How was your trip to the Accademia, by the way? Did you take any photographs of *David*?'

Izzie lingered in the doorway, watching all fifteen members of the Somersby Singers pile into the building, their voices competing with the Christmas music drifting through the air as they filled their friends in on their various morning activities, laughter reverberating around the stone walls, along with the scraping of chairs as everyone prepared for their first rehearsal in Tuscany.

'Hey, Izzie, there you are! I thought you weren't coming!'

She smiled at Gianni, as he stepped forward to drop kisses on her cheeks. As usual, he was wearing the skimpiest denim shorts she had ever seen on a guy this side of the 1970s, but his choice of workwear did not detract from his attractiveness. If he stood in a line-up that included Mario Lopez, Robert Pattinson and George Clooney, she would struggle not to choose him as her dinner date. However, the broad welcoming grin he had greeted her with slipped from his lips when he saw the look on her face.

'Izzie? Are you okay?'

Izzie was just about to spill the whole episode in detail, but she stopped herself. Gianni had endured enough stress over the perilous future of Villa Limoncello that she didn't want to add to his worries. He had been even more keen than Luca to make sure that the Snowflakes & Christmas Cakes course went smoothly and had spent most of the previous week draping fairy lights and Christmas decorations around the eaves of the barn to make it as festive and welcoming as possible, as well as ordering and collecting everything on her long list of crafting supplies. If she told him that one of their guests had almost been decapitated by a falling plant pot then she suspected it might force him towards the brink of his sanity. The disaster had been averted, Nick seemed unconcerned, and she should leave it at that.

'Yes, yes, everything's okay, thanks, Gianni.'

Except everything was not okay, because as much as she tried not to think about it, her instincts told her that someone could have assisted that plant pot's journey south and it could only be one of the other four people staying at the villa.

Chapter Five

The patio outside the limonaia

Colour: Smoky espresso

Izzie watched Gianni disappear from view on his decrepit quad bike that was more like an oversized bluebottle than a sleek stallion. She was about to make her own way back to the villa, craving a few quiet moments to herself in the *limonaia* to reflect on what had happened before giving Luca a call, when she saw Nick poke his head out of the door and her heart dropped like a stone down a well. But it wasn't her he was looking for.

'Phoebe? Are you intending to grace us with your presence this afternoon or is your phone just too interesting to tear yourself away from?' asked Nick, glaring at Phoebe, who was leaning against the outside wall, scrolling through her messages, her forehead creased in concentration, obviously lost in a virtual world and temporarily forgetting their tight timetable. 'Phoebe!'

'Oh, yes, sorry, it's work. I just need to—'

'You need to take your place inside!'

Nick had started to return to the studio when his eyes snagged Phoebe's outfit.

'Where's your Somersby Singers polo shirt?'

'Oh, I—'

'Oh, my God! Is it too much to ask for you to toe the line just this once?'

Izzie stared at Nick, his dark brown hair billowing like a cloud of candyfloss around his exasperated face, the choir's obligatory emerald-coloured polo shirt clashing horribly with the burgundy velvet jacket he was wearing with his beloved conductor's baton sticking out of the top pocket.

'I wouldn't care so much if you were up to scratch with the last two verses of "Joy to the World"!'

'I told you, Nick, I've been snowed under at the office. I've just finished a complex fraud case and a complicated pharmaceuticals merger. I might not have had much time to practise at home, but I've never missed a single rehearsal, despite having to go back to the office afterwards to prepare for hearings at the County Court or the Crown Court the next day!'

'Well, it's not good enough, Phoebe, I want you to—'

'Look, I don't have to listen to this! I'm not nine, I'm *thirty*-nine!'

And to Izzie's surprise, Phoebe shoved her phone into her handbag and stormed off in the direction of the villa, leaving Nick gawping in her wake.

'Phoebe!'

'Where's Phoebe running off to?' asked Dylan, appearing in the doorway, his arm slung casually around his guitar, his eyes filled with concern as he followed Phoebe's retreating figure through the avenue of grapevines.

'I've sent her to get changed into her polo shirt! Now, come on, we've already lost thirty minutes of rehearsal time!'

Nick disappeared into the studio, but Dylan hesitated on the threshold, unsure whether to follow Nick or to chase after Phoebe. Izzie saw the indecision stalk across his face, along with something else she didn't immediately recognise, until he shrugged and went inside, where Nick was already shouting for quiet and asking everyone to take their places for a first run-through of their repertoire.

Izzie heaved a sigh of relief that her duties for the day were over. Her feet ached, she had a thumping headache, but all she wanted to do was grab a coffee and settle down in the *limonaia* with her folder to check she had everything organised for the following day's craft demonstration. Despite the trauma of the last hour, a pleasurable prickle of anticipation meandered through her veins – glass-painting was one of her favourite Christmas craft activities and she hoped Gianni had managed to source everything she'd put on her order list.

She stepped onto the terrace, her mind on the various designs for the Christmas baubles, wondering if she should have a little competition for the best decoration, when a flash of emerald caught her eye. She glanced to her left and saw Phoebe, slumped in one of the cane chairs outside the *limonaia*. She was wearing her polo shirt, but her expression screamed frustration.

'Oh, hi, Phoebe, are you okay?'

'Apart from the indignity of being sent back to the villa like a naughty schoolgirl?'

Izzie smiled. 'Would you like a coffee before you go back?'

'Got anything stronger?'

'How about a glass of wine?'

'Perfect! Sorry, Izzie, I don't want to put you to any trouble.'

'It's no trouble.'

Izzie went into the kitchen, grabbed a bottle of Chianti and two glasses, and took a seat next to Phoebe on the patio outside the glasshouse. She poured them each a small measure of the rich, fruity wine and handed one over to Phoebe, who tasted it like a seasoned expert.

'Mmm, delicious! I feel better already.'

'Good. Is Nick always such a hard taskmaster?'

'Yes, but as Jennie says, he's excelled himself this Christmas season.' Phoebe took another generous gulp of her wine and sighed. 'But, if I'm honest, I do understand why he's doing all this: the strict schedule, the demands that we practise every week without fail, even wearing these stupid polo shirts in the worst colour imaginable. I'd be exactly the same if I was in charge, I know I would. I'm like that at work with our new trainees – demanding perfection, always drumming the RFT maxim into them.'

'What's RFT?'

'Right first time. Saves hassle, saves time, saves money.'

'So, what do you do for a living?'

'I'm a commercial litigation lawyer. Actually, my whole family are lawyers – mum, dad, brother, uncle – so it was sort of expected that I would follow in their footsteps.'

'Sounds like you're not so sure it was the right path.'

'Actually, when I was at school what I really wanted to be was a singer/songwriter, but when I floated the idea of applying for a place at a conservatoire instead of at law school my parents were horrified. I'm ashamed to say that I took the least rocky route and joined the rat race. Four years studying at uni, two years' training contract at a respected City law firm, then the last fifteen years climbing the slippery slope towards associate partner at a Legal 500 company in Leeds.'

Phoebe paused to take another sip of her wine.

'Would you believe that this is the first holiday I've had in ten years? Once you're on the corporate treadmill, it's hard to jump off. What if someone slides their feet into your shoes whilst you're away from your desk? I've seen that happen to so many people, especially female colleagues who take maternity leave. After a while, work becomes the only thing you have in your life – I've been labelled a workaholic more times than I can remember.'

'Do you have a partner?' asked Izzie, swirling her wine around her glass before enjoying the taste of rich ripened cherries with a top note of dried oregano, balsamic vinegar and maybe a hint of smoky espresso in there.

'You're joking, right? I don't even have time to shop for a holiday wardrobe, never mind someone to spend the few spare minutes I can carve out of a day with. Look at me, reduced to wearing my business suits because I don't have anything else, how crazy is that? And, as you might have noticed, I've never had time to learn how to cook, or bake, and please, keep me away from the staple gun tomorrow!'

A flash of something Izzie couldn't decipher stalked across Phoebe's expression but it was gone in a second. She knew there was more to Phoebe's explanation of her hectic lifestyle than she was divulging. And yet, Izzie empathised with her. She understood what it took to rise through the ranks and knock on the boardroom door because her ex-fiancé, Alex, had been on the same conveyor belt, hoping to be noticed amongst all the other would-be partners at *his* law firm, keen to put in all the hours necessary to accomplish his dream. Some weeks she would only see him on a Sunday afternoon, and even then he was scrawling through a file of papers, preparing for a court case or a meeting with clients the following morning. She wondered briefly whether he had achieved his goal.

Izzie switched her gaze from the depths of her wine glass to Phoebe, to ask her which firm she worked for, maybe even if she knew Alex, but Phoebe was clearly floating along in a different universe, her eyes fixed on a point on the horizon where the velvety green slopes met the azure of the sky.

'Six months ago, reality hit me with ferocious slap. I'll be forty next year and I realised that if I don't find someone to share my life with in the next couple of years, well, I'd be looking at my dreams of having a family in the rear-view mirror. So, I decided to take action; I signed up to a couple of dating agencies.'

'Sounds like fun.'

'Far from it; every date was a complete disaster. Then someone suggested I joined a community choir to reconnect with my love of music, so I did and I found that I loved it!'

'So how did you end up coming over here?'

'Nick gave me… I mean, he gave everyone, an ultimatum.'

To Izzie's surprise colour flooded Phoebe's cheeks and she started fiddling with the stem of her glass. For the first time, Izzie noticed that instead of the neat French manicure she had expected, Phoebe's nails were bitten down to the quick, the skin around her cuticles scraped away, raw and jagged.

'What sort of ultimatum?'

'Well, not really an ultimatum, per se. He just said that surely we could all manage to find five days in our busy lives to devote to making our Somersby Singers Christmas concert the best ever.'

Phoebe was now actively avoiding meeting Izzie's eyes. She swallowed the last gulp of her red wine, gathered her designer handbag and jumped up from her seat, a smile plastered on her lips.

'Thanks for the drink and the chat, Izzie. I'd better get back to the studio or else I'll definitely find myself in the doghouse! *Ciao!*'

And before Izzie could reply, Phoebe dashed from the terrace and headed towards the gazebo, her stilettos crunching through the gravel. Izzie remained on the patio, ruminating on everything she had heard. Something had happened between Phoebe and Nick, and she wondered what secret Phoebe was keeping and why.

Then something else occurred to her.

No, surely not.

But what if…

No!

It was no good, the seed had been sown. What if Phoebe was responsible for the falling flowerpot?

Chapter Six

The kitchen, Villa Limoncello

Colour: Clinical white

Izzie's stomach performed a somersault of dread as she tossed back the remains of her wine, gathered their empty glasses and returned to the villa. She slumped down at the scarred kitchen table and, exhaling a long sigh, thoughts ricocheted around her brain until she felt dizzy. How could this be happening? But as her heartbeat slowed from canter to trot, she began to put what had occurred into perspective – surely this was nothing more than an unfortunate accident.

Wasn't it?

She decided to investigate. She jumped out of her chair and made her way to the gallery at the top of the stairs, pausing at the tall, shuttered window that looked out over the wonderful view of Tuscan countryside. The cicadas continued to chirp their daily soundtrack, the sun continued to send shards of golden light down onto the hillside, and the church bells continued to chime on the hour. She leaned over the windowsill to inspect the three remaining terracotta pots for damage or movement, but they were exactly where she expected them to be. She bent closer to scrutinise the ring of soil where the missing flower container had sat for years and her suspicions grew.

Could someone have nudged it on its way? But who would do such a thing? And why? And what if Nick hadn't been the target…

Thankfully, before she could explore that particular scenario any further, her pocket began to buzz.

'*Ciao!*'

A blast of relief spun through her body as she made her way back down the stairs to the kitchen and flicked on the kettle – something her mother swore by whenever stress made an unscheduled visit, and there was no one more experienced with that scenario than her parents. In the weeks and months following Anna's passing, Izzie had sometimes thought that they were running a Cornish beach cafe, such was the demand for coffee, tea and cake.

'Izzie! Why didn't you call me? Gianni says there's been an accident involving one of the guests!'

She recognised the tightness in Luca's voice, the fear that once again, misfortune had come to call at his beloved Villa dei Limoni. She filled him in on what had happened, downplaying the proximity of the miss, assuring him that Nick had brushed it off as an unfortunate mishap and was more concerned about the rehearsals running to schedule.

'Who told Gianni, by the way?'

'Phoebe – she thought you'd told him when you saw him at the studio. Why didn't you?'

'I didn't want to worry him. You know how anxious he's been lately about the vineyard's first harvest, then fretting about whether the wine will live up to the Rosetti Chianti, not to mention the fact that the situation with Meghan is far from ideal. I know how much he misses her when she's back in the UK.'

'Look, Izzie, if the villa has to be sold, then Gianni will have to deal with it. It won't be the end of the world – he'll walk into another job.'

Izzie detected a faint tremor in Luca's voice that put her on her guard. It was the first time she had heard him talk about the possibility of the villa being put up for sale. They had spent the last six months doing everything they could to avoid that eventuality and it would break her heart, and Gianni's, if it had all been for nothing. Nevertheless, at the end of the day, it was Luca's decision.

'Luca, what's going on? Is there something you're not telling me?'

'Can we leave this conversation for later? I've got ten tables of hungry diners to feed and Carlos has just informed me that he's got an appointment at the dentist! I'll come over to the villa later, okay?'

'But Luca...'

The line had gone dead. She placed her phone on the table, bewildered at the cooling of their relationship. She felt a headache coming on – probably the lunchtime dalliance with the demons of red wine – so she fixed herself a coffee, added a dollop of cream and took it out to the gazebo. She sank into one of the director's chairs and spent the next ten minutes meandering down her memory's superhighway, relishing the times she had spent in Luca's company: firstly, the wedding held in the villa's gardens when they had shared a passionate embrace and she had promised to stay on to help renovate the villa and run courses for the discerning traveller, and then there were the wonderful times she had spent in the kitchen at Antonio's, where Luca had taught her how to make an omelette, his muscular body pressed into hers as he guided the whisk in her hand.

She thought, too, of the romantic gestures he had made, like enlisting Francesca's help to source a particular rose that carried the same name as her sister so he could create an amazing cake with the sugared petals scattered on the top, a gesture which even now brought tears to her eyes. Or the time when they had zoomed down a hill together on the Vespa, her arms held aloft like Rose in *Titanic*.

Okay, so she had been disappointed when Wine & Words didn't go ahead, but she had spent two fabulous weeks in San Vivaldo helping with the grape harvest and upgrading the barn in preparation for the wine-tasting and creative writing courses. During that time, she had grown closer to Luca with their encounters becoming ever more intense. Yet now, a mere two months later, his distance was hurtful and confusing.

Then an uncomfortable thought strayed into her mind – could Luca have met someone else whilst she'd been away in London? It would certainly account for the cooling of his attitude towards her, but then why meet her at the airport? Why go to the trouble of sourcing such a thoughtful and *personal* gift? Why…?

Thankfully her phone buzzed to stop her from descending that particular spiral of doom.

'Hi, Meghan! It's great to hear from you. How's things? How's Jonti?'

'Ah, Isabella Jenkins, ever the duchess of distraction. Gianni called. He told me what happened to the choir leader, Nick Morgan, is it?'

'Yes, but it's all good. In fact, I think I'm the only one who's upset about what happened.' Izzie made an attempt to laugh, but it came out like a hiccup.

'Was it an accident?'

'It looks that way. The flowerpots are really old. I think the one that fell must have just crumbled away. There was nothing much left of it when it landed on the terrace.'

'Well, that's a relief. You've got enough on your plate with organising and presenting the last-minute Christmas craft tutorials without turning amateur detective like you did last time! So, tell me what you've got planned for tomorrow's session?'

'I've got these amazing glass baubles from a factory in a little town south of here, and Gianni has promised to erect a Christmas tree in the gazebo, complete with fairy lights, for us to display the baubles on.'

'And the Thursday session?'

'I thought I'd join forces with Francesca and demonstrate how to make Christmas wreaths and floral table displays. Remember the chandelier she made for Louisa and Stefano's wedding?'

'Yes, that *was* stunning. I can't wait to see you on Saturday and Jonti is so excited he's like a cat on a hot tin roof! Have you warned Carlotta that he's expecting her to come up with a match made in heaven?'

Izzie laughed for the first time since the flowerpot debacle and it felt good. She adored Meghan, always ready with a word of encouragement, a snippet of gossip or the offer of advice. She was the best friend a woman could ask for, and she had been her rock during those dark times when there had been no light at the end of the tunnel. She, and Jonti, had supported her at Anna's funeral, at her memorial service, on birthdays and anniversaries when all she wanted to do was bury herself under the duvet and shut out the hard, cruel world. It had been Meghan, too, who had suggested she came to Tuscany – to help Brad, her film director brother, with a location shoot – where she had found solace.

'Carlotta can't wait to meet Jonti. She says she feels like she knows him already.'

'So, have you made a decision yet?'

Izzie gulped at the surprise turn in the conversation; no beating about the bush for Meghan – she was an expert in firing questions from left of field. She inhaled a deep breath to give herself a few moments to marshal her arguments and present an eloquent reply about how she was weighing up her options, factoring in every eventuality and possibility. However, she knew all that would be pointless because Meghan had already made up her mind about what Izzie should do. Whilst she knew her friend only had her best interests at heart, she'd hoped to avoid this conversation at least until the course had finished. It would be much better if Meghan was sitting next to her, relaxing with a glass of Vin Santo in the *limonaia*, Izzie's favourite place in San Vivaldo if not the whole of Tuscany – a place where all her worries seeped away into an oasis of tranquillity and all anxieties became inconsequential.

She fingered the handle of her coffee cup, trying to come up with a response that would satisfy her friend so that she would let the subject drop.

'Izzie?'

The phoneline crackled, which made Meghan seem much further away than snow-bound London, and a spasm of regret shot through Izzie's heart – she would have loved to have her best friend at her side that week while she delivered the crafting part of the Snowflakes & Christmas Cakes course.

'No, I haven't. Not yet, and Harry did give me until the end of the week to think about it.'

'But what's there to think about?'

'Meghan...'

'Okay, so it's a very generous offer, but with your skills and expertise that's only to be expected, and I admit that the creative director title does have a certain ring to it, not to mention the fact that he's offering you a share in the company to go along with it. But it's six months too late! If Harry had come up with his proposal in May, before his corporate clod of a son fired you...'

'Darren didn't fire me, he made me redundant.'

'Without Harry's authority! You know, Darren Hambleton is the most short-sighted, unimaginative, egotistical person I've ever had the misfortune to come across. Do you know what he said to Jonti last week when he was putting the final touches to another one of those clinical whitewashed shoe boxes he's flooding the capital with, which he has the audacity to call luxury homes?'

'Meghan, can we—'

'He told him to paint the door handles with white gloss so they didn't stand out so much against the chalk-coloured walls! Do you really want to go back to that? Back to the snoring boring life of magnolia and ivory drabness?'

'That isn't what Harry's suggesting. It's a completely separate project he's planning in South Cornwall. Harry's bought an old farmhouse with lots of outbuildings that he's renovating into holiday homes. He'll do the building work and I'll be in charge of the interior design to make sure the décor reflects the seaside vibe, not the monochrome minimalism Darren prefers in the capital. Anyway, Darren's no longer in charge of Hambleton's London portfolio. I told you, he'll be based in Dubai after Christmas.'

'Regaling those lucky people with his corporate clichés and obnoxious bullshit, no doubt. Lucky them!' said Meghan sarcastically.

Darren Hambleton had never been Meghan's favourite person, even less so after he'd dispensed with Izzie's services because he thought she brought too much flair to Hambleton Homes interiors.

'Look Izzie, I know this is a chance for you to go back home to St Ives, to be near your parents, to reconnect with friends after everything that's happened with Anna, and I'm delighted that you're giving it serious consideration, I really am. But I also know how much you love Villa Limoncello, how much being there has helped you come to terms with your loss. It's really great to see the old Isabella Jenkins poking through that veil of grief you insisted on draping yourself in. Organising and presenting Tuscan retreats is the perfect role for you – you're a natural!'

'You didn't say that in July!' laughed Izzie.

'True. If you and Luca hadn't donned your deerstalkers and unmasked the food-poisoning culprit, then I reckon the Italian health inspectors would have closed you down before Villa Limoncello had the chance to shine.'

'Exactly!' said Izzie firmly.

'What do you mean?'

'Nothing, nothing.'

'What does Luca think about it?'

Izzie experienced a squirm of discomfort. How could she explain to Meghan about the growing chasm between them, about how she felt he was keeping something from her, secrets that didn't involve her, how she felt he was pushing her away by leaving the decision about Harry's offer to her and refusing to have any input. Of course, she knew that could just be to allow her the space to come to her own decision about her future, but how could she make such a choice without knowing all the facts – particularly what would happen if she stayed on in Tuscany, with Luca.

'Luca's giving me the space to make my own decision.'

'But Luca loves you! Anyone who sees the way he looks at you knows he does; I know it, Gianni knows it, Carlotta knows it, Francesca knows it, even the woman who designed those amazing silver earrings he bought you to cheer you up after the Wine & Words course was cancelled knows it! If he doesn't love you, why is he commissioning handmade jewellery with cute red glass hearts on? I would have preferred a ring, but hey ho!'

'Meghan!'

'Look, Izzie, all I'm saying is just talk to him…'

'Sorry, Meghan, I have to go. The guests are on their way back to change for dinner.'

'Izzie…'

'Love you, talk later. *Ciao*.'

'Okay, *ciao*, darling.'

Izzie swiped the disconnect button with a sigh of relief and leaned back into her chair. Guilt danced across her mind; there was another hour to go until Nick released his prisoners… oops, fellow choir members so they could shower and change for that evening's dinner at Antonio's Trattoria, and at least Meghan had been truthful enough to make her views clear. However, after everything that had happened that day, she was exhausted and she just didn't have the strength to talk to Meghan about her feelings for Luca, or his for her.

Was Meghan right? Did Luca love her? And if he did, would that sway her decision about going back to Cornwall, her childhood home, the place where she'd grown up, with her twin sister at her side?

Her head felt like it was about to explode as she oscillated between confidence and doubt. With difficulty, she shoved the recurring questions from her mind – after all, there was a lot to get through before Friday arrived and Harry would need his answer.

She strolled back to the kitchen, stopping to collect a couple of lemons from the *limonaia* on the way, where she filled a washing-up bowl with soapy water and made a start on washing the kitchen floor to work away her anxiety demons.

Chapter Seven

The swimming pool, Riccardo's B&B

Colour: Sparkling aquamarine

'*Santa Claus is comin' to town, Santa Claus is comin' to town…*' sang Izzie as she scrubbed the terracotta floor tiles where Sofia had spilt a dish of honey that morning, her bottom in the air as she swayed from side to side to the jaunty Christmas music.

'Izzie?'

'*Santa Claus is…* Oh my God! Luca!'

Izzie scrambled up from the floor, dropped her cloth in the sink and whipped off her yellow Marigolds, her cheeks glowing as she turned to face him.

'What are you doing here?'

'Well,' he grinned, 'that was certainly the most unusual welcome I've had to the Villa dei Limoni since I bought it!'

'I thought you were at Antonio's?'

The amusement that had twinkled in his eyes disappeared and he grew serious.

'I need you to talk me through what happened earlier.'

In as few words as possible, Izzie detailed the incident in the least emotive language she could and then they trotted up the stairs together to take a look.

'What do you think?'

Luca ran his fingers through his hair, causing it to stick up in random tufts, then scratched at the back of his neck as he considered the situation. He had changed out of his chef's jacket into a pair of contour-hugging dark denim jeans and a pale apricot polo shirt that highlighted his muscular biceps and sun-kissed skin to perfection. A whiff of his citrussy cologne floated in the air and mingled with the fragrance from the geraniums in the pots on the windows sill.

'I don't want to read something into the situation that isn't there, and from what you've said it sounds like Nick feels the same, but I can't see how one of these pots could have fallen without some assistance.'

'They're very old…'

'Even so, they've been here for years.'

'But who would do such a thing?'

'I don't know.'

'And…' Izzie paused, fearful of uttering the next sentence.

'And what?'

'Can we be sure that Nick was the target?'

'Izzie, why on earth would anyone want to harm you? Only the other four guests were in the villa at the time, and if it wasn't an accident, it has to be one of them and you only met them yesterday. I don't suppose you saw anything at the window?'

'No, no, I didn't see anything or anyone. I was too busy rushing over to make sure that Nick was okay, and if he didn't have such good reflexes who knows what would have happened. Oh my God, someone could have died!'

'I don't think so, the pots here are too small to do any serious damage, but they could certainly have caused a nasty injury. But there's something else gnawing at that brain of yours, isn't there? Come on, tell me.'

Izzie paused. Whenever life tossed random grenades in her path, her go-to solution was to grab her trusty notebook and start making a plan, a well-thought-through to-do list of how to deal with it. Order – that was the answer to all life's chaos and her thoughts were circling like vultures eyeing their prey. But her purple folder was downstairs on the kitchen table so she would just have to fly solo for once.

'It's just something Phoebe said earlier.'

'Phoebe?'

'Yes, she popped back to change into her Somersby Singers polo shirt and we had a chat. Did you know she's a lawyer – which didn't surprise me when she told me – but she actually wanted to be a singer/songwriter.'

'And?'

'Well, when the conversation turned to why she came over here, I got the impression she was holding something back, that she had some sort of secret that only Nick was privy to.'

'What sort of secret?'

'Not sure – she seemed to bristle with restrained fury, but mingled with fear.'

'So you think she could have nudged the flowerpot from the windowsill as some sort of revenge, or maybe to turn the tables on the fear factor?'

Izzie didn't say anything; she had no evidence that Phoebe would do such a thing, except that expression on her face like a cornered tiger. Could she have lashed out?

'Where was Phoebe when it happened?'

'In the villa, getting ready for the choir rehearsal – all four of the guests were. It could have been any of them, or all of them!'

'Who was first on the scene?'

'That would be Phoebe, followed by Dylan with his guitar.'

'And the others?'

'I think Sofia and Jennie arrived together, but I don't think we can include Jennie. She's like a mother hen, always making sure everyone is okay. I mean, who carries a fully stocked first aid kit in their handbag? And she was really kind when…'

'When what?'

'When I nearly fainted.'

Luca took a step closer to Izzie, laced his fingers through hers and gave her hand a squeeze. He held her gaze, and, for a few glorious seconds, his lips hovered within inches of her mouth, his breath tickling at her cheek and causing her whole body to tremble with anticipation.

'Izzie, I…'

But, again, he seemed to wrestle with an invisible demon and pulled back.

'I think we should take these pots to the *limonaia*. Just in case.'

As Luca removed the remaining flowerpots from the windowsill, the movement sending wafts of floral perfume into the air, disappointment and confusion rolled around Izzie's thoughts. Now she was certain there was something going on with Luca, and she wasn't going to stand around wondering, guessing, leaping to increasingly bizarre conclusions. She had grown emotionally stronger over the six months since she had met him and she knew that in circumstances such as these, the best course was to face these issues head on: to raise her chin, meet his eyes and ask him the questions that were rampaging through her mind on a tickertape.

'Luca, what's going on? And don't say "nothing" because I know there's something you're not telling me.'

Luca paused, indecision written across his face.

'Luca?'

Suddenly his hesitancy evaporated. He placed the flowerpots onto the floor, and reached out to grab her hand, a gesture that caused her heart to give a nip of pleasure.

'Come with me.'

He guided her down the stairs and out through the kitchen door to the terrace.

'Where are we going?'

'Always the questions. Trust me!'

Luca gave her his familiar smirk, his eyes alight with laughter and mischief. Izzie loved how spontaneous he was, loved how he always had something up his sleeve to bring a smile to her face.

Why did everything have to be so complicated? What had she, or Luca, done to deserve a lead role in the Great Flowerpot Fiasco? Why couldn't she have spent her week in Tuscany appreciating the complexities of Italian patisserie, taking advantage of the aura of serenity and calm Villa Limoncello instilled in all its residents, and building on her relationship with Luca, and the other friends she had made in San Vivaldo: Gianni, Carlotta, Francesca and Oriana? Once again it looked as if she would have to don her metaphorical deerstalker to uncover exactly what had happened that afternoon, otherwise the villa would have another blemish on its character and she couldn't allow that to happen.

They had reached the crumbling stone wall that separated Villa Limoncello from the beautifully renovated B&B next door owned by the bestselling crime author Riccardo Clarke, its perfect proportions and immaculate gardens making Villa Limoncello look like Cinderella before she met her fairy godmother.

'Luca, stop! I don't think Riccardo's home. He emailed me before I came over here to say he was going to be in the UK this week to meet his agent and won't be back until Friday afternoon. Did I tell you he's started to write again? Not a crime thriller this time, but a travel biography, would you believe, a sort of Peter Mayle meets Gino D'Acampo.'

'That's great news.' Luca grinned, helping her scramble over the ivy-choked boundary wall between the two properties.

'So what are we doing sneaking around his garden?'

Luca didn't answer; instead, he led her through a trellised archway, which in summer was entwined with the bright yellow roses Riccardo's late wife had planted before cancer left its malicious calling card, and paused in front of the large rectangle of perfect aquamarine twinkling like a miniature lake of diamonds in the late afternoon sun.

'Luca, I—'

But it was too late, he had linked his arm through hers and launched them both into the swimming pool. Izzie let out a cry of alarm when the less-than-warm water hit her body, spluttering with shock as she pushed her dripping hair from her eyes.

'Oh my God, I can't believe you just did that!'

She spun round and attempted to walk back to the steps, unsure whether to laugh or cry. But Luca was by her side in an instant, laughing at her indignant expression, splashing droplets of water in her face. She retaliated, scooping up wave after wave and throwing it over his head until he managed to grab hold of her wrists, coil his arm around her waist, and pull her towards him, only pausing when her lips were level with his, the delicate whisper of his warm breath on her earlobes sending Izzie's emotions into overdrive.

'You know, Izzie, life in San Vivaldo was pretty uneventful before you came to town. For a woman who adores orderliness, you certainly lead an event-filled life – it's been a continual rollercoaster ride since you confronted me about running you off the road.

And you know what? I wouldn't have you any other way. *Grazie mille.*'

'What for?'

With his liquorice curls plastered to his cheeks, and his wet shirt moulded to his body like a second skin, Izzie thought he had never looked so handsome. She wrapped her arms around his neck and floated in his arms, enjoying the gentle sway of the water and the whoosh of heat his proximity caused spreading out to her every extremity – those shivers rippling the length of her spine had nothing to do with the temperature of the water.

'For being here, for organising and presenting the courses, for the amazing transformation you've created at the villa and the barn, for that lethal concoction you insist on labelling authentic limoncello. It's been an amazing six months and I've enjoyed every single minute of it.'

Izzie could feel the 'but' hanging in the air like a firework ready to explode, and her heart sank to the bottom of the swimming pool. What was going on!

'Luca...'

'Izzie...'

She raised her eyes to meet his gaze, to urge him to tell her why he was acting so weirdly, but just as she opened her mouth, his lips were on hers, gentle at first, exploring, probing, then becoming more insistent, sending spasms of electricity through her veins as she gave herself up to a crescendo of pleasure. She reached up to lace her fingers through his hair and pull him even closer, to feel the hard contours of his body pressing into hers, and her heart told her everything she needed to know about her feelings for Luca Castelotti.

Now that she was in Tuscany, the thought of returning to her former existence of monochrome ordinariness, where she'd lived on coffee and toast and had only managed to beat the daily struggle to six o'clock by relying on her carefully crafted lists, was inconceivable. Did the label creative director and the offer of an annual bonus in the form of company shares make up for what she would be giving up? Surely not!

But could she be sure her feelings were reciprocated?

From the way Luca had just kissed her, she was tempted to answer that question with a resounding yes, but she knew there was something he was hiding from her and until he told her what that was, she couldn't make her decision about Harry's offer. So, for the time being she would concentrate her efforts on solving the mystery of the flying flowerpot – it wasn't how she had hoped to spend what could be her last week at Villa Limoncello, though.

Best-laid plans? They weren't worth the paper they were written on!

–

Luca changed gear in his beloved Spider and raced along the winding roads that lead from the Villa dei Limoni to San Vivaldo, his thoughts not on the gorgeous Tuscan countryside flashing by the windows, but bouncing around his head like caged lottery balls.

However, after taking a corner a little too sharply, he slowed down and pulled in at the exact spot where he had inadvertently run Izzie off the road all those months ago when he'd come across her riding the sugar-pink Vespa he'd thought was safely stowed in the villa's outbuilding. When he thought back to that day and remembered the way her vivid blue eyes had flashed with indignation as she confronted him over his second-rate driving skills, he couldn't prevent a smile from twisting his lips.

With a sigh, Luca reached into the glove compartment and removed a black velvet box tied with a silver ribbon. He flicked open the lid and stared at the contents. Having seen the delight on Izzie's face when he'd presented her with the hand-crafted silver earrings before she went back to London after the Wine & Words debacle, he'd rushed back to see Valentina to ask her to design a matching necklace, complete with a tiny red glass heart at its centre. It was a stunning piece of jewellery, and the perfect gift for what he had planned to say to Izzie when he gave her it at the end of the Snowflakes & Christmas Cakes course.

With every fibre of his body he had wanted to tell Izzie that he loved her, that the six weeks she had been away had been the most desolate of his life, weeks when the colour seemed to have disappeared from the world only to return when she had stepped into the arrivals hall at Florence Airport; that his heart had soared at the sight of those vibrant Titian curls, the sparkle of happiness in her eyes, and her wide beaming smile.

He adored the way she strived to speak Italian as often as she could, how she expressed her boundless creativity with such panache at the villa and in the Painting & Pasta classes she'd run in the summer, how incredibly supportive she had been when he was accused of food poisoning by one of the guests. Whenever they were together, taking the Vespa out for a spin, indulging in an impromptu dip in Riccardo's swimming pool, cooking up a storm in the kitchen at Antonio's or the villa, he could feel the sparks of electricity flash between their bodies, the intensity of their attraction that he couldn't ignore.

He could pinpoint the moment when he had fallen in love with her to the time he had taken her in his arms and asked her to dance with him, despite the fact there'd been a shower of summer rain and they'd both ended up soaked to the skin – or maybe it was because of that!

But how could he tell Izzie how he felt about her now?

After everything Izzie and her family had been through, he didn't want to complicate things, or influence her in any way, whilst she made her decision about whether to take Harry Hambleton up on his offer to be the creative director of his company – a position that would enable her to return to her childhood home in Cornwall, the place she had grown up with her twin sister by her side.

And how could he live with himself if he was the cause of depriving Izzie's parents of their one remaining child, as well as the chance of a lifetime for Izzie to expand her career and maybe start her own interior design business again – something he knew she would love to do now that she was at last emerging from the chrysalis of grief.

No, he couldn't do that.

So, he'd decided the best thing to do was to take a step back to give Izzie the space she needed without him colouring her vision for her future. And if that meant he had to hide his feelings for her, then so be it. This was a decision she had to make on her own, even though he thought his heart would break if she decided not to stay.

Chapter Eight

The kitchen, Villa Limoncello

Colour: A cornucopia of colours

The next day, Izzie woke in her sunflower-bedecked bedroom to the sound of an energetic dawn chorus. It was one of the things she had missed whilst she'd been back in London, the constant musical accompaniment to life on a Tuscan hillside: the croaking frogs, the church bells, a lone Vespa struggling up the incline. She dashed in and out of the shower, grabbed a hoodie and made her way to the kitchen, relishing the peace and calm as she fixed herself an espresso and took it outside to the terrace.

Six thirty – it really was the best part of the day.

She strolled through the garden, smiling as the woody lavender stalks tickled her shins, and made her way down to the studio to make sure everything was ready for the crafting session that was due to get underway at ten a.m. She had been surprised that all five of their guests had opted to join in – even Nick!

Within minutes she had arrived at the formerly dilapidated barn that she, Luca, Gianni and Meghan had shed blood, sweat and tears to renovate. In the short time they'd had before the anticipated arrival of their Wine & Words guests, they'd managed to make it into a useable space that oozed Tuscan charm; rustic yet practical, stylish yet comfortable, and as Tuscany could get cold in the winter – even snowy – it was warm and cosy, too, perfect for Christmas crafting sessions.

Izzie unlocked the paint-blistered wooden doors and slipped inside. She opened her trusty folder and conducted a final check of her to-do list for the first of their Christmas-themed sessions, her mood lifting with every tick accomplished. Last of all, she removed five laminated instruction cards and set them next to a pile of raw materials for each of the guests to refer to as she talked them through the step-by-step instructions until they ended up with a set of personalised glass baubles that would hopefully take pride of place on their family's Christmas tree for years to come.

A helix of excitement twisted through Izzie's body as she fingered the little jars of glass paint, the selection of paintbrushes and her favourite piece of equipment in her armoury: her glue gun. After spending three years at the RCA, then five years running her own interior design studio, this was exactly the sort of activity she adored – inspiring others to create treasures for their own homes.

She sent a silent missive of thanks to Gianni for sourcing the materials on her list in such a short space of time. He had even managed to get hold of a selection of styrofoam spheres – which she planned to transform into tree decorations – squares of felt and fabric that they could cut into festive shapes and embroider, and a box of wooden shapes that could be painted and threaded with string.

She got to work unpacking the craft trunk that she'd brought with her from London when she came over in September before the Wine & Words course had been cancelled. She had stored it in a cupboard in the outbuilding next to the *limonaia* and when she got back home, she'd spent a fabulous weekend with Meghan and Jonti trawling the capital's flea markets, boutiques and haberdasheries to fill up a brand-new trunk for the project she'd been engaged to do for her friend Alicia. They'd had a wonderful time splashing out on spools of multi-coloured ribbon and Victorian lace, on transparent tubes crammed with buttons, pearls and beads, hanks of yarn – mohair and angora – printed paper, even edible glitter and cake sprinkles. Anything and everything that could be used by a busy interior designer to turn a bland, magnolia Knightsbridge townhouse into an individual, character-filled home.

She pressed the play button on the CD player, and, humming along to 'Let it Snow', she set out six separate sets of materials: one for her to use during her demonstration, and one for each of her students. Then she placed a variety of alternative items that could be used as Christmas decorations in the middle of the table for them to help themselves to: thick sheets of foil wrapping paper, miniature wooden picture frames, coloured cardboard and tissue paper, along with dishes filled with beads, sequins, pom-poms and a box containing scissors – plain and pinking – a snail-shaped cushion with pins, needles and safety pins, a Stanley knife, twists of embroidery thread every colour of the rainbow and finally her glue gun and her staple gun.

Standing back to survey her hard work, a warm, festive feeling seeped into her heart. It had been almost three years since she'd experienced the uptick of emotions when Christmas came around, but hopefully this year things would be different. She had an idea. She checked her watch – maybe there was just enough time. She sprinted back to the kitchen, smiling when she saw the ancient bicycle propped up against the villa's wall, a cute little nose peeking out of the wicker basket.

'Hi, Pipo!'

She ruffled the little dog's ears and received a friendly lick for her trouble.

'Izzie!'

Carlotta grasped Izzie's shoulders and placed the customary two kisses on her cheeks, a waft of lily-of-the-valley perfume rising into the air around them.

'*Buongiorno*, Carlotta. How's breakfast coming along?'

'*Tutto è finito!*'

Carlotta waved her hand towards the kitchen table that was groaning under a cornucopia of Italian breakfast goodies, the sleeves of her bright satsuma-coloured kaftan flapping like angel wings at her wrists. With her pale silver hair cut into a sharp-angled bob, she carried her sixty years well and Izzie suspected that with her daily cycle ride from San Vivaldo to the villa, Carlotta was probably in better shape than she was. Not only was her friend a fantastic cook, having catered villas in the area for the last twenty years, she was also the go-to person for relationship advice, but Izzie had no intention of navigating that particular minefield before she'd had her second, or even third, coffee of the day.

'How's Vincenzo?'

'Busy fixing his nephew's Fiat so I said I would go over to Siena with a picnic basket when I've finished here. I've prepared lunch – it's in the fridge ready just to uncover and serve.'

Carlotta paused as she finished slotting a batch of utensils into their allocated spaces in the drawers and draped the tea towel, which had been slung across her shoulder like a pashmina, over the oven rail.

'Is everything okay, Izzie?'

Oh, God! groaned Izzie inwardly. She should have known she couldn't keep secrets from Carlotta – she not only knew everyone in San Vivaldo but she also knew everything that went on. Nothing was off-limits. Perhaps she should ask her to ditch the picnic idea and stay on at the villa to help her unravel the secrets their guests were keeping. Carlotta would have the inside scoop before they'd finished their first coffee break, before moving on to possibly even introducing them to their future partners – although she knew that Nick was already married.

'Everything is fine, thanks.'

'So you think it was an accident?'

'Ah, you've spoken to Gianni.'

'No, Vincenzo told me.'

'And he spoke to Gianni?'

'No, he spoke to Francesca last night.'

'Francesca?'

'Yes, and she heard what happened from Roberto.'

'Roberto who supplies the Vespas?'

'Yes, he plays football with Gianni on Monday nights.'

Izzie sighed. She didn't know why she was surprised – life had been very much the same in St Ives when she and Anna were growing up. Everyone in their neighbourhood knew everyone else and their extended families; they celebrated each other's birthdays, attended their weddings, their anniversary parties, and everyone pulled together when tragedy struck – like when they had lost their beloved primary school teacher as she pedalled to work one sunny morning. The whole village had mourned her sister's passing, but it had been particularly devastating for Anna's pupils, who had adored their kind, funny, generous reception class teacher who had championed their efforts and guided them through the labyrinth that was school life with humour and grace.

'Yes, it was just an unfortunate accident. There was no harm done and Luca's removed all the pots from the windowsills upstairs and put them in the *limonaia* for the time being.'

'Okay,' said Carlotta, her face reflecting her scepticism. 'So, there's no patisserie session morning?'

'No, Luca asked me to organise a Christmas crafts class down in the studio. We're making decorations for the tree Gianni has put up in the gazebo.'

'You know, in Italy we don't always have a Christmas tree in our homes.'

'No tree? Why not?'

'We have a *ceppo* instead.'

'What's a *ceppo*?'

Carlotta handed Izzie a tiny cup of thick, dark espresso, leaning back against the sink as she blew on her coffee to cool it.

'It's a wooden frame, designed in the shape of a pyramid, with several tiers or shelves. On the bottom tier we usually display a small nativity scene, then on the other shelves there's gifts of fruit, or candy, or little toys. The whole thing is decorated with coloured paper, silver pine cones and tapered candles, and then at the apex we usually hang a star.'

'Wow! I wish we had more time for the crafting side of things, I would love to make one of those.'

'What do you have planned for the Thursday session?'

'I've arranged for Francesca to come over with…'

'Oh, hi?'

Sofia lingered in the doorway, her earphones dangling around her neck like a hi-tech necklace, clutching a pink journal with a picture of a unicorn on the front.

'Come in, come in, breakfast is ready,' said Izzie, indicating the sumptuous spread of Italian pastries, slices of local cheeses and ham, freshly squeezed orange juice and a huge brown tea pot. 'Sofia, this is Carlotta Bellini. Carlotta, this is Sofia Bianchi, a soprano in the Somersby Singers choir. Would you like espresso, caffè latte, cappuccino or good old English breakfast tea?'

'Orange juice is fine, thanks. By the way, I don't think the others will be down for a while. They all put away *a lot* of wine last night, even Nick who said he wasn't going to indulge! Hypocrite!'

Sofia slid into a seat at the table and helped herself to a warm *cornetto*, sending a cascade of flaky pastry and powdered sugar tumbling down the front of her cropped denim jacket which she wore with the sleeves shoved up to the elbows.

'*Buongiorno, Sofia.*'

'*Buongiorno, Carlotta, è bello conoscerti.*'

'*Ah, tu parli italiano!*'

'*Si, sono nata qui.*'

'Gosh, I had no idea you spoke Italian!' exclaimed Izzie, staring at Sofia, although, now she came to think about it, she had no idea how she could have missed the Mediterranean features – the smooth caramel-hued skin, the long wavy mahogany hair, the dark amber eyes, not to mention her inherent sense of fashion.

'My mum was Italian – she grew up in a small village just outside Milan, although she moved to Yorkshire to live with my aunt Rosa and uncle Freddie after I was born.'

Izzie saw a streak of pain shoot across Sofia's young face and she recognised its cause immediately. When you lose someone close, you develop in-built sensors to spot others who share your suffering, those who have fallen to the bottom of that long dark shaft and are in the process of crawling back out again by their fingernails. Her heart contracted with sympathy and she reached out to squeeze Sofia's hand.

Sofia peered at Izzie over the rim of her glass, tears sparkling along her dark lashes. Carlotta took a seat on Sofia's other side and offered her a tissue.

'Mum passed away four years ago – breast cancer. I'd just finished my A levels and it was the hardest thing I've ever had to deal with. I miss her every day, but I have Aunt Rosa.'

'*E tuo padre?*'

'I never knew him. Mum met him one summer during a university exchange for music and drama students – apparently it was a whirlwind romance and she didn't find out she was pregnant until he'd left to go back to his studies in London. You probably won't believe me, but I was never curious about him. I had Mum and Aunt Rosa and Uncle Freddie, and my two crazy cousins, Fabio and Benito – we were a family. But when Mum died, I, well… I did start to wonder and Aunt Rosa offered to help me look into my family tree and… well…'

Emotion bubbled over and Sofia dabbed at her eyes with Carlotta's tissue, gulping down her orange juice to steady her nerves as she pulled her journal towards her and started to fiddle with the glitter pen.

'Do you write?' asked Izzie, keen to move the conversation away from what was clearly a very painful subject.

'Yes, I do!' Sofia's eyes lit up immediately. 'Well, I dabble – I'm actually writing a stage play. I work in the costume department at the Theatre Royal in York, which I absolutely love. Mum and Rosa used to run a bridal boutique and I grew up amongst all the wedding dresses and veils and tiaras and shoes and all the stories of romantic encounters. I would scribble them down in my diary, add extra twists and turns to them, change the endings sometimes, imagine where the couple would go on their honeymoon, how many children they'd have, that sort of thing. When I graduated from college, I was thrilled when I was offered a job in the theatre – it was a dream come true – and I can write at the weekends.'

'*Mi piacerebbe leggere il tuo romanzo quando è finito!*' said Carlotta, patting Sofia's hand. 'And I hope you have success in your search for your father.'

Izzie saw a flicker of unease dash across Sofia's face but before she could press her further on the progress of her search, Sofia had changed the subject. Izzie sighed – not another of their guests with secrets. Had Sofia found her father? Had she contacted him? If so, what had happened? If not, why not? She shook herself – none of this was any of her business, but her heart did go out to Sofia.

'So, what are we making in the craft session today?'

Sofia reached for her glass of orange juice, her hand shaking so much she spilled a few drops onto the table.

'Sorry! Sorry! God, I'm just so clumsy at the moment – I don't know what's happening to me! Mum was the same, though. Aunt Rosa was always really strict with her about not taking her coffee into the boutique.'

'*Nessun problema!*' Carlotta smiled, jumping up from her seat to collect a dishcloth from the sink. She wiped up the spillage, then doused the table with anti-bacterial spray. Izzie smiled too, remembering the events of the

Painting & Pasta course in the summer after which both she and Carlotta had been super-vigilant with hygiene matters.

'Yes, what *do* you have planned for us this morning, Izzie? I can't wait to get stuck in,' exclaimed Jennie, bowling into the kitchen, her canvas bag looking even more voluminous, if that were possible. She showed no signs whatsoever of a late night or overindulgence in the local wine. 'Oh, hi there, I'm Jennie Parker.'

Jennie shot her hand out to greet Carlotta, her smile turning to curiosity when Carlotta took it then leaned forward to deposit kisses on her cheeks. Izzie grinned. With her mother hen tendencies, Jennie reminded her of Carlotta and she knew the two women would get on like a house on fire if Carlotta wasn't rushing off to meet Vincenzo.

'*Buongiorno, Jennie, mi chiamo Carlotta*.'

'Ah, the famous Carlotta. I'm thrilled to meet you! I've heard all about your matchmaking skills – perhaps I might be in need of a little sprinkle of your magic!' Jennie laughed, but Izzie heard the strain in her voice. She knew Jennie was recently divorced and with her two boys at university, she could imagine that her nest felt very empty. She suppressed a giggle as she pictured Jennie with her oversized bag tending to a local Italian guy's every need.

Carlotta smiled. 'Then perhaps you would like to join Vincenzo and me at Pani's cafe in the village on Thursday night?'

'I'd love that! Gosh, Sofia what will I wear? Do you think you could take a look at the outfits I've brought with me and see if you could add a bit of your fabulous sparkle? I'll need to look my best if I want a handsome Italian man to whisk me off for a romantic moonlit drive through the Tuscan countryside in his Ferrari!'

All four women laughed and Izzie was relieved to see the earlier shadow of discomfort in Sofia's eyes had vanished and she was enjoying the switch in the conversation away from her personal life.

'Hey! It's nine thirty! Don't you think we should be making our way down to the studio?' came the booming voice of Nick, his appearance filling every corner of the kitchen with high-octane energy. 'Where are Phoebe and Dylan? Have they had their breakfast already?'

'We're here,' said Dylan, ambling into the kitchen, for once minus his guitar, his shoulders slumped, his hair dishevelled, looking like he'd slept in his clothes.

'In body, if not in mind!' mumbled Phoebe, striding over to the coffee machine to grab an espresso, which she downed in a single gulp before refilling her cup for a second injection of caffeine. In complete contrast to Dylan, she was as polished as always, her hair in a sleek ponytail, her make-up perfect and wearing a gorgeous crease-free shirt that matched her piercing blue eyes, currently hidden behind dark glasses. 'Remind me to give the grappa a miss tonight, will you? I feel like death.'

'Well, I hope you'll have recovered your senses *and* your voice for this afternoon's rehearsal. I want everyone at the top of their game because from the showing yesterday we have quite a few wrinkles to iron out.'

Nick picked up a plate, loaded it with slices of Tuscan bread, cheese and prosciutto, and carried it out to the terrace with his battered leather music satchel clenched under his arm, that day's waistcoat a mixture of blue and green paisley giving him the appearance a well-fed peacock.

'I don't know about you three, but I think I might have gone from a tenor to a bass this morning!' groaned Dylan, dropping his head into his hands and rubbing the bridge of his nose in an attempt to alleviate the pressure between his eyes.

'Here, take one of these and you'll be as right as rain,' said Jennie, rummaging in her bag and producing a sachet of powder, which she handed to Dylan at the same time as Phoebe put a cup of black coffee in from of him.

'Do you have another one of those, Jen?' asked Phoebe sheepishly.

'Of course!' Jennie beamed and handed one over.

'Thanks, you're a life saver! I am not, repeat *not*, ever drinking alcohol again!'

'Until tonight?' asked Dylan, sending a smile in Phoebe's direction that left Izzie in no doubt whatsoever that Carlotta's matchmaking skills had already started to work their magic for two members of the choir, even though they hadn't realised it yet.

Chapter Nine

The studio, Villa Limoncello

Colour: Rudolph red

'Okay, so welcome to Villa Limoncello's very first Christmas Crafts session. This morning we'll be creating a selection of decorations to hang on the Christmas tree. Gianni has put up a tree in the gazebo for us to decorate and take some photographs, then you can take them home with you when you leave.'

'Oops, sorry, Izzie,' gasped Sofia, jumping up from her chair to retrieve the set of white styrofoam balls she had sent skittling to the floor.

Phoebe giggled until she saw the stern expression on Nick's face. She stopped abruptly, her hand flying to her mouth like a chastised schoolgirl, her expression of mirth frozen in situ, which caused Jennie to laugh, Dylan to smirk and Nick to roll his eyes in frustration. Izzie decided that the best thing to do was to rush on with her introduction.

'I thought we could start with these gorgeous glass baubles that Gianni's sourced from one of the famous glass-making companies we have here in Tuscany. And for those of you who would prefer to steer clear of working with glass' – she shot a quick glance in the direction of Sofia – 'I have these polystyrene balls that can be decorated with a selection of sequins, beads, pearls and pom-poms.'

Izzie held out the various sized balls to show everyone.

'I've got plenty of silver and gold glitter spray if you want to decorate these pine cones or the fir tree branches that Gianni cut from the Christmas tree this morning. There are templates over here that you can use to make wooden, cardboard or felt decorations in the shape of snowmen, reindeers and Christmas stockings. I'm also going to demonstrate how to make a cornucopia filled with golden chocolates, or you can turn it upside down and make it into a Santa Claus hat. All these items can be hung on your tree, but they can also be attached to presents as personalised gift tags, or you might prefer to save them until Thursday's crafting session when we'll be expressing our creativity with floral wreaths that can be used to adorn your front doors at home or as table decorations. I've also got slices of oranges and lemons baking in the oven if you want to make a more fragrant decoration with these cinnamon sticks and a length of floristry twine.'

'Wow, put me down for one of those,' said Jennie, picking up a stick of cinnamon and inhaling. 'Delicious. And is this sheet music? What's this for, Izzie?'

'Oh, yes, I thought you would like that. It can be used to make decorations, too. I usually brush cold coffee over the paper to give it a sepia look, then I either roll it into scrolls and tie with red ribbon, or fold it into fans, or make it into cones to put sweets inside. So, let's get started. If you'd all like to pop on your Villa Limoncello aprons, select a square of red felt fabric and, using the template, cut out a semi-circle like this.'

For the next twenty minutes, all that could be heard between Izzie's instructions were the dulcet tones of Bing Crosby as he sang songs from *White Christmas*, keeping everyone calm as they got to grips with using a glue gun to produce a conical shape from the soft material. Sofia and Dylan had chosen to make Santa hats, topped with a white pom-pom and finished off with a cotton wool fringe around the rim. Nick, Jennie and Phoebe, on the other hand, stuffed their decorated cornucopias with the gold foil-wrapped chocolates Izzie had bought from Oriana's *pasticceria* the day before. They each added a loop of red-and-white ribbon and presented their masterpieces to one other with a huge amount of pride and enthusiasm.

'Great start!' Izzie smiled, gently removing the staple gun from Sofia's hands because she had just managed to staple an off-cut of her square of felt to the red gingham tablecloth that protected Gianni's wine-tasting benches.

'Sorry!' she giggled.

'How have you not been fired yet?' laughed Phoebe, dangling her cornucopia from her index finger and considering it as though it was a work of Renaissance art. 'Or do the actors not mind about having sewn-up sleeves or non-working zips?'

'You know, when I'm in the theatre workshop, I seem to be able to channel my inner sewing bee with no problems at all. It's like I'm performing a role in a play, that it's not real life, it's a fantasy where I'm confident and proficient and dexterous!'

'Who taught you to sew?' asked Dylan, finishing off his Santa hat with a generous spray of fake snow.

'Oh, my mum and my aunt always seemed to have a pair of scissors in their hands when I was growing up and they let me have all the off-cuts to make clothes for my dolls, who, I would add, were the best-dressed Barbies in the playground! By the time I was twelve, I was making things for myself, and then for my friends. I was thrilled when my drama teacher asked if I would like to help with the costumes for our end-of-term play – it was a dream come true! Mum was so proud when she came to see it.'

'You're so lucky that your family were supportive of your dreams,' said Phoebe, her face clouding. 'All my parents wanted me to do was read law reports and the *Financial Times*!'

'Okay, I think it's time to take a coffee break before we make a start on the glass painting. You can either paint the outside of these gorgeous glass baubles, or you can fill them up with paper confetti, or hundreds and thousands, or maybe some of these sequins or beads. If you choose the polystyrene balls, or one of these perfumed wooden balls, they can be decorated with absolutely anything that takes your fancy – let your creativity fly!'

'I'm definitely investing in one of these glue guns when I get back home!' said Jennie, selecting a series of white styrofoam balls in descending sizes. 'In fact, I think I should get together a basic sewing kit – pins, needles, scissors, thread, buttons, maybe some knicker elastic – just in case.'

'I think that's an excellent idea, Jen. You never know when there's going to be a stitching emergency!' commented Dylan, his tone completely serious.

Izzie suppressed a giggle as she imagined Jennie taking up a James Bondesque stance with her glue gun, ready to fight a rampaging troop of mannequins intent upon unravelling her hand-knit jumpers, then blowing on the tip before storing it back in her hip holster – made out of Liberty-print fabric.

'Does anyone need anything from the villa?' asked Nick, wriggling out of his apron and back into his flamboyant waistcoat for the three-hundred-yard trip back to the house. He removed his beloved baton from his back pocket and stuck it behind his ear – all he needed now was a black beret and he could give Picasso a run for his money.

'I'll come with you,' said Dylan, setting aside his stash of Christmas decorations, each one perfectly executed with not a stray dollop of glue or errant stitch in sight. 'I'm sick of these cheesy Christmas songs. I've got a CD in my rucksack that I helped my brother and his band to produce a couple of months ago which I think you'll like. *Ciao!*'

'*Ciao*,' chorused the women as the door swung shut on their conversation.

'Ah, he's such a caring person, as well as an accomplished and versatile musician,' sighed Jennie as she attached a brigade of reindeers, all with enormous red pom-pom noses, to a length of crimson and green ribbon to create a very attractive Christmas garland.

'Who? Nick?' laughed Phoebe.

'No, Dylan! It's lovely to see him take some time for himself now that Jack and Martha are both at university. It doesn't surprise me at all that he's the most accomplished of all of us at the craft stuff. You have to be practical and adaptable when you're bringing up children.'

'Bringing up children?' asked Izzie, pausing in her depiction of a gift-laden sleigh in glass paint to glance across at Jennie. Dylan couldn't be more than early thirties – thirty-five at the most – much too young to have a child at university, let alone two.

'Yes, it's a sad story, I'm afraid, Izzie. Dylan's mother and father died in a hot-air balloon accident whilst on holiday in Egypt celebrating their twenty-fifth wedding anniversary. He had just turned eighteen, his sister was twelve, and Jack was only eight. Absolutely tragic. But Dylan, bless him, stepped up and became their carer, with a little help from his grandparents. Poor lad, gave up his place on a music degree course and got a job at a local high school in their IT department, but he never gave up on his dream to become a professional musician.'

'Dylan encouraged both Jack and Martha to continue with their musical studies, even helping them to start a band so they could have an outlet to express their emotions,' said Phoebe, taking up the heartbreaking story as the women continued to stick sequins and bows and feathers on their Christmas baubles, the pile in the middle of the table becoming ever taller. 'And, instead of playing gigs at uni, he uploaded his music to his YouTube channel and he's got thousands, no, hundreds of thousands, of followers.'

Phoebe paused, holding a finished bauble aloft, the colours sending a rainbow of light onto the whitewashed walls of the studio.

'But the thing I think he's most proud of is the digital media company he built up whilst staying in night after night to look after his brother, which showcases the talents of all those kids who don't have the luxury of private music lessons, those who are self-taught – naturals, Dylan calls them. He helps them to produce their tracks and then uploads them to his website. I don't think he earns much from it, but it does okay. He's an amazing musician, Izzie, and just wait until you hear him sing!'

'I told him that he should audition for *X Factor* or *BGT* last year,' added Sofia, sitting back in her chair to survey her decorations, her nose wrinkling in disappointment. 'But he just laughed, told me he had no intention of doing something as old-fashioned as TV. Of course, Nick was scathing about people who enter talent contests, but that's easy to say for someone who's had every possible advantage going to progress his musical career.'

'Does Nick have children?' asked Izzie, handing round coffees from the percolator and a plate of mince pies which, along with the plates and mugs, she had trundled down to the studio in Gianni's wheelbarrow earlier that morning.

'No. I think that's why he pushes the Somersby Singers so hard – all his hopes and dreams are wrapped up in the choir instead of his offspring.'

'Don't he and Sarah want kids?' asked Phoebe, taking a tentative sip from her coffee. 'Oh, sorry, that was a bit of a personal question.'

'Oops!' cried Sofia, as the plate of mince pies clattered to the floor, cracking on impact and sending the pies scooting under the table. Her hands flew to her mouth, her fingers trembling at her lower lip, and her face drained of all colour. She pushed back her chair, ready to drop down to start tidying up the mess when Izzie intervened.

'It's okay, Sofia, just leave it. I'll sort it!'

She retrieved the dustpan and brush from a cupboard in the corner and within moments the shards of crockery and crumbs of pastry were cleared away. Izzie smiled ruefully – the lengths people went to avoid eating her mince pies!

'I don't think it's a secret, Phoebe,' Jennie continued, flicking a worried glance at Sofia, who was still as pale as overworked pastry, 'but Nick would be mortified if he knew we were gossiping about his private life, especially as I work at the surgery where Sarah's a patient. However, I can tell you that Sarah loves children, but it just hasn't happened for them. It doesn't for some people, you know.'

'Nick really *is* focused on the choir, isn't he?' said Izzie, keen to move the conversation onto more neutral ground.

'Too much!' declared Phoebe, reaching into Izzie's Tupperware box for a mince pie and stuffing it into her mouth whole, her cheeks bulging like an overfed hamster, a gesture which filed Izzie's heart with happiness.

'Nightmare,' added Sofia, some of the colour returning to her face as she finished off her cappuccino and set down her mug with infinitesimal care. 'He's like a musical slave driver except he cracks his baton instead of a whip!'

Phoebe burst into laughter at Sofia's joke, sending flaky pastry crumbs across the table. Jennie rolled her eyes at all three of them, extracted a packet of wet wipes from her bag, handed one to Phoebe and wiped the debris away from the table with another.

'Nick just wants everyone to have the opportunity to shine!' she said, defensively. 'You know, his father was a world-renowned cellist – that's very big shoes to fill. Personally, I think he's brave even poking his nose above the parapet in the same field. He's forty-three and it's only in the last five years that he's found the confidence to do what he's been wanting to do his whole life.'

'Which is?'

'Conduct. And he's so keen to do it himself, without people saying he's riding on his father's coat-tails, that he adopted his wife's surname for professional purposes.'

'What does Nick do for a living?' asked Izzie, her heart giving a nip of sympathy for Nick – someone else who had avoided following his dreams for fear of falling short of familial expectations.

'He's a drama teacher at the local high school where Dylan teaches, and at the weekends he helps Sarah to run her children's theatre school – you know, ballet, tap, jazz, musical theatre, acting classes, that sort of thing. I think they also do cheerleading!'

'I totally get that he can't help being a perfectionist,' mused Phoebe, holding up a bauble only for every one of the buttons she'd stuck on with the aid of the glue gun to slide off and scatter onto the table. 'But we're performing in front of the residents of the local care home, or the congregation of the local church, not the Royal Albert Hall. They won't care whether we're note-perfect or not – and, if we don't tell them, half the audience probably won't notice if our outfits don't match, and the other half won't be able to hear us!'

Sofia giggled, but Jennie looked scandalised.

'No matter who our audience is, Phoebe, it's our responsibility to deliver as flawless a performance as we can – we should take pride in our choir! We want people to say that the Somersby Singers are sensational!'

'Yes, miss!' replied Sofia, and gave her a mock salute.

Jennie rolled her eyes.

'Where do you think Nick and Dylan have got to?' said Phoebe. 'I've got a bit of a headache coming on so I wouldn't mind a short siesta before this afternoon's rehearsal.'

'I'll go and see if…' began Jennie, putting down her knitting needles.

'No, you stay and finish your decorations,' said Izzie. 'I'll go, I need to collect the baked orange and lemon slices from the kitchen – they should be cold by now.'

She made her way outside and strolled towards the villa along the avenues between the grape vines, their conversation causing her head to spin. Her thoughts filled with her sister, but also with the timely reminder that she was far from alone in having lost someone she loved. Sofia had lost her mother, Dylan his parents in a dreadful accident, Jennie was divorced, even Nick had suffered a loss by omission.

In some weird way, their stories gave her a modicum of solace, that life could and did continue – not in the same way as before, in a different way, but not without happiness.

Chapter Ten

The gazebo, Villa Limoncello

Colour: Christmas-tree green

Izzie checked inside the villa, but she couldn't find Nick and Dylan and assumed she must have missed them. Maybe they'd taken a different route back to the studio. She filled a dish with the wonderfully fragrant orange and lemon slices, grabbed an extra bag of cinnamon sticks and a reel of thick brown parcel string, and made her way back through the garden, pausing when she heard voices coming from behind the Christmas tree in the gazebo.

'That's blackmail!'

'Don't be so melodramatic! All I'm asking is that you ditch the so-laid-back-you're-almost-horizontal attitude and put a bit more effort into your performance.'

'Otherwise you'll blabber about my personal life?'

'I don't know why you want to keep it quiet. What's there to be ashamed of? If it were me, I'd be singing about it from the rooftops!'

'I'm not ashamed! I just don't want my private business splashed all over the local press or buzzing its way through the village grapevine, or circulating the school corridors or the staff room, either, that's all.'

'How you think it won't eventually filter out is—'

'Look, Nick, this is none of your business. And if you had any secrets, I wouldn't dream of threatening their exposure just to secure your attendance at my choir practice!'

'*Sober* attendance.'

'You had just as much to drink last night as I did, if not more.'

Izzie could hear the snap of anger in Dylan's voice as she stood like a participant in a game of musical statues, eavesdropping on their argument. She knew she should move on and leave them to it, but some invisible force kept her glued to the spot, or it could have been what her sister used to call 'nosiness' and she used to call 'a healthy interest in other people's lives'.

'The difference is I can get up the next morning, on time, and with a clear head and a spring in my step, whereas you could hardly string two words together until Jennie came to the rescue with one of her miracle hangover potions!'

There was a pause and Izzie wondered whether Dylan was sizing up Nick for a well-directed punch on the nose for the sarcastic tone he had used. However, when he did eventually speak his voice was surprisingly conciliatory, if not apologetic.

'Okay, okay, I admit I might have overindulged. I'm sorry, I'll be more restrained on the alcohol front from now on.'

'And you'll speak to Phoebe?'

'I'm not her keeper, Nick. Anyway, why are you so stressed out about this? We've done lots of concerts over the last five years, why does this one mean so much to you? We'll all sing our hearts out, you know that, and every one of us will perform to the best of our abilities. Is there something I'm missing?'

'Only that I want us to blow the competition out of the water!'

'What competition? The Salvation Amy band? The choir from the WI? The local primary school children?'

'All of those…'

'Oh, God, Nick, I give up. I promise to reign in my alcohol consumption and to engage my very best voice, but I want a promise from you in return.'

Silence.

'Nick?'

'Okay, okay, your secret's safe with me! Now, let's get these Christmas craft shenanigans finished, so we can have lunch and start our choir practice on time this afternoon!'

Izzie didn't want Dylan and Nick to discover she had been listening in on their conversation so she dashed off towards the vineyard, the scattered seashells that Gianni swore helped the vines to grow crunching beneath her feet like crumbled biscuits. When she arrived at the studio, she was a little out of breath.

'Oh, there you all are! We were wondering whether we should send out a search party,' said Jennie, her bejewelled glasses bouncing against her chest as she reached out to grab the packet of cinnamon sticks from Izzie before it tumbled to the floor.

'Just had a couple of calls to make,' muttered Dylan, sending a narrowed glance in Nick's direction. 'We're here now – what's next, Izzie?'

'Okay, so I've got these baked orange slices for anyone who wants to attempt a more aromatic decoration. I've also found these beautiful wooden discs, which you can decorate and then personalise with a loved one's name and hang on the tree as a memory, or you could paint these miniature picture frames, then when you get home you could add a photograph or a picture that brings a smile to your face.'

Time flew by as everyone embarked on their own Christmas decoration project. Just as it was with the previous day's patisserie session, Jennie and Nick were the most proficient crafters; Jennie had even managed to knit a series of tiny red bobble hats, to each of which she attached a mini pom-pom and a curl of ribbon.

'I've made hundreds of these over the years for the premature baby unit at our local hospital.'

'Is there anything you're not involved in?' asked Nick, glancing up from the glass bauble he was painting with a selection of musical notes and instruments.

'Not much. I love getting involved!'

'What about dancing?'

Everyone was so immersed in their own craft project that Izzie was the only one to catch the glint in Nick's eye as he smirked in Jennie's direction. She looked across at Jennie, expecting her to launch into a story about the Zumba or salsa classes she attended at the gym, but instead, to her surprise, she saw Jennie's cheeks flush with heat and a shadow of dread stalk across her expression, her body crumpling back into her chair like a deflated balloon. When Izzie looked back at Nick, he had averted his eyes, but the corners of his mouth were pulled back in a gesture of satisfaction and she knew he had sent some sort of message to Jennie.

First Phoebe, then Dylan, now Jennie. Clearly, Nick had made it his business to discover his fellow choir members' triggers, secrets they would rather not have broadcast to the world. She couldn't understand why Nick would do such a horrible thing, and she was upset on their behalf that he was using those tactics to ensure they toed the line with their choir contribution.

Had Nick threatened Jennie, too, like Dylan? But what with? Exclusion from the choir? And what was her secret? She didn't think kind-hearted Jennie could have too many skeletons lurking in her closet. But then, as Meghan always said, it was usually the people you least expected who had the most exciting pasts. Perhaps that was the case with Jennie before her family had gobbled up all of her time and energy?

Oh God! Secrets – that was everyone apart from Nick!

But, didn't everyone have secrets?

And was one of the group keeping a secret about a nudge they had given to a certain flowerpot as revenge for Nick's unrelenting pressure on them to spend every spare moment, not relaxing and recharging their batteries before a series of challenging Christmas concerts, sampling the local cuisine and learning how to make limoncello as they had expected, but singing their hearts and lungs out?

'Okay, it's one o'clock. I think we should wrap things up and go and have lunch. Has everyone enjoyed their morning of Christmas crafts?'

'Yes, thank you.'

'*Sì.*'

'Yay!'

Izzie smiled and the mischievous elf on her shoulder whispered something in her ear, causing her to add, 'Well, if I've whetted your appetite for all things crafty, then you might like to take a trip to Florence while you're here to visit the Christmas market that's being held on the piazza outside the Basilica di Santa Croce. There are over fifty stalls showcasing a wide range of crafts by local artisans, from decorated candles and soaps to wooden figurines and carved musical boxes. There's lots of foodie stalls, too.'

'Wow, we can't miss that!' declared Sofia, sending Nick a belligerent glance. 'Let's drive over there after this afternoon's rehearsal. Izzie, will you come with us?'

'Of course, I'd love to.'

'What about Luca?' asked Jennie with a glint in her eyes as she gathered up the remaining craft paraphernalia and helped Izzie to store her trunk and storage boxes in the cupboard, whilst Nick and Dylan set up the studio in readiness for the arrival of the rest of the choir for that afternoon's practice. 'Will you ask him to come, too? It'll be wonderful to have a local guide to tell us all about real Italian Christmas traditions.'

'I'll ask him, but he's usually busy with the restaurant early evening.'

'Okay, so shall we meet at seven on the front steps… Oh, erm, no, shall we say the terrace?' said Phoebe, clearly not wanting a repeat of the previous day's incident.

'Perfect. Now come on, we need to change into our polo shirts.'

Jennie linked Phoebe's and Sofia's arms and they set off towards the villa, chatting excitedly about shopping for authentic Tuscan Christmas gifts, whilst Nick and Dylan brought up the rear, their arms filled with everyone's decorations.

'Here we are!'

The group stopped at the gazebo and spent a few minutes hanging their decorations on the branches of Gianni's Christmas tree before disappearing into the dining room for their lunch of home-made minestrone soup and focaccia dotted with rosemary, followed by dessert comprising of a huge *torta della nonna* with a generous dollop of mascarpone sweetened with icing sugar and flavoured with limoncello. Suitably replete, the choir dutifully retired to their rooms to change, excitement about the upcoming trip to Florence rippling through the air.

Izzie took her time clearing away the lunch plates, then washing and drying them by hand as the villa still did not have a dishwasher. When the kitchen had been returned to its pristine glory, she cut herself a slice of the *torta* and took it into the *limonaia*, where she savoured every mouthful of the delicious Italian dessert whilst inhaling the ambient aroma of the lemons that grew in huge ceramic pots all around the glasshouse.

The villa's previous owner had amassed a wide variety of lemon plants, some with skin the consistency of porridge, some sporting green stripes, and some that were almost spherical. Many were old, and a few had been there for over two hundred years! She remembered Gianni telling her the story that when Maria Rosetti had passed away, a curator from a prestigious botanical institute in Florence that housed lemon trees said to date back to the Medici family, had arrived to catalogue the trees and rescue the most valuable specimens before they were lost forever.

Izzie glanced at her watch. Luca would have finished the lunch service at Antonio's by now, so she whipped her phone from the pocket of her jeans and stared at the screen. She couldn't think of anything she would rather do than mooch around the stalls of the Santa Croce Christmas market with Luca by her side. It would be the perfect time, away from the villa and the restaurant, to talk to him – except they would not be alone.

She sighed. Never mind, it was only Tuesday – she had until Friday to carve out a slice of time for their chat. In the meantime, she planned on enjoying their trip to Firenze, a city Anna had adored so much she'd chosen to plan her hen weekend there, which sadly had never happened. Izzie had been reluctant to visit the Tuscan capital ever since, fearful of prodding at painful memories, worried about ghosts from the past lingering in the cobbled alleyways.

But a visit with Luca in the summer had made the place come alive and she adored its narrow streets, its shady courtyards and piazzas, its stunning architecture, churches and statues, its wonderful pavement cafes. She knew Anna would have loved to have explored every nook and cranny, linger over an Aperol spritz and watch the sun sink slowly over the Ponte Vecchio. Izzie was proud that she was fulfilling their dream, certain that her sister was looking down on her with a broad smile of approval, urging her to explore the city in the wintertime, to soak up the festive atmosphere, to squeeze every ounce of enjoyment out of every minute of her life and create enough memories for both of them – and so that was exactly what she intended to do.

'Hi, Luca.'

'*Ciao, Isa… bel… la.*'

'The guests have asked if you'll step into the role of tour guide for the evening and accompany them on a trip to the Santa Croce Christmas market. What do you think?'

'Fabulous idea, but I didn't think they had time in their schedule for any sightseeing?'

'I think Nick would have had a mutiny on his hands if he'd refused. Luca, I think—'

'Okay, you take the hire car and I'll meet you on the Basilica's steps at eight o'clock. I'll give Constantino a call and ask him to reserve us a table for dinner. *Ciao!*'

'*Ciao*,' she murmured, feeling the chasm between them stretch a little wider.

She heard the villa's guests making their way through the garden and towards the studio, their voices rippling through the air as they sang a rendition of 'Deck the Halls', but even their joyous melody of *fa-la-la-la-las* couldn't lift her spirits. With a heavy heart, she meandered back towards the kitchen to finalise the ingredients they would need for the next morning's demonstration of *cantucci di Prato* and gingerbread biscuits.

Chapter Eleven

Pasticceria da Oriana

Colour: Tangerine dream

Izzie lingered on the terrace outside the kitchen door, soaking up the rays of sunshine streaming down from the cerulean sky and drinking in the picturesque view in front of her. Of everything she could credit with helping her to emerge from the blanket of gloom she'd hidden beneath since losing her sister, there was one thing that ranked above all else on that list.

Sunshine.

Sunshine was the therapy she'd been unable to avoid. Seeing her life switch from Technicolor to monochrome overnight, her parents had urged her to seek bereavement counselling, to talk to someone about her pain, but the thought of spilling the raw agony that nestled in her heart to a stranger terrified her. So, she had bottled it all up, only taking the trip down to Cornwall to see her mum and dad when she absolutely had to because she hated seeing the same anguish that she felt reflected on their faces. Staying away meant she didn't have to deal with it, didn't have to be faced with a barrage of memories everywhere she turned.

She had switched her previously carefree days to a more rigid routine, setting her alarm for the same time every morning, climbing into the same outfit, collecting a skinny latte from the same cafe on the corner, going through the motions of a day at work, then falling into bed at the same time every night; no diversions, no decisions, less chance of having to summon up the energy to make choices and experience the emotions that would entail.

Of course, that coping technique had washed away her creativity sprites and left her with a dull, drab, colourless life which had filtered through into every aspect of her existence until her business was in trouble and her fiancé was at his wits' end. Alex had done everything he could to break her out of the cocoon of sorrow she'd retreated into, begging her to seek help, but in the end, they'd agreed it would be better to go their separate ways. Although she was ashamed to admit it, Alex leaving had been a relief; their relationship was just one less thing to worry about and she had been pleased when Jonti had reported last year that he was seeing someone else – Penelope – whom she liked but whose fashion choices Jonti constantly lamented.

She closed her eyes and tipped her face towards the sky, feeling her worries drain away. Her lips curled into a smile as she tuned into the cacophony of nature going about its daily business all around her, and her nose twitched with delight at the puffs of lavender and rosemary rising from the pots on the terrace steps. Now that she was there in Tuscany, surrounded by the serenity offered by Villa Limoncello, the benefits of Harry's offer receded into insignificance – a project that was someone else's dream, not hers.

Meghan's voice burst into her thoughts and she knew her friend was right – as usual, Meghan knew her better than she knew herself sometimes. It was an amazing offer, and had Harry issued it six months ago when she had plodded through her days as a home stager for Hambleton Homes, sticking to the company's brief that minimalism was the Holy Grail, then being given complete design autonomy could have been the catalyst that broke her free of her snoring boring existence.

But time had marched on. She was no longer that person and she knew with absolute certainty that her place was in Tuscany, organising and presenting courses at Villa Limoncello and until that could pay her wages, she would look for a job at one of the local cafes or restaurants so she could pay Luca rent for her room. With her decision finally made, she felt as if the block of concrete that she'd been carrying around on her shoulders had melted away; she felt light-headed, buoyant, happier than she had been for weeks. When the guests left on Friday, she would sit down with Luca, and Gianni, and draw up an itemised business plan for the following year to turn Villa Limoncello into a destination that would be the envy of the whole valley.

Optimism flowed as she thought of the courses they could offer – not just cookery classes, wine-tasting holidays and writing retreats, but photography sessions, yoga retreats or perhaps even a tennis academy. And if things went well, maybe Meghan could relocate to help with the running of the estate on a more permanent basis if her search for a job with one of Florence's fashion houses didn't work out. The inclusion of a potential yoga retreat at Villa Limoncello sent her thoughts scooting to her friend Oriana, San Vivaldo's patisserie princess.

Izzie made a decision.

A trip to San Vivaldo was exactly what she needed! Humming the chorus from 'I Wish it Could be Christmas Everyday', she spun on her heels and went in search of the little pink Vespa that had become her companion since arriving at the villa. She loved it – even the helmet that made her curls look like she'd sustained an electric shock when she took it off! She couldn't wait to see Oriana to chat through her decision to stay on in Italy, to ask for her advice on the classes she had planned, and to treat herself to a slice of her amazing tiramisu.

As she navigated the twists and turns of the roads that led up to the hilltop village, her contentment spiralled. The Snowflakes & Christmas Cakes course was back on track and, whilst there were still three days left to go and anything could go wrong, she was optimistic that the first Christmas course would be a success, if she discounted the freak accident with the flowerpot as it seemed everyone else was doing.

She parked the Vespa in a space right outside Oriana's *pasticceria*, a palace of sugary magnificence that drew the eye to the plate glass window to drool over the kaleidoscope of culinary gems on display. It was more like a high-end jewellery shop than a village bakery, with row upon row of colourful pastries, boxes of sugared almonds and slabs of nougat all wrapped in cellophane and tied with festive ribbons. She pushed open the door and inhaled the sweet caramelly aroma, tinged with roasted pistachios and a top note of vanilla.

'*Ciao, Izzie!*'

Izzie leaned forward to greet Oriana, marvelling at her lean muscular figure, courtesy of the daily yoga routines she taught in the studio behind the shop. It was the perfect partnership – an hour of yoga then a guilt-free treat from the store on the way home.

'*Ciao*, Oriana, do you have time for a coffee?'

'Sure, come through to the studio.'

Izzie followed Oriana, her back ramrod straight as she led her to the rear of the bakery, her glossy mahogany hair swishing against her shoulder blades as she walked. She was so immaculately turned out that she could have easily graced the cover of a magazine without any additional tweaks, but her attractive features and toned muscles belied her ability to cut through all extraneous nonsense and deliver straightforward nuggets of advice or solutions. She was an environmental crusader, a vociferous locavore and a lover of vegan desserts which had thrilled some of Villa Limoncello's previous guests. Izzie also had Oriana to thank for rescuing her from the most embarrassing mistake of her life when she had been under the impression that the film shoot she'd thought she was organising for Meghan's brother was in fact a real-life celebrity wedding.

'How's the course going? I heard there'd been a bit of a hiccup.'

Whilst Oriana prepared their coffees, Izzie recounted the details of the flowerpot incident before moving swiftly on to talk about that morning's craft session.

'Ergh, what's this? It's not coffee!' she exclaimed, peering at the pale-yellow water that smelled suspiciously like cat's pee.

'It's chamomile tea, infused with peppermint! And it's much better for you than all that espresso you consume – I'm surprised you get any sleep,' Oriana laughed, dropping down onto one of the bright green bean bags next to Izzie. 'Did Luca use the *panforte* tartlet recipe yesterday?'

'Yes, the guests loved them.'

'It was one of my mother's recipes. She'll be thrilled. What's on the menu for tomorrow?'

'*Cantucci di Prato*, and then tiramisu with a Christmas twist on Friday before everyone leaves for home and the first of their Christmas concerts on Saturday night.'

'Quite a few of the choir members have called in to the patisserie after their various activities, and I must say they seem to be a very committed bunch. I thought they were here to have fun, sample the local wine, indulge in the culture and art, and the skiing, increase their harmony in both senses of the word.'

'Nick, the choir leader, is a perfectionist.'

'Ah, I can identify with that particular character trait. Nothing wrong with aiming for excellence,' laughed Oriana, sipping her tea, glancing at Izzie over the rim of her cup. 'So, how are things with Luca?'

Izzie rolled her eyes. No wonder Oriana and Meghan got on so well. They were both proponents of the maxim 'cut straight to the chase' when wanting the inside track.

'Great. We're learning how to work in tandem when we co-present the courses. I think Monday morning's session went really well, so I hope the others do too. I've spent weeks trying to perfect my recipes, but I'll definitely not be winning a place at Le Cordon Bleu in Paris any time soon! I've also been thinking about other ideas for classes at the villa. How would you feel about hosting a yoga retreat? Or presenting a course on vegan cookery?'

'Have you spoken to Luca about your ideas?'

'No, not yet, but…'

'But what?'

Oriana crossed her slender legs, encased in skinny white jeans, and pushed up the fluted sleeves of her tangerine blouse. However, in Izzie's opinion, the best item of her attire was the *Pasticceria da Oriana* apron, white with a tiny pink angel embroidered on the front.

'Well, I've made a decision.'

'What about?'

'About the job my old boss has offered me.'

'Creative director?'

'Yes.'

'And…'

'I'm not going to take it.'

'You're not?'

'No, I want to stay here, Oriana. I want to devote all my time and effort into making Villa Limoncello the best venue in the area for retreats, courses, maybe even start a tennis academy, or host a volleyball competition, or a netball match, when we get around to renovating the courts. What do you think?'

Izzie experienced a wriggle of concern when Oriana didn't leap up from her seat to embrace her, to tell her how pleased she was that she was staying on in Tuscany or bombard her with a myriad of other suggestions.

'I'm glad you're staying, Izzie…'

'You don't seem very excited.'

Izzie scrutinised her friend's face and saw she was struggling with something.

'What's the matter?'

'I really think you should talk to Luca before you call Harry.'

'I've tried to talk to Luca, Oriana, believe me, but, well, he's acting a bit…'

'A bit what?'

'Weird, you know, distant, aloof, cool. Every time I try to guide the conversation around to the future, he changes the subject or does something crazy.'

'Crazy?'

'Like yesterday, for instance, he grabbed my hand and plunged us both into Riccardo's pool – fully clothed!'

'Ah, that's so romantic!'

'Romantic? It was freezing!'

'But I'm sure Luca's scorching hot body heat kept you warm as you floated together in a sizzling passionate embrace, the ripples of the water caressing your skin and whipping your desire into a frenzy of—'

'Oriana!' Izzie laughed, enjoying the burst of attraction that spun all the way out to her fingertips whenever Luca was the focus of a conversation. 'Anyway, what I'm saying is, one minute he's buying me sunflowers and a cute knitted donkey hat, and the next he's zooming away in his Spider like a bat out of hell!'

Izzie saw Oriana's eyes cloud over and her stomach dropped.

'Is there something you're not telling me? Have I blundered into another massive mistake?'

'Well...'

Oriana paused again, indecision stalking across her face as she fiddled with the handle of her mug before placing it on the floor next to her bean bag and turning to meet Izzie's eyes. She parted her lips, then closed them again, clearly wrestling with her conscience.

'Oriana! Tell me what's going on! All this secrecy stuff is driving me nuts!'

'What secrecy stuff?'

'It seems like everyone around me is hiding some deep dark secret that they're at pains to conceal – apart from Gianni, that is. At the moment, I think he's topping the league as the most open and straightforward person I know. But, getting back to my question – what's going on with Luca?' And then it hit her. Oh God, surely not. 'Has he... has he met someone else?'

Oriana obviously hadn't been expecting their conversation to swerve off on quite such an obtuse tangent because her eyes widened and her jaw dropped.

'No! No, Izzie, it's nothing like that. Oh, my God, I told him he should tell you when he picked you up from the airport!'

'Tell me what?'

'I'm so sorry, Izzie, Luca's selling the villa.'

For a moment, Izzie wasn't sure whether she had heard right.

'Sorry, Izzie.'

She opened her mouth to say something but her thoughts had scattered, bouncing in confusion around her head, and she couldn't put together the words to express her shock. Okay, so she knew things were difficult after the Wine & Words course had been cancelled, but selling the villa? After everything they had done to breathe new life into the house and the studio? Why? Why would Luca do that? Then, her brain reconnected to its modem and the full implication of what Oriana had just told her dawned.

Gianni!

'But what about Gianni? What about his olive trees and his vineyard? He's just had his first successful *vendemmia*! His wine is going to be the best Chianti Tuscany ever tasted!'

Her heart gave a painful squeeze. She just couldn't bear to think of the look on Gianni's face when he found out about Luca's decision to sell, but then equally she couldn't believe he didn't know already – if Oriana did. Luca was his best friend; they had travelled together, side by side, along life's twisted highway since kindergarten.

'You need to talk to Luca, Izzie.'

'Does Gianni know?'

'Yes, he—'

'So why didn't *he* say something?'

'I suppose he thought it was up to Luca to tell you. But, Izzie, he's not selling the vineyard or the olive grove and studio, just the villa and the gardens.'

'And the *limonaia*,' whispered Izzie, imagining her favourite place in the world being turned into a sumptuous conservatory in which discerning holidaymakers took their evening aperitifs whilst gazing at the best view in Tuscany.

What would happen to the lemon trees? Some of them were rare and others had called the glasshouse their home for over two hundred years! Oh God, she couldn't bear to think of them being thrown into a skip with everything else in the villa that bore the label 'careworn'.

'Izzie, why don't you go over to Antonio's now and talk to Luca about all this? The lunch will have—'

'Do you know if he's found a buyer yet?'

'I'm not...'

But Izzie could tell from Oriana's expression that he had. He'd probably sold it to one of his former banking colleagues keen to add another asset to his portfolio of luxury items. Dilapidated villa in Tuscany – tick. Tennis court – tick. Columned gazebo – tick. Ancient *limonaia* – tick.

Suddenly, she was ambushed by a whoosh of emotion. Tears prickled at her lashes, and despite being grateful to

Oriana for putting her in the picture – again – she was beginning to feel claustrophobic in the windowless yoga studio as a plethora of questions started to circle her brain. She desperately needed to escape from her friend's sympathetic gaze otherwise she feared she might crumble into an inelegant mess on her polished wooden floor. So, forcing a smile on her lips, she abandoned her mug of herbal tea and pushed herself out of the beanbag's embrace.

'Thanks for the tea, Oriana.'

'Izzie, wait, why don't I come with you to the trattoria?'

'No, no, it's fine. I'll go and have a chat with Luca before I go back to the villa.'

'Are you sure you're okay?'

'Of course, and thank you. Thank you for telling me, Oriana, especially before I rang Harry to turn down his offer. You saved me from a grovelling telephone call.'

'Izzie…'

They had arrived on the threshold of the shop, mercifully empty of drooling customers. The wonderful display of Italian pastries, crunchy biscotti, panettone dotted with chocolate or sultanas, and Christmas confectionary had completely lost its lure for Izzie.

In fact, she felt nauseous.

Whilst she was shocked that Luca was selling the villa, financially at least, it had probably been inevitable. No, what had stunned her to the core was the fact that he hadn't told her, hadn't sought her thoughts or her support after taking such a difficult, and no doubt painful, decision. Okay, Luca owned the villa, not her, but she had, mistakenly as it turned out, thought she had meant more to him, thought they had a deeper connection than a mere passing friendship or someone who visited occasionally to present the creative side of their courses.

Sadness swept through her body as she turned to hug Oriana goodbye and stepped out into San Vivaldo's cobbled piazza. Despite her assurances to Oriana, she couldn't face having the conversation with Luca right then. She needed time to process the new information, but even more importantly she needed the space to reassess her feelings for the man who had come to mean so much to her, but who clearly didn't feel the same way.

Chapter Twelve

Piazza Santa Croce, Firenze

Colour: Nutmeg brown

'Wow! This place is fabulous!' declared Jennie, bundled up against every weather eventuality in her sensible velvet-collared coat, a pair of neat leather gloves and a woollen beret set at a jaunty angle. With her trusty canvas bag hooked over her shoulder, her eyes shone as she surveyed the wooden, chalet-style stalls in the Piazza Santa Croce.

'I'm glad I brought my credit card!' laughed Phoebe, who looked like she was about to address a business conference in her navy gaberdine trench coat that Izzie recognised as Prada. 'Oh, God, I haven't been shopping for months, I can't wait!'

'Me neither!' declared Sofia, giggling as Nick and Dylan exchanged an eye roll.

Unlike the women, who had dressed with practicality in mind, Nick had chosen to wear a beautifully cut cream-coloured dinner jacket with emerald green lining and a matching paisley cravat, looking every inch the would-be celebrity choir conductor. At least he'd left his baton at villa!

Izzie stood at the back of the excited group, listening to Luca explain a little about the history of the magnificent Basilica di Santa Croce that presided over the Christmas market, including the fact that it was the final resting place of Michelangelo.

A sharp nip had invaded the air, but that wasn't why Izzie's body and senses were numb. She had tried her utmost to act naturally, to keep a smile on her face, to nod in all the right places but, ironically, she was aware that she was acting in exactly the same way as Luca had been acting since she'd arrived in Tuscany: standoffish, aloof and jittery. Whilst before Oriana had informed her of Villa Limoncello's imminent sale, she would have wanted nothing more than to break away from the rest of the group and spend her time in Florence mooching around the market with Luca as her personal guide, now she was keen to stick with the group and avoid Luca's question-filled gaze, fearful that once she spoke to him about his decision, it would be true.

Avoidance, for the time being at least, was her preferred way to deal with the news until she'd had time to come to terms with the fact that her future was not going to be in Tuscany, or with Luca.

'Hey, look at this!'

Jennie broke away from the group to investigate the stall selling all things wooden, from tiny alpine houses to cooking utensils such as spoons, spatulas, whisks and rolling pins, from decorated place mats to hand-turned bowls and cruet sets. There were even a couple of guitars hanging from the eaves which caught Dylan's eye.

'I'm going to buy one of these chopping boards for Maggie at the surgery!'

When Jennie had made her purchase, they moved on, exclaiming at the range of foodie treats on offer: the local cheeses, the nougat spotted with pistachios and almonds, the Italian breads, the German sausages, the apple strudel, the huge candy lollipops. They marvelled at the craftsmanship of the painted glass ornaments, the paper lanterns, the fresh-flower-filled soaps and candles, the hand-decorated Russian dolls. Everywhere Izzie looked there was something new to discover, accompanied by the delicious scent of Christmas fragrances: warm mulled wine, cinnamon, cloves, baked orange peel, all to the backing track of animated conversation in a variety of languages.

'Oh, wow, aren't these gorgeous!'

Phoebe had stopped at a stall selling handmade jewellery, the necklaces, bracelets and rings sparkling under the twinkling lights that framed the kiosk making it look like a fairy-tale grotto. Whilst the women oohed and ahhed at the earrings adorned with crystal snowflakes, the men investigated the adjacent stall, piled high with heavy hessian sacks containing every spice an avid student of culinary delights could wish for – paprika, cumin, cardamom, dried oregano, star anise, whole nutmegs and nobbles of ginger.

'Okay, so is everyone ready to eat?'

'Yes, I'm starving!' declared Sofia, surreptitiously sneaking a pretzel into her coat pocket.

'*Bene*. I've booked a table at Ristorante Constantino, which is just a few streets away.'

The group followed Luca as he guided them through the maze of narrow, cobbled alleyways that Florence was famous for, the sand-coloured façades of the buildings decked in garlands of fairy lights or projected images of Christmas scenes as part of the annual luminaire.

'Hey, Luca what's this?'

'Ah, yes, that's a *presepe* – a nativity scene. You'll see them all over Florence, in churches, shops, banks, restaurants, even the railway station has one. Every Italian family has a *presepe* in their home at Christmas, and every one is different. Some are simple and feature Mary, Joseph, the three wise men, the shepherds and their flock, an ox, a donkey and an angel, but some families really go to town, staging a whole village in their living room complete with lights and music, rivers and waterfalls and peopled with a wide cast of characters.'

'Characters?'

'*Sì*,' laughed Luca, really getting into his stride as he relayed his festive traditions. 'I have a friend whose family include painted wooden figurines of a wine merchant, a fisherman, a pizza maker, a butcher, a baker…'

'A candlestick maker?' teased Jennie.

'Possibly. Anything goes; my cousin's girlfriend's family have plaster models of sports stars and actors, such as

Leonardo DiCaprio, and they add to their collection every year, combing the stores for quirky figures to include the following Christmas. But one thing remains the same – Baby Jesus is only added one minute before midnight on Christmas Eve.'

'Well, that makes sense,' said Dylan, pausing to stare into the window of a shop selling a jumble of musical instruments.

Fortunately for the rest of the group, it was closed and a few minutes later they had arrived at a narrow doorway that sported a rectangular brass plaque but otherwise would not have advertised itself as a restaurant. However, as soon as Izzie stepped through the door, the warmth enveloped her, along with the delicious perfume of red wine, roasted garlic and fresh ciabatta, and her stomach rumbled. A muted ripple of conversation drifted around the stone walls of the main dining room, but the group was shown to a covered courtyard at the rear of the restaurant where a table had been prepared with pristine white table linen and sparkling cutlery and glassware.

The meal was delicious, but Izzie struggled to eat, the whole event passing by like a scene in a dream. She laughed at Dylan's stories about the exploits of his brother's band, smiled when Nick talked about the Christmas pantomime his drama students were putting on for local children who would not otherwise get to see a show, and sympathised with Sofia's attempts at writing her own stage play. Every time she chanced a peek in Luca's direction, he seemed to be staring at her, his eyes narrowed as though he could read everything that was spinning through her mind, that he knew that she knew.

When the *cantucci* and Vin Santo were being handed round, Izzie demurred, preferring to stick to the rich, red local Chianti that Nick had selected to accompany their meal as she listened to Phoebe tell Jennie about a divorce case one of her friends had handled.

'And, do you know what the wife did when she found out about his adultery?'

'No?'

'Well, before her ex came round to the house to collect his belongings, she painstakingly unpicked the lining from every one of his Savile Row suits and threaded the hems and cuffs with anchovies before re-sewing them up and replacing them back in the suit carriers that she'd generously sorted out for him. It's such a small thing, but it gave her a modicum of satisfaction.'

'I wish I'd had the courage to do something like that,' murmured Jennie, her voice cracking slightly on the last word.

'Oh my God, Jennie, I'm so sorry. I completely forgot…'

'It's okay, Phoebe, Tim and I are still on civil terms – just. Although when he told me that he and Lydia are spending Christmas at a five-star hotel in the Caribbean, I nearly bashed him over the head with my cycle helmet. You know, we were married for almost twenty years and we never once had a foreign holiday. Oh, the boys didn't mind, they loved camping in mud-soaked fields in the middle of nowhere, hoping for clear skies so they could use their father's latest telescope to stare at the stars. Obsessed, they were! I always thought they'd go off and study astronomy at university.'

'What are they studying?' asked Izzie, relieved to see the distress melt away from Jennie's friendly face now the conversation had turned to her twin boys.

'Ben is studying law at Durham and Daniel is studying accountancy – neither of them wanted to follow their dad into pharmacy. In fact, since they found out about his affair with his secretary, they've avoided visiting him in the holidays. I've tried to talk to them about it, tried to reassure them that their father's love life has no bearing on his relationship with them, but Ben in particular is appalled.'

'Jennie, it's up to Ben and Daniel whether or not they want to see Tim,' said Phoebe gently, placing her hand on the older woman's arm. 'They'll be twenty-one next year – they're men who know their own minds and can make their own decisions.'

'But they'll always be my little boys. I know they're both forging ahead with their lives and I'm overwhelmingly proud of them, but I miss them so much, especially now that Tim's gone. The house sometimes feels like a mausoleum without their happy, cheerful voices singing along to that god-awful music they listen to, or their heavy feet hammering on the stairs, or the laundry piled high on top of the basket instead of inside!'

Tears sparkled along Jennie's lower lashes, but she flicked them away in irritation, taking a sip of her Chianti to steady her emotions.

'I know it's the natural progression of life, and I would be mortified if they thought their mum was sitting at home, in her empty nest, surrounded by memories and dashed dreams, feeling sorry for herself.'

'But you're not! You're sitting in a restaurant in Florence with a bunch of fabulously talented singers, drinking prosecco and munching on *cantucci*! You have a busier schedule than I do, and that's saying something! Aren't you off on a charity trek to Machu Picchu in March? Then you have that cycle ride across India with the girls from the gym. If you and Tim were still together, would you be doing any of those things?'

Jennie laughed. 'Of course not! We'd probably have bought a motorhome and be trailing around all the Dark Sky Parks of the British Isles!' She shivered at the very thought, which made Phoebe and Izzie giggle. 'I want you to know how grateful I am to you, Phoebe, and all the other members of the Somersby Singers.'

'What for?'

'For the wonderful camaraderie, for the joy that singing in the choir gives me, for that rush of adrenalin I feel before the first note is expelled, for the elation that buzzes through my veins when we're in full voice, for the happiness I see reflected on everyone's faces – ours and the audience's. I love how we all lead such diverse lives, but when we're singing, we come together as one;

all our troubles just seem to evaporate for that one perfect moment.'

'It is amazing, isn't it?'

'I don't think I could have got through the last year without you all.'

And this time it was Phoebe who had to dab away her tears.

Chapter Thirteen

Ristorante Constantino, Firenze

Colour: Marble grey

When every last drop of Chianti, and a full bottle of grappa, had been drained and the dinner finally came to an end, all five guests were in exuberant spirits and readily agreed to Luca's suggestion that they take a moonlit saunter through the streets and piazzas of Florence, to marvel at Il Duomo and Giotto's beautiful bell tower, to take photographs of the forest of Renaissance architecture that filled the city, and to soak up the vibrant atmosphere that seemed to resonate through the medieval stones.

'*Ciao, Constantino! Grazie mille!*' the group chorused as they left the *ristorante*, pausing briefly on the threshold to inhale the cool night air after the warmth of the restaurant before ambling down the cobbled alleyway in the direction of Piazza del Duomo.

Luca took the lead, continuing his tour guide role, chatting to Jennie, Phoebe and Sofia about growing up in such an amazing city, whilst Dylan and Nick argued about their favourite Italian operas and Izzie, struggling into her coat, brought up the rear, her thoughts on other things. A mere twenty metres down the street, Izzie came to an abrupt halt, shock ambushing her progress as her heart crashed against her ribcage, causing her to catch her breath.

'Oh my God! Nick!' she cried, her hand flying to her mouth. 'Are you, are you… okay?'

She rushed forward and Nick spun round towards her, a quizzical look on his face.

'What…'

'Argh!' screamed Sofia and Phoebe in unison.

'What's going on?' asked Dylan, standing shoulder to shoulder with Nick, looking from Izzie to Phoebe and back again.

Then he saw it too, and instead of jumping to the conclusion that Izzie, Phoebe and Sofia had, he burst out laughing, as did Luca when he inspected the back of Nick's previously pristine cream jacket which now had a slash of what Izzie had thought was blood – although she had no intention of admitting that to anyone – but which was in fact a generous splatter of red wine. It was a mistake anyone could make, she reasoned to herself, particularly against the backdrop of the earlier flowerpot incident.

'Will someone enlighten me, please?' blustered Nick, his puzzled expression shifting to one of concern with a soupçon of annoyance.

Fortunately, Jennie swiftly rode to the rescue.

'Sorry, Nick. It looks like someone's spilled a glass of red wine down the back of your jacket whilst we were having dinner in the restaurant.'

'Ahhh...' giggled Sofia, exchanging a smirk with Phoebe and Izzie.

'We have to act quickly or it'll stain. Take it off.'

Jennie bustled over to a vacant table outside a tiny trattoria where she spent a few seconds rummaging in her bag as Nick removed his jacket and inspected the damage, his forehead creasing into parallel lines. Izzie didn't care if Dylan and Luca thought she was crazy – it definitely looked like blood to her!

'Here we are,' declared Jennie, whipping out a tiny glass bottle filled with white powder.

'I don't think the answer is to get Nick high,' laughed Dylan, wriggling his eyebrows.

Jennie ignored his attempt at humour and got to work with the bicarbonate of soda and a bottle of water she also carried with her in her Tardis-like bag whilst the group looked on in fascination, especially Luca.

'I could do with you in my *ristorante*!'

Within minutes, the stain had vanished, and Nick thanked Jennie profusely, having confided the fact that the dinner jacket had cost over a month's wages when he'd bought it, something he hadn't mentioned to Sarah, telling her instead he'd picked it up in a charity shop.

'Your secret is safe with me.' She beamed, clearly delighted to have been able to help. 'Now, shall we get back to our tour?'

'Yes, let's!' declared Sofia, linking Jennie's arm with hers.

Izzie walked alongside Jennie and Sofia, listening but not joining in with their conversation, thoughts bombarding her brain. She knew accidents happened in restaurants, but surely the waiters in Constantino's were much too adept to inadvertently splatter a patron's jacket with Chianti. She had seen them weave in and out of the tables, their platters of food held high, as dexterous as Olympic gymnasts. Did that mean that the wine-spilling incident was not an accident, that someone had *intentionally* chucked a glass of notoriously difficult-to-remove red wine at Nick's very expensive designer jacket?

If that was the case, then it had to be one of the four people currently admiring the marble statues in the Piazza della Signoria. They all had secrets they were anxious to keep – she knew that already. Was this one of them sending a second, wine-infused warning to Nick to keep quiet?

No, no, no, she chastised herself. What had happened with Nick and the kamikaze flowerpot was making her jump to ridiculous conclusions – the spillage had to be just an unfortunate coincidence because the alternative didn't bear thinking about. She shoved her suspicions into the crevices of her mind and resolved to enjoy what was left of the evening without reading calamity into innocent scenarios.

'Why are there so many statues of naked guys?' asked Sofia, giggling as she rushed up to embrace one of them before handing her phone over to Dylan so he could take a picture of her for her Instagram page.

'Hey, I'll have you know that these are works of art created by some of Italy's finest Renaissance sculptors!' said Luca with mock indignation.

As they strolled across the Ponte Vecchio, Phoebe and Dylan split away from the group to lean over the parapet and look down to the River Arno below, their heads, smooth blonde-on-black curls, tipped towards each other as they chatted, as though they inhabited a world where no one else mattered. Izzie saw the way Dylan looked at Phoebe when he thought she wasn't looking, and she wondered why no one else had noticed.

Something else that caught her eye was the way Sofia made a concerted effort to avoid Nick, sticking resolutely to Jennie's side at the market, making sure she grabbed the seat between Dylan and Luca at the table at the restaurant, and now, as they paused for Phoebe to drool over the gold jewellery in the shop windows on the bridge, hooking her arm through Izzie's. But then Nick did give the impression of a sturdy oak overshadowing a young sapling. Leaving aside the jacket incident, that evening he'd been boisterous company, keeping everyone entertained with his knowledge of the exploits of the Medici family, the reasons the dynasty had died out, as well as regaling them with anecdotes of his summer placement at the Giuseppe Verdi conservatory of music in Milan whilst studying for his degree, even singing on the stage at La Scala.

Eventually, they arrived at the train station where they had parked the hire car and started to pile in, the whole group laughing as Sofia managed to stumble from the kerb and fall into the arms of a very handsome passing stranger.

'Izzie?'

Luca reached out to stop her from squeezing into the back seat next to Phoebe. She smiled at him, raising her eyebrows in question.

'How about a nightcap? I can take you home in the Spider later.'

'Ooh,' came a chorus of comedic heckling from inside the car, before everyone dissolved into alcohol-fuelled giggles, apart from Dylan, who was their designated driver.

Izzie rolled her eyes at them, but her emotions were trouncing her decision-making abilities. What should she do? Go home with her guests so she could avoid a very difficult conversation until she'd had time to sleep on everything Oriana had told her that afternoon and she came up with a well thought-through plan? Or go for a drink with Luca to hear what he had to say?

'Please, Izzie.'

His eyes, the colour of rich espresso, held hers, willing her to say yes, and despite her reservations, there had only ever been one answer.

'Okay, thank you.'

As the hire car zipped away into the traffic, Izzie smiled at the choral refrain.

'*Buonasera!*'

'*Buona notte!*'

'*Ciao!*'

'*Arrivederci!*'

She linked her arm through Luca's and they strolled along the wide pavements towards a tiny cafe off one of the side streets where Luca was greeted like a long-lost member of the family, handed a bottle of amaro and left in peace. Izzie watched him pour two glasses of the golden liquid, then decided to jump in before he had chance to select their topic of conversation – she had to know what Luca's take was on what had happened at Constantino's.

'What do you think of the Chianti incident?'

'What do you mean?' Luca wrinkled his nose in question.

'Do you think it was an accident?'

'Yes, what else could it be? Accidents happens in busy restaurants.' There was a pause whilst Luca studied Izzie's expression and realised what she was thinking. 'You think someone did this on purpose, don't you?'

'I…'

'Because of the falling plant pot?'

'It's… well, it's a possibility.'

'That someone is targeting Nick for some reason?'

'Maybe,' she murmured, suddenly realising how ludicrous it sounded when someone said it out loud and, with a surge of relief, she resolved to let it go. 'No, you're right, sorry, I'm just overthinking things.'

Silence descended. Izzie took a sip of her drink, watching Luca's fingers toy with his glass until eventually he raised his gaze to meet hers, his eyes filled with anguish. Of course, she knew what he was going to say and she suddenly wanted to make it as easy as she could for him.

'Izzie, there's something I need to tell you.'

'It's okay, Luca, I know.'

'You do?'

'Yes, Oriana told me this afternoon.'

'What did she tell you exactly?'

'That you're selling the villa.'

She watched Luca run his palm over the dark stubble on his chin, and the scorch of pain that flashed through his eyes caused a tumbling sensation to rush through her body.

'I'm sorry, Izzie, I should have told you. I planned to talk to you on the way back from the airport, then last night when we ended up in Riccardo's pool, but well... I just couldn't find the right words.'

'So, have you found a buyer?'

'Yes, one of my former colleagues from the bank has made me an offer.'

She knew it! But the fact she had been right gave her no satisfaction whatsoever. Her breath caught in her throat, but she forced her head to rule her heart – after all, selling the villa *was* the sensible solution. Luca had bought Villa dei Limoni as a home for him and his then fiancée, Sabrina. When he'd unveiled his investment, Sabrina had been horrified that he wanted to quit the corporate rat race for a more relaxed lifestyle in the Tuscan hills and she had refused to live in a run-down old villa, so Luca had closed it up and not set foot in the house for two years.

No one in San Vivaldo, apart from Gianni, who had agreed to manage the vineyard and olive groves, knew who had bought Villa dei Limoni from the American guy who had inherited the property from his distant relation,

Maria Rosetti. It was the American who had changed the name of the place to Villa Limoncello in the hope of making it more marketable to his wealthy compatriots seeking their own little slice of Tuscan paradise.

Luca hadn't stayed in the banking industry, but had decided to follow his life-long dream of becoming a chef and owning his own restaurant – much to the dismay of his parents, and his fiancée, who had moved on to a relationship with one of Luca's more financially ambitious friends. So, all Luca was doing was what he should have done two years ago when Sabrina refused to contemplate spending her life there – selling the place to someone who *did* want to live within its idyllic walls.

Except Izzie had fallen in love with the villa, with its quirky bedrooms decorated in a riot of sunflowers, or roses, or lavender – walls, ceiling and doors – and its pretty formal gardens filled with honeysuckle and bougainvillea and magnolia bushes, its whitewashed gazebo where she'd taught her summer painting sessions, the cute wishing well, the *limonaia*… and with its owner, Luca Castelotti.

Stop – wait!

But it was true. She'd fallen in love with the Villa dei Limoni's handsome, thoughtful, funny, spontaneous owner who had taught her that loss and grief, like love and joy, were all part of life's rich tapestry, and now, just as she had learned to accept that and move on, she had to force herself to focus on a different future, one probably in Cornwall.

'I know you're upset, Izzie. Tell me what's going through your mind?'

But how could she tell him that only that afternoon she'd decided to turn down Harry's offer, that she wanted to stay on in Tuscany when that wasn't an option any more? It would just make Luca feel bad and what was the point of that? No, she would squeeze every last ounce of enjoyment out of the remaining time she had in Italy, and gather as many memories as she could before she launched into a new chapter of her life.

'Nothing, nothing, it's all good.'

'I'm sorry, Izzie, but this way you can take up Harry's offer and be with your family. It's what they want, isn't it? It's an exciting prospect, don't you think?'

'Yes, yes, it is,' she managed, not wanting to look Luca in the eye, fearing that if she did, the white lie she had just told him so that her own scuppered dreams wouldn't weigh on his conscience would unravel. After everything he'd done for her, she couldn't, and wouldn't, add to his problems. 'I've actually got lots of ideas for the project – chalk-white walls, fresh beachside colours for the paintwork, rush matting on the floors. I can't wait to get started.'

'That's great. Okay, shall we get going?'

Outside, the night air was sharp, mingled with a sweet tang of roasted tomatoes and garlic. As they made their way back to the station, Luca slung his arm around Izzie's shoulders and she snuggled into the crook of his arm, relishing the warmth and the whiff of his cologne and the tannin of his leather jacket. Looking up to the star-filled sky, she experienced an overwhelming certainty that her sister was watching her, urging her not to let that moment pass.

So, when they arrived in the Piazza Santa Maria Novella, she stopped, stretched up onto her tiptoes and kissed Luca, savouring the way her body reacted when he kissed her back, but failing to see the expression of deep sadness in Luca's dark brown eyes.

Chapter Fourteen

The kitchen, Villa Limoncello

Colour: Crunchy gingerbread

Izzie tightened the strings on her apron before taking her place at the head of the farmhouse table in the middle of Villa Limoncello's kitchen. That morning, when she had flung open her bedroom shutters to greet the new day and breathe in the morning air, a feeling of complete serenity had suffused her soul. Yes, she was upset that Luca was selling the villa, but it was up to her to be supportive of his decision, to bolster his spirits and to make sure the remainder of the course went without a hitch.

With a spring in her step and a jaunty Christmas tune ringing in her ears, she reminded herself how lucky she was, how fortunate to even have had the opportunity to spend time there, to come to terms with the grief that had threatened to strangle the life out of her, and to make the friends she had – just because the villa was being sold didn't mean she couldn't come back to San Vivaldo for a visit.

At exactly ten o'clock, their guests presented themselves at the scrubbed wooden table in the kitchen for their second patisserie class. A ripple of Italian opera circled the room as Izzie busied herself removing the cling film from the bowls of ingredients she'd prepared at six thirty that morning, which would form the basis for creating the *cantucci di Prato* that Luca would be demonstrating, as well as a batch of her special-recipe gingerbread that they would cut into snowmen and reindeer shapes, then decorate with piped icing before wrapping them in cellophane and ribbon to give as gifts.

When she'd finished her task, she glanced around the table and realised for the first time that the atmosphere was subdued, the conversation either muted or non-existent, and their guests were clearly unable to meet each other's eyes.

'Does anyone know where Jennie is?' asked Luca, looking even more attractive that morning with the cuffs of his linen shirt – in a gorgeous pale lemon colour – rolled up to his elbows to reveal strong muscular forearms covered in a ripple of dark hair that sent Izzie's senses into overdrive. 'Phoebe?'

Phoebe exchanged a glance with Dylan and then sent a scathing glare in the direction of Nick, who had the grace to blush.

'I don't know whether she's coming to the class this morning,' said Phoebe, her voice tight with anger. 'I did give her a knock to see if she wanted to have breakfast with me and Sofia on the terrace, but she said she was going to give it a miss.'

'And it's all Nick's stupid fault!' blurted Sofia, her tiger-like eyes blazing.

'What's going on?' asked Luca, pausing in the middle of emptying a bag of pistachios onto a baking tray as he prepared to launch into his demonstration of how to prepare the first of their recipes.

No one replied, but everyone stared expectantly at Nick.

'Izzie, do you want to go upstairs to see if she's okay?'

'Sure…'

'No, I'll go,' said Sofia, dropping the slab of white chocolate she'd been breaking into chunks and flouncing out of the room.

'Would anyone like to enlighten us?'

'Nick? Do you want to tell Izzie and Luca what you did last night – in front of the whole choir?' snapped Phoebe, her upper lip curling in disgust.

'Not really,' he muttered.

It was the first time Izzie had seen him display reluctance when invited to take the floor, his face bathed in embarrassment. Even that day's waistcoat showcased a rainbow of muted blues and purples, and his beloved baton was nowhere to be seen. His eyes were baggy and bloodshot, and when he reached up to run his fingers through his hair his hand trembled.

'Then I will!' said Phoebe, her hands on her waist as she turned to confront him. 'You should be ashamed of yourself, Nick. What you did was unforgiveable and totally uncalled for!'

'I apologised – I don't know why I said it – it was probably the grappa or the—'

'What happened?' interrupted Luca, keen to prevent a full-blown altercation from breaking out in the kitchen.

'One the way back to the villa last night, we decided to call in at the hotel in San Vivaldo for a nightcap with the others, and one of us indulged in so much grappa that they lost all control of their manners,' said Dylan, who for the first time since he'd arrived in Tuscany did not have his faithful guitar by his side. Instead he stood next to Phoebe, facing down Nick, who seemed to shrink from the animosity flowing in his direction.

'I said I was sorry…'

'But what I want to know is why pick on Jennie?' continued Phoebe, taking up the accusatory baton from Dylan. 'She's the nicest, most generous, kind-hearted person in the whole choir and quite frankly if it wasn't for her loyalty to the Somersby Singers, we would never be where we are. You might be a talented musician, Nick, but you are an atrocious people-person. Do you have any idea how many of our current members would have quit if Jennie hadn't been there to smooth over the cracks?'

Nick looked down to his feet and shook his head.

'Almost everyone! In fact, I wouldn't plan on there even being a Christmas concert this year…'

Phoebe's final sentence woke Nick from his shamed reverie, and his eyes shot to hers in panic.

'We can't cancel the concerts! We can't! I've given my word! We have to do this, we have to—'

'You should have thought about that before you let your mouth go,' said Dylan, spinning round a chair so he could sit astride it and look Nick straight in the eye.

'I know, I know, and I'm truly sorry.'

'It's Jennie you need to grovel to, mate.'

'I tried last night, and then again this morning, but she wouldn't answer her door. Tell me what I should do and I'll do it, just don't threaten to cancel the shows – you can't do that to me.'

'You might not have a choice,' said Sofia, appearing at the kitchen door, her journal tucked under her arm, glitter pen behind her ear. 'Jennie's taking a shower – she told me she'd be down a little later and we should start the class without her.'

'Will someone please tell me what's going on!'

'Good old Nick here blurted out Jennie's deepest darkest secret in front of the whole choir and half the hotel staff last night,' said Phoebe, sliding into a chair next to Dylan and helping herself to a glass of Izzie's home-made lemonade.

'She was so upset, and who can blame her? You are a complete moron, Nick.'

'True, true.'

Izzie understood why they were reluctant to repeat the disclosure but she thought she would burst if someone didn't tell her what Nick had said. Ever-worsening scenarios spiralled through her brain until she had Jennie down as an axe murderer.

'Actually, I think it's fabulous, and if it were me, I'd be shouting about it from the rooftops,' said Sofia, bending down to the floor to retrieve the wooden spoon she had nudged from the table, dropping her pen in the process.

'What's fabulous?'

'Before Jennie got married and became a suburban housewife and the mother of twin boys, she was a burlesque dancer at a club in Soho. I googled her this morning, and apparently, she was exceptionally talented. However, as she's kept her dalliance with showbiz quiet all these years, she clearly didn't want her past broadcast in public! She was mortified last night, ran out of the hotel, and took a taxi straight back here. When we got back, she didn't answer her door.'

Nick stood at the far end of the table, his hands shoved into his pockets, his head lowered, his expression reflecting his contrition.

'If I were Jennie, I'd tell you where you can stick your stupid choir. In fact, you know what? I quit. I don't want to be part of anything with a leader who is such an ar—'

'It's okay, Sofia, it's okay. I'm fine.'

Jennie lingered in the doorway, her eyes red-rimmed from crying but otherwise presenting the same neat exterior that everyone was used to: her chestnut hair flicked up at the sides to reveal a glimpse of her pearl earrings, a tasteful red cashmere sweater upon which she had embroidered a silver snowflake and added crystal gems to give it some extra sparkle.

'The last thing I want is for people to quit the choir, especially you, Sofia.'

Izzie saw the look that passed between Jennie and Sofia but try as she might she couldn't decipher its meaning. God, not another secret!

'We've all worked too hard to give up on the Somersby Singers now. Anyway, I'm really excited about our concert on Saturday night, aren't you?'

Jennie hugged Sofia to her, whispering something inaudible in her ear, and then moved on to embrace Phoebe and Dylan before stopping in front of Nick, who stood awkwardly, his eyes filled with terror that his beloved choir might be crumbling before his eyes.

'I admit I was upset last night, Nick. When you interviewed me for a place in the choir, I told you about my former career in confidence and I'm saddened at the cavalier way you've disclosed a secret that only my husband was a party to for the best part of twenty-five years.'

'Jennie, please, I offer you my sincerest apologies. I had no intention of…'

'It's okay, really. It's a part of my life that I chose to keep to myself because I was the wife of a respected pharmacist and the mother of two impressionable boys. I didn't want to risk loose gossip getting out of hand and embarrassing them. But you know what? My past is an important part of who I am, or who I was at the time, and I have to admit that I loved every single second of it, the glitz and the glamour, the feathers and the fabulousness of performing on stage with the other artistes. Being in that industry made me feel so alive, so in control, so desirable. I'm not ashamed of it, in fact, now that I'm divorced and my sons have their own lives, I might just be tempted to go back to it!'

Sofia giggled. 'Really?'

'So, I accept your apology, Nick, and I think we should all move on. I'm sure Izzie and Luca are keen to show us their Christmas recipes. What do you have planned for us this morning?'

And with her head held high, Jennie took her place at the table between Sofia and Phoebe, secured her apron around her waist and smiled in expectation at Luca.

'So today we'll be making *cantucci di Prato* – which are miniature anise-flavoured almond biscotti traditionally served at the end of the meal with a glass of dessert wine such as Vin Santo. I'll also be demonstrating a twist on this Tuscan delicacy, *cantucci al pistacchio e cioccolato bianco*, which are made with pistachios instead of almonds and a generous handful of white chocolate. Then, Izzie will take us through her recipe for gingerbread biscuits which we'll be decorating with a Christmas theme. Okay, so first we make a pyramid of flour, like this, then we add the sugar, eggs, baking powder, lemon zest and a pinch of salt, mixing it all together on our individual pastry boards with our hands until we have a soft dough.'

As the morning of culinary endeavour progressed, the atmosphere in the villa's kitchen softened, with Jennie making it clear to everyone that she had forgiven Nick for his impromptu exposé of her past – even helping him to roll out his lumpy attempt at Izzie's gingerbread and showing him how to hold a piping bag to decorate his reindeer's antlers. The smell of warm spices and sweet pastry spread through the air as their biscuits baked, and the room reverberated with animated chatter as everyone talked about their favourite Christmas traditions.

'Last year, when Ben and Daniel came home from university for Christmas, they insisted on organising a real Christmas tree and they brought back the most enormous fir tree I've ever seen. Of course, it wouldn't fit in the lounge, so do you know what they did?'

'What?' asked Sofia, smiling at the obvious delight on her friend's face.

'Well, they might be about to graduate with first class honours in their chosen fields, but when it comes to common sense, they could do with a few more lectures! Ben fetched a handsaw from the garage and instead of cutting off a few inches from the bottom of the trunk, he sawed a foot from the top! That year we had a Christmas bush! It was hilarious – certainly a conversation starter at our New Year's Eve party!'

'At home, we never had a Christmas tree,' said Luca, laughing at Jennie's story. 'We had a *ceppo* instead – it's a sort of wooden pyramid of shelves that's filled with sweets and gifts and decorated with pine cones and candles – and we also had an Urn of Fate, where we take it in turns to draw out a present.'

'Wow, that sounds fun!'

'Also, in Italy, instead of writing a letter to Father Christmas asking for a long list of gifts, children write a letter to their parents telling them how much they love them. The letters are placed under the mother and father's dinner plates on Christmas Eve and are read after the meal.'

'Now that's a tradition we could do with adopting!' Jennie smiled, nodding her approval.

Leaving their *cantucci* to cool on wire racks, they all retired to the dining room to feast on Carlotta's home-made lasagne. And when every morsel had been consumed, instead of rushing everyone off to the studio to rehearse, Nick allowed them to return to the kitchen to fill cellophane bags with their *cantucci al pistacchio e cioccolato bianco* and tie the tops with red and green ribbon. Izzie handed out snowflake-shaped wooden tags and, using Sofia's glitter pen, they wrote the names of their lucky recipients. To everyone's surprise, Jennie, who had again made two perfect batches, presented hers to Nick along with a conciliatory kiss on the cheek.

'Okay, everyone,' she laughed, her warm brown eyes sparkling. 'If we don't get going, I think Nick might explode and I don't want to add to Izzie and Luca's workload any more than we have done already.'

Izzie watched them leave for their afternoon rehearsal and then fell into the almost choreographed routine she and Luca had devised to clear away the culinary utensils and implements, wash them, dry them and then return each one to their rightful place in the cupboards.

'Okay, now we've finished up here, I've got a surprise planned for you, *Isa... bel... la*.'

'What sort of surprise?'

'If I told you that it wouldn't be a surprise!' Luca smirked, the cute dimples appearing in his cheeks as his eyes sparkled with mischief. 'One tip, though – you'll need to bring your hat!'

Chapter Fifteen

Abetone, Tuscany

Colour: Snow white

Bundled up in a sunflower-yellow ski jacket, a pair of borrowed snow boots and the quirky knitted hat and gloves combo Luca had given her at the airport, Izzie stared out of the window of Luca's Alfa Romeo as they threaded their way through the tiny Tuscan villages on their way to his 'surprise'. In the distance, she could see snow-topped mountain peaks poking through the forests of fir trees that cloaked the hillside. It was like a scene from a Christmas card, except for the bulbous silver clouds that appeared in the sky as they climbed higher and higher up the Apennines.

'Looks like it's going to snow! Do you think we should change our plans?' she asked.

'Don't you like snow?'

'I love the snow if I can enjoy it from the inside of a cosy winter hideaway with a log fire burning and plenty of hot chocolate topped with whipped cream and those tiny marshmallows! You know, I hate to admit it but I always just assumed that Tuscany basked under a blanket of year-round sunshine!'

'This is Abetone – there's usually snow here from December to April, so it's one of the most popular ski resorts in the area. There's over eighty kilometres of ski slopes from gentle nursery slopes to diamond runs for the more experienced.'

'Oh my God, we're not going skiing, are we?'

Luca laughed, but he didn't answer her question, which sent her spirits bouncing to her fleece-lined boots. Before she could say anything else, Luca swung the Spider sharply to the left and they came to a halt in the car park of a hotel crouched at the base of a leisurely incline and covered in a pristine swathe of snow that glistened in the intermittent sunshine. To Izzie's surprise it looked just like an Alpine ski lodge, with a pitched wooden roof and whitewashed façade, complete with bright red shutters – chocolate-box perfect.

'This hotel belongs to Fabrizio, a friend of mine from university. I'll introduce you to him later.'

'Why later?'

'Because we're going to have some fun first. Come on!'

Luca jumped from the driver's seat and raced around to her side of the car, pulling her out of her seat in his eagerness to show her what he had planned in that snowy winter wonderland. Izzie smiled at his enthusiasm, slid her palm into his and allowed him to guide her towards the veranda at rear of the hotel. She heaved a sigh of relief when she saw it housed a collection of wooden tables and benches where snow lovers were enjoying a well-deserved cappuccino and the most fabulous view of the valley.

'Wow, the scenery is amazing, and so is that aroma of freshly brewed coffee!'

But it was as if Luca hadn't heard her because instead of heading for the empty table in the far corner and ordering them a gingerbread latte each, and maybe a slice of that delicious-looking *castagnaccio* sprinkled with pine nuts, he made his way to the bottom of the snow-covered hill.

'Come on, this way.'

Sporting a trendy black-and-orange ski jacket with matching hat pulled down over his dark curls and a pair of reflective sunglasses, he looked like he was about to take part in an Olympic cross-country skiing challenge. Izzie groaned inwardly; she fervently hoped their afternoon did not involve anything so rigorous. If she were honest, whilst she appreciated the beauty of the panorama spread before her, she preferred the warmth of the sunshine on her face, maybe the odd palm tree and a symphony of cicadas rippling through the air. The silence up here in the mountains was so loud it made her ears buzz and the heavy pewter sky was beginning to feel oppressive.

'Where exactly are we going?' she puffed as she trudged behind Luca up the admittedly gentle slope behind the hotel, through whose windows she could see visitors enjoying an afternoon of relaxation in the swimming pool and indulging in spa treatments.

'Not far.'

With her breath laboured, she plodded higher, the end of her nose smarting in the icy temperature, but at least the rest of her body was toasty. When they finally reached the brow of the hill, the area flattened out and she saw a tiny wooden cabin sitting against a battalion of pine trees like an oversized cuckoo clock. Then she saw what was parked up in front of it and realised what Luca had planned.

'No way! A sledge? Are you kidding me? I haven't been on a sledge since I was ten years old!'

'Come on!'

Luca sprinted towards their waiting toboggan and Izzie stumbled in his wake, her arms and legs flailing to keep herself upright in the ankle-deep snow. She eyed the ancient wooden contraption, sceptical that it would even make it to the bottom of the hill without falling to pieces. Also, looking back down at the hotel from their vantage point, the gradient looked much steeper than it had on the way up.

'Luca, I'm really not sure about this.'

'You'll be fine. Just channel your inner ten-year-old child!'

Luca stooped down to pick up the rope, and waited for her to climb onboard. She hesitated, but what choice did she have? She could either whizz down the icy slope with Luca's arms around her, or refuse and stomp back down the hill by herself, which didn't appeal either.

'Oh, God, I think I'm going to regret this.'

She took her position at the front of the sledge and Luca sat behind her, scooting in close and wrapping his legs around her thighs, clutching hold of the rope so he could control their descent. She could feel his warm breath on her cheek and his muscular chest pressed into her back and a tingle of pleasure sizzled through her veins.

'Ready?'

'Ready.'

Moments later, they had tipped over the lip of the hill and were whooshing through the air, slowly at first, then gathering speed. A feeling of total exhilaration spread through every single part of her as they sailed down the hill, skipping over tiny hillocks, landing with a bump, then continuing their rollercoaster journey until they skidded to stop at the bottom and a sensation of absolute joy burst into her heart.

'Ya… aa… ay!'

Luca leaped from the sledge, his face wreathed in delight as he dragged her upright, drawing her into his embrace until their noses touched. Izzie expected him to kiss her, but instead he stooped to the ground, gathered a handful of snow and flung it at her.

'What the…' she spluttered with surprise. 'Okay!'

Izzie crouched down and scooped up the largest snowball she could manage, and threw it with as much strength as she could garner at his retreating back, but it went sailing past his head. Luca spun round, grinning with mischief, and began to walk towards her. She took flight, stumbling in her unfamiliar snow boots until he caught up with her, grabbed her by the waist and shoved her into the snow.

'Hey!'

Luca fell down on top of her, his eyes scorching deep into her soul for what seemed like an eternity. She felt as though the rest of the world had zoned out and her complete attention zoomed into his lips, only his lips, as they descended onto hers. A cascade of emotions obliterated all ancillary thought and her heart blossomed at the affinity she felt resonate between them, lying there in the crisp Italian snow, as she kissed the most amazing man in Italy – until his warm lips were replaced by a face full of snow.

'Oh my God, I can't believe you just did that!'

She rolled from beneath him and scrambled to her feet, sprinting away towards the veranda of the hotel with droplets of snow melting and trickling down her collar. She made it as far as the car park when a well-aimed snowball glanced off her shoulder and she ducked behind his Spider for cover, her face burning from the unfamiliar exertion, her breath coming in intermittent spurts.

'Izzie…'

Luca caught up with her, holding his empty hands in the air, then moving forward to cup her cheek with his hand, his expression suddenly serious.

'Izzie, I want you to know that—'

'Hey, Luca, *bello vederti, amico*!'

Luca expelled a sigh and shook his head ruefully as he stepped forward to greet his friend Fabrizio with an affectionate embrace. If George Clooney had a younger brother, his likeness was standing in front of Izzie, his warm brown eyes filled with amusement as he realised he'd inadvertently interrupted a romantic interlude. Izzie liked him immediately.

'*Fabrizio, posso presentarti Isabella Jenkins.*'

'*Ah, Izzie, è bello conoscerti finalmente.* I've heard so much about you. Come on, come inside. I've reserved a cosy corner next to the fire and Natalia has baked some of your English mince pies which we are serving to our customers with mascarpone sweetened with a little limoncello. I hope you'll approve!'

'*Grazie, Fabrizio.*'

Luca hooked his arm around Izzie's shoulders and they followed Fabrizio into the hotel to a quiet table right next to a floor-to-ceiling window that looked out over the snowy scene – a real winter fairy tale of snow-capped peaks, pine trees dusted with icing sugar snow, and cute wooden lodges dotting the hillside. If Izzie hadn't known they were in Tuscany, she would have thought they were in the land of apple strudel and yodelling. She pulled off her hat and gloves and wriggled out of her bulky yellow coat, her fingers and toes tingling as they thawed and became accustomed to the warmth.

'So, how was your first experience of Tuscan winter sports?' Luca grinned, after saying goodbye to his friend and relaying their order to a waitress in rapid Italian. 'Are you ready to tackle a black run?'

'No way! Sledging is about my limit!'

All around them, couples and families lingered over their drinks, chatting about their accomplishments in a variety of languages, spirits high as the day's spurt of adrenalin dissipated. Within moments, the promised plate of mince pies and a plate of Italian pastries were placed in front of them, along with two tall mugs of rich hot chocolate, the aroma of sweet cocoa causing Izzie to close her eyes in ecstasy.

'What are these?' she asked, helping herself to a thick, snow-white biscuit, which to her surprise was softer and more chewy than the biscotti and *cantucci* she was used to.

'They're *cavallucci*, which translated means "little horses". They're made with local Tuscan honey, walnuts or hazelnuts, and flavoured with aniseed and candied orange, then liberally dusted in icing sugar – as you can see.'

'Why are they called "little horses"?'

'Well, they date back to Renaissance times and there are a number of theories. The one I like the best is that they were made for the servants who worked in the stables of the country houses around Siena. After all, it is where the Palio is held every year!'

'Mmm, they're melt-in-the-mouth amazing. I think we should definitely include these in our next Delicious Desserts course at Villa Limoncello. Oh, sorry, I...'

Izzie's heart sank at her momentary lapse of memory. Of course, there wasn't going to be another course, or there might be, but neither she nor Luca would be part of it. She wanted to broach the subject of the sale of the villa, but the day so far had been perfect and she didn't want to spoil the feeling of calm that had enveloped them in their private corner of the luxury ski hotel by reminding Luca he was losing the villa, so she changed the subject.

'What were you about to say to me in the car park when Fabrizio arrived?'

Luca hesitated, staring into the dregs of his hot chocolate as if the answers to all life's problems could be found at the bottom of the mug. When he eventually met her gaze, her heart gave a jolt of surprise at the distress she saw there.

'Oh, nothing that can't wait until later,' he hedged, flicking his eyes to the ornate gold clock on the wall above the fireplace, then to the darkening skies out of the window. 'Come on, I think we should be getting back to San Vivaldo or we might end up being stranded here in the mountains.'

Izzie couldn't think of anything she would like better than to get stuck in a cosy, snow-bound skiing retreat with Luca, but of course that wasn't an option when they had guests back at Villa Limoncello to take care of. After waving goodbye to Fabrizio, she slotted her arms into her jacket and followed Luca to the door, bracing herself for the short trek to where they'd left the car.

'Look, it's started to snow!'

She tipped her head backwards, and for a few precious moments she watched a flurry of featherlike snowflakes drift down from the sky and settle briefly on Luca's curls before melting into raindrops. She turned to offer him a smile, but instead of sharing her delight in nature's recurring beauty, he had scooted into the driver's seat of his Alfa Romeo, revving the powerful engine as he waited for her to follow suit before crawling out of the car park, his subsequent attention claimed for the effort needed to navigate the mountain roads in the snow.

Izzie knew that their journey home would have been the perfect time for her to tell Luca how she felt, to ask him if there were any other alternatives to selling the villa, or, failing that, to plead with him to reconsider his decision. But, after their afternoon of strenuous activity, and with the heat of the car's radiator, she was asleep within minutes, only waking when they arrived at the villa, where they were greeted by their guests on their way out to dinner in the village.

Chapter Sixteen

The studio, Villa Limoncello

Colour: Holly-berry red

When Izzie tentatively opened the shutters of her bedroom window the next morning, she had expected to see the whole valley draped in a soft blanket of white, but overnight the smattering of snow had vanished, leaving a sharp crispness in the air watched over by a translucent blue sky. She pulled on a sweater with a huge white snowflake on the front that Meghan had given her for Christmas the previous year, and teamed it with skinny black jeans and her Ugg boots. She dragged a comb through her hair, dampened her curls with a splodge of coconut oil, then skipped down the stairs to kickstart the day with an injection of caffeine.

Francesca had texted her the previous evening to confirm she had managed to source everything on Izzie's shopping list, including the wire rings and cathedral candles for that day's wreath-making session, and again Izzie could feel the niggle of excitement at the prospect of spending a whole morning indulging in a cornucopia of Christmas crafts. Interior design was truly where her heart lay and she wondered briefly whether she should consider running a few classes in Cornwall when she returned home.

The thought of moving back to St Ives held mixed emotions. She missed her parents and she knew how excited they were about Harry's proposal, despite reiterating that they only wanted her to do what made her happy. On the other hand, she would miss Italy, too, and the friends she had made there. Could she stay, even after the villa was sold? However, that morning wasn't the time to start the process of weighing up the pros and cons, so she pushed her vacillations into the back of her mind and focused on that day's tutorial.

She ran her pencil down the checklist in her purple folder marked 'Thursday morning', ticking each box as she went, enjoying the whoosh of accomplishment when she had a full house. Styrofoam wreaths like huge white doughnuts, multi-coloured pipe cleaners, wide ribbon in a plethora of shades, even red-and-white striped candy canes and boiled sweets, as well as a box of metal jingle bells to add something musical to their creations.

'*Buongiorno*, Izzie! Where do you want these?' asked Francesca, bursting into the studio holding two enormous white cardboard boxes filled to the brim with sprigs of fresh holly and mistletoe, branches from fir and olive trees, pine cones and huge bouquets of glossy foliage, some left in their natural state, others sprayed with silver or gold paint.

'Here, let me help you!'

Izzie took one of the boxes and placed it on the table, before turning to greet her friend with the customary kisses. As soon as she had met Francesca, who had supplied the bouquets and floral arrangements for the celebrity wedding that had been held at the villa in May, they had clicked. With her pink-tipped hair and penchant for lacy vest tops and a tangle of silver jewellery, San Vivaldo's floral maestro reminded her of Meghan, but it was Francesca's West Country burr that had sealed the friendship. It had turned out that her mother had grown up in Devon and had met her father whilst interrailing in the Eighties, fallen in love with Florence and the guy who ran the local plant nursery. As a consequence, Francesca could switch from high-speed Italian, complete with hand gestures, to English laced with a broad Devonshire accent as the situation demanded.

'So, how many avid Christmas crafters do we have descending on us this morning?'

'Five, I think. And I thought we'd have a bit of a competition to make things interesting. We can display the wreaths over by the Christmas tree in the gazebo and ask Gianni to judge them.'

'Gianni?' laughed Francesca, her eyes dancing with amusement. 'Are you sure? He might have made the best Chianti the world has ever tasted, and he might be able to sing an aria like an angel, but he's no art critic. Why don't you ask Oriana to do the honours?'

'Good idea. I'll give her a call later.'

With Francesca's help, Izzie set out six styrofoam rings – one for her to use in her demonstration, and the others for the students to decorate as they wished – then piled the rest of the accessories in the middle of the table: a mound of foliage, dishes of sequins, beads and buttons, spools of ribbon, lace and Christmas string, boxes of corks and wooden discs and pine cones, along with canisters of glitter spray, tubes of glue, scissors and wire cutters.

'Hi, Izzie, are you ready for us?' asked Jennie, sticking her head around the studio door, her jazzy glasses nestled comfortably between the white pom-poms that depicted a cascade of snowballs on that day's hand-knitted cardigan.

'Absolutely, come in, come in. Take a seat at the table in front of one of the wreaths.'

'Wow, this all looks amazing! Thanks so much for doing this – I know it was a bit last minute. Were you planning on offering any more craft-based courses next year? What about pottery or upholstery, or stencilling, or more glass-painting, or maybe something with a spring theme like decorating chocolate eggs?'

Izzie opened her mouth to reply, but found that her pool of positivity had dried up.

'I'm sure Izzie will email everyone with the schedule for next year,' said Francesca smoothly, handing out cups of coffee as the rest of the guests arrived, chatting about last night's dinner and their plans for their wreaths that morning.

Izzie flashed Francesca a grateful smile and, when everyone was seated at the table, she channelled her inner Kirstie Allsopp and launched into her presentation.

'Okay, so this morning is all about creating Christmas wreaths that you'll be proud to hang on your front doors at home. Francesca will give you a quick lesson on using the floristry wire and the clippers, and then I encourage you to go all-out with your creativity.'

'Wow, I adore this fluffy pink tinsel!' said Sofia, reaching out to grab a frilly garland, wrapping it round her neck like a feather boa and striking a seductive pose.

'We're decorating the wreaths, not ourselves, Sofia,' said Nick, wearing his schoolteacher face, which caused Phoebe to roll her eyes at Sofia behind his back.

'Also, I thought we could have a bit of a competition.'

'A competition?'

Nick's ears, and mood, perked up at the sound of that. He pushed his shoulders back and puffed out his chest, causing the buttons on his emerald-green waistcoat – this one embroidered with musical notes and treble clefs in gold thread – to strain under the tension.

'I have to warn you that Sarah and I have been finalists in the village Christmas tree decorating competition three years running, so I'll be utilising everything I've learned. Are we allowed to phone a friend for ideas, Izzie?'

'I encourage you to use everything at your disposal,' she laughed.

'Well, you'd better be at the top of your game, Nick,' said Jennie, perching her glasses on the end of her nose and peering over the top of them, her peach-coated lips turned upwards into a wide smile, 'because I'll have you know that I've been the chair of our WI's craft committee for the last five years, so the challenge is definitely on!'

Nick laughed, and Izzie was delighted to see that any remaining animosity there might have been between the pair over Nick's unfortunate slip of the tongue had extinguished and they seemed closer than before. She wasn't surprised that Jennie had forgiven him so swiftly – she was clearly not the sort of person to hold a grudge for long.

'Okay, I'll let Francesca take the rostrum and guide you through the techniques.'

'Thanks, Izzie. So, everyone has a styrofoam ring in front of them which you can decorate with anything you like, using the glue gun: baubles, ribbons, pom-poms, multi-coloured pipe cleaners, tinsel, even corks or these cute miniature photo frames. If you want to try something quirkier, might I suggest these gorgeous red-and-white candy canes which would go really well with red Santa hats or green elf hats made out of this felt fabric.'

A splutter of giggling erupted and everyone turned to look at Sofia, whose cheeks had turned pink.

'What's tickling you?' asked Jennie, her smile filled with affection.

'Oh, it's just a story my mum and my aunt used to laugh at.'

'Tell us, we could do with a good laugh!' said Dylan, leaning back in his chair and placing his ankle on his thigh, his pleated leather bracelets dangling from his wrists as he combed his fingers through his hair – probably the first time it had been brushed that day.

'Well, I want you to remember that Mum and Aunt Rosa were brought up in Italy, and that English is their second language. Okay, so, like you, Izzie, they both adored all things fabric-related – actually, before they started their bridal boutique, they looked into opening a haberdashery. Anyway, one day they were shopping in one of the department stores in Leeds, and, as usual, they headed straight for the haberdashery section. I'd asked Mum to get me some material for a school project, so she went up to one of the shop assistants and said in a really loud voice, "Is this the department where I can get felt?"'

The room burst into laughter and Sofia beamed, delighted that she'd been able to share a precious memory of her mum with her friends. Izzie understood exactly how she was feeling because, with the help of Luca's sage advice, she had recently learned that instead of avoiding every mention of her sister's name for fear of stirring up painful memories, she had to embrace the fact that Anna was still an important part of her life and would continue to be so until its end.

'Francesca, what are these?'

'They're floristry rings in case you prefer to design something more traditional. You can twist some of this holly, ivy or mistletoe around the wire, and then add a few pine cones and cinnamon sticks with the orange and lemon slices Izzie baked on Tuesday for a really fragrant approach.'

'Mmm, these dried oranges smell amazing!' said Jennie, picking up a slice of the citrus fruit and inhaling.

'Or perhaps you'd like to insert a disc of Oasis into your wire ring, like this, so you can make a wreath using these magnolia leaves, or these branches Gianni has brought for us from the olive trees and fir trees grown around the villa's grounds, and a few of these dried sage leaves and stems of rosemary.'

'Rosemary?' said Sofia, picking up a sprig. 'I thought you used this to cook with?'

Francesca laughed. 'Actually, rosemary has been used to celebrate winter festivals for centuries. It's said to signify remembrance, family and friendship, and helps to strengthen brain and memory function – in ancient Greece, students would even weave it into their hair in the hope it would help with exam success. But my favourite bit of rosemary folklore is that if you breathe in its fragrance on Christmas Eve it'll bring happiness over the coming year.'

'Okay, so that's me decided!' declared Phoebe, grabbing a handful of the aromatic herb and stowing it away in her handbag. 'I need all the help I can get!'

The group laughed, but Izzie saw there was a serious edge to her exclamation. She remembered Phoebe's inadvertent reference to Nick issuing an ultimatum when they had been chatting on the patio outside the *limonaia* on the first day and she knew there was something worrying her. And no wonder! Having witnessed the way Nick had divulged Jennie's closely guarded secret, Phoebe had every right to be fearful of something similar happening to her. Izzie wondered what snippet of confidential information Nick had gleaned about Phoebe's life that she was terrified of being aired.

'Have you decided what sort of wreath you're going to make?' Jennie asked Sofia, who was busy raking through a box of baubles, picking out all the pink and silver ones of varying shapes and sizes.

'Yes! Don't you think these go together really well? Can I use the glue gun, Izzie?'

'Of course, it's on the bench over there, along with the staple gun if anyone needs that, but there's also wired tinsel, brown parcel string and darning needles. Oh, and there's a roll of double-sided sellotape somewhere, too.'

'What about you, Dylan?' asked Jennie.

'I'm going for a drinking theme! I love these Chianti corks and I think they'll look great with a few of those blue and gold sleigh bells to add colour, with the added benefit that it'll be musical too!'

Izzie smiled at Dylan's enthusiasm. In fact, he seemed more engaged in the tutorial than he had been previously, and she was pleased to see that once again he'd left his guitar behind instead of having it either slung around his neck or perched on an adjacent chair like a trusted friend or guardian angel.

'What do you have planned, Nick?'

'I thought I'd create something from these wooden discs, maybe use a few of the pine cones with the holly leaves and make some hessian bows, then spray everything with that fake snow. I love a bit of fake snow!'

The group spent the next three hours chattering away about their forthcoming choir concerts, which of their songs still needed attention, whether Nick would let them customise their polo shirts or agree to them wearing jeans instead of plain black dress trousers, before moving on to their respective families' Christmas traditions.

'What do you think?' asked Jennie, whose finished wreath looked like something you could buy in Harrods, the fragrance from the baked oranges and cinnamon sticks, as well as the pine cones she had studded with cloves and star anise, making it the most aromatic of all the entries.

'It's gorgeous.' Francesca smiled, handing Jennie a length of scarlet ribbon to attach to the back of her wreath to form a hanger so she could display it in the gazebo for the judging ceremony.

'Thank you, but I think I've got some tough competition.'

She pointed to Dylan's wreath, a perfect circle of wine corks studded with blue jingle bells that jangled when he held it aloft, beaming at the well-deserved compliment.

'Thanks, Jennie. Thank you too, Francesca, I actually really enjoyed this session.'

'Me too!' agreed Nick, holding his entry at arm's length and contemplating its greatness as if it were a Michelangelo sculpture. His wreath was different again: a ring of overlapping wooden discs that had been decorated with hand-drawn musical instruments. 'I can't wait to show Sarah what I've managed to create without her input!'

At the other end of the Christmas wreath spectrum was Sofia's attempt, a fantasy of frilly silver and pink tinsel, intertwined with matching baubles, and then liberally doused with Izzie's glitter spray and finished off with a silver heart she'd cut out of foil.

'I love your wreath, Sofia, it's so fresh and quirky. It'll brighten up your aunt's front door no end!'

Sofia grinned at the vote of confidence. 'Thanks, Jennie. I'm going to upload a couple of photos to my Instagram page.'

'Why don't you wait until they're all on display in the gazebo – it'll make a much better photograph,' suggested Nick, already striding towards the door. 'Come on, I'll help you.'

'Oh, no, I don't want to...'

'It's no trouble.'

'It's a great idea.' Jennie smiled, blatantly ignoring the look of horror on Sofia's face at the possibility of having to spend time with Nick on her own. 'Don't forget your coat.'

'Thanks,' muttered Sofia, wriggling into her fleece-lined denim jacket and following Nick out of the door, pausing briefly to exchange a strange look with Jennie when she thought no one was looking.

Izzie's curiosity was piqued – there was definitely something going on between Jennie, Sofia and Nick – and her suspicions were confirmed when she saw Jennie mouth the words, *Tell him*.

Chapter Seventeen

The studio, Villa Limoncello

Colour: Shady grey

Jennie helped Izzie and Francesca finish tidying up the detritus from their morning's endeavour, then she scooped up her wreath and slotted it carefully into her canvas bag before turning to Phoebe.

'Dylan, Phoebe, are you coming?'

Phoebe was so engrossed in scrolling through the messages on her phone that she hadn't heard Jennie's question.

'Phoebe?'

'Oh, sorry, what did you say?'

Izzie noticed that her complexion had lost its habitual radiance, and so did Jennie.

'Is everything okay?'

'Oh, yes, just an email from the office, that's all.'

'You youngsters work far too hard!' exclaimed Jennie, hitching the handles of her bag higher up her arm as she loitered at the studio's door. 'You're supposed to be on holiday this week – why can't they respect that and leave you alone so you can recharge your batteries? Surely there's someone else in that law firm of yours who can handle things until you get back? None of us are indispensable, you know!'

But instead of bolstering Phoebe's spirits, Jennie's comments had the opposite effect, and to Izzie's surprise Phoebe burst into tears.

'Well, it turns out that you've hit the nail on the head. I'm *not* indispensable!'

'Oh, darling, I'm so sorry. I didn't mean…'

Jennie looked aghast, dropping her bag to the floor and rushing towards Phoebe to comfort her, but Dylan got there first and crouched down at the side of her chair.

'Phoebe? What's going on?'

'I…' began Phoebe, her eyes flicking from Jennie to Izzie and Francesca before coming to a stop on Dylan, whose face was bathed in concern.

'I'll catch up with you later, Izzie.' Francesca smiled, clearly anxious to allow Phoebe some privacy.

Izzie nodded and smiled her thanks to her friend. 'Phoebe, please, tell me what's happened?'

Phoebe fiddled with her phone as she pondered on how to explain. 'Oh, it's just such a complete nightmare.'

Izzie reached out and took Phoebe's hand in hers and gave it a squeeze. 'If you talk to us, we might be able to help.'

'I don't know where to start.'

'Well, my mum always told Anna and I when we said the same thing that we should start at the beginning and keep going until we get to the end.'

'Good advice,' muttered Dylan, clearly at a loss as to what had cause Phoebe's meltdown in the middle of a crafting session, but Izzie could see from the look in his eyes that his reaction was more than that of a concerned friend. He was in love with Phoebe and she wondered whether she should make her excuses and join the others in the gazebo and leave Dylan and Phoebe to talk alone. She had just started to raise herself from her chair when Phoebe began to speak.

'You'll think I'm a fool.'

'That's not even a possibility.'

'Okay, so... I've just been informed that I'm being transferred to a different department at work. Less complex cases, less responsibility, less...'

'But I thought you were hoping to be promoted to associate partner in the new year?'

'I was.'

'So what's happened?'

And it all came tumbling out.

'Well, as you know, I've been a committed workaholic for years and in the summer it all seemed to be paying off when Giles Denby, that's our senior partner, called me into his office. He told me that the equity partners were holding a board meeting to decide who should be made an associate partner in the new year and that my name was on a list of five potential candidates. I was overjoyed – it's exactly what I've been working towards. So...'

Phoebe gulped in a breath and Izzie remained motionless, not wanting to break the spell that had descended over the studio and bestowed the vaulted room with a feeling of safety in which to spill confidences. All that could be heard was the faint tinkle of festive music from the CD player in the corner and the chiming of a distant church bell telling everyone in the valley that it was lunchtime.

'So, as I hadn't had a social life for months, I decided to celebrate by treating myself to a spa weekend with a couple of girlfriends, joining the community choir, and registering with a few dating websites. I went out with a couple of guys…'

A streak of discomfort shot across Phoebe's face and her cheeks coloured as she kept her eyes diverted from either Izzie or Dylan.

'And after a few unsuccessful attempts, I met this guy called Nathan and we went on a few dates…'

Izzie remembered her conversation with Phoebe earlier in the week when she'd talked about dating and she had assumed that someone had broken her heart, but it was worse than that, much worse.

'We seemed to just click, and after not being in a proper relationship for years, I started to see him most weekends, then it was every weekend, then it was during the week. I'd only known him for three months when he moved in with me in September. I admit that the sensible lawyer part of my brain was screaming caution, but the romantic dreamer in me was loving every moment we spent together – the bouquets of flowers Nathan sent to the office, the impromptu picnic lunches, the last-minute theatre tickets for my favourite shows, weekends away at cute pubs in the countryside.'

'So what happened?' asked Dylan, his jaw set rigid as he prepared himself for what had obviously not ended happily ever after.

'I can hardly believe it was me who did this but...'

By now Phoebe had started to wring her hands so aggressively that Izzie had to slide her palm into hers to calm her, offering an encouraging smile.

'Tell us what happened?'

'Nathan asked me to lend him some money. He spun some story about one of his relatives who lived in Buenos Aires being seriously ill and that he really needed to visit her before the inevitable happened. Of course, I agreed straight away and gave him my debit card to pay for his flight. I even went to see him off at Heathrow!'

'And?'

'I never saw him again.'

'Bastard! Sorry, Jennie. So, he didn't pay you back?'

Phoebe didn't answer Dylan's question for a long time, simply allowed her eyes to rest on his face.

'What?'

'It's worse than that.'

'How can it be worse!'

'Nathan had my bank account details and he completely wiped me out of every penny I had – he took thousands.'

'Oh, my God! Did you report him to the police?'

'Of course I did, but it turned out that he'd used a false name, and all the stuff he'd told me about where he was from, where he went to uni, details about his family and friends, none of it was true.'

'Oh, Phoebe, that's just awful! I'm so sorry,' said Izzie, handing Phoebe a spare paper napkin to dry her eyes, trying to imagine what it must have been like for her to find out she'd been the target of such a cruel scam. 'But what's all this got to do with your promotion?'

'Of course, I had to tell Giles what had happened, and he was really supportive, helping me to deal with the police, and the bank. My parents were livid. In fact, I'm glad Nathan *had* left the country or I think my father would have hunted him down and dragged him kicking and screaming to the nearest prison.'

'So...'

'As I said, Giles was supportive, but one of the other partners, Andrew Stainsworth, who was championing his own candidate, said I was a gullible idiot and that I couldn't be trusted as a partner in a law firm if I could be conned out of so much money so easily. He intimated that the same thing could happen to a client!'

'That's despicable!' declared Dylan, whose face had filled with colour in indignation. His eyes flashed with restrained anger and he was clearly struggling to keep a lid on his emotions. 'Do lawyers have a trade union they can complain to?'

Phoebe laughed, but there was no joy in her voice. 'Oh, don't worry, Giles shot him down straight away, but the seed was sown. They had the board meeting yesterday and the vote did not go my way.'

'That's not fair...'

'I might not have got the position anyway. Harriet is an extremely competent solicitor who's had a couple of very successful cases in the Court of Appeal this year. But I admit I'm devastated – it's just another blow on top of everything else, that's all.'

'Well, perhaps it's time you jumped off that corporate treadmill and started to chase your musical dreams instead,' suggested Dylan, taking Phoebe's other hand into his and meeting her gaze.

'Dylan…'

Izzie suddenly realised that she was surplus to requirements, so she joined Jennie in slipping quietly out of the studio, leaving Dylan to help Phoebe pick up the pieces of her shattered career and mould her life into something different.

Chapter Eighteen

The limonaia, Villa Limoncello

Colour: Sherbet lemon

'That was another delicious lunch, Izzie.'

'Thank you, but today's feast is all down to Carlotta and her friend Vincenzo, who happens to be a committed locavore.'

'What sort of religion is that? I've never heard of it,' said Sofia, cramming the last piece of her *cantucci* into her mouth and licking the ends of her fingers with exaggerated delight.

Izzie laughed. 'Vincenzo's mantra is that as much of our food as possible should be sourced in the local area. He's an expert forager – the mushrooms and asparagus and all the herbs in that risotto came from fields within a kilometre of San Vivaldo, and the apricots used in the tart you had for dessert were collected in summer from the trees over by the tennis court and preserved in bottles, like the cherries and the gooseberries.'

'I think I'd struggle to adopt that lifestyle at home,' said Nick, rubbing his well-padded stomach in satisfaction. 'Although Sarah *is* keen on recycling and reducing our plastic consumption, and we don't eat as much red meat as we used to either – so I'd be grateful if you didn't mention that huge T-bone steak I had at the trattoria last night when we get back home.'

'Your secret is safe with us,' laughed Phoebe, the dark smudges beneath her eyes that had been a permanent feature when she'd arrived at the villa now almost unnoticeable. Her eyes sparkled and Izzie thought she looked five years younger and certainly one hundred per cent happier. She wondered if she and Dylan had kissed in the studio and made a note to tell Carlotta there might be another success story to add to her ever-lengthening list.

'Thanks, Phoebe, I appreciate that!'

Izzie knew she wasn't mistaken when she saw the spectre of guilt stalk across Nick's face, and in that moment she realised that Nick had known about Phoebe's relationship problems and in some way used his knowledge to ensure she didn't skip rehearsals despite her heavy work schedule. There was something ironic in him now asking Phoebe to keep his steak-eating crime to herself, and it was testament to her new-found acceptance of her situation that she'd agreed so willingly.

'Okay, if everyone's had their fill, I want a full dress rehearsal down in the studio in one hour.' A groan of complaint reverberated around the dining room and Nick rolled his eyes, but there was warmth in his expression. 'And if everything goes well, I'll let you finish an hour early to get ready for our expedition to San Gimignano this evening.'

'Yay!' cried Sofia, celebrating their good fortune by reaching for another one of Izzie's gingerbread snowmen. 'I'm really excited about going to San Gimignano. My friend Archie is so jealous – apparently Assassin's Creed was filmed there so he wants me to take lots of photographs for him.'

'I don't think I've heard of that film,' said Jennie, gathering together their empty plates and carrying them towards the kitchen.

'That's because it's a video game,' laughed Dylan.

'Oh, right. However, I feel I should point out that I think the town is more famous for its medieval architecture and its gelato! Come on, the sooner we get started, the sooner we can leave on our trip.'

'It's okay, Jennie, you can leave the tidying up with me.'

'Are you sure? I don't mind helping.'

Jennie caught a glimpse of Nick's raised eyebrows and relented. 'Okay, thanks, see you later.'

'If everyone could be on the terrace for six o'clock, that would be great. I've organised taxis so no one has to drive.'

The group disappeared down the garden path towards the studio, Dylan and Phoebe talking about the world of live music and song-writing, Jennie asking Nick about his previous trip to San Gimignano, and a surprisingly subdued Sofia following on behind looking like a lost lamb. It was becoming ever clearer to Izzie that Sofia would do anything to avoid being alone with Nick, although he was completely oblivious to it, living as he did in a parallel world filled with operettas and arias and musical theatre.

Izzie exhaled a long sigh of relief. Why on earth had she thought running courses in the gorgeous Tuscan countryside where every day would be filled with creative endeavour coupled with a generous dose of animated chatter, friendship and laughter – not to mention delicious patisserie – would be easy? Throw together a group of friends away from their natural habitat and any kind of drama could ensue!

She craved the sound of a friendly voice and she knew exactly what she had to do. She headed back into the kitchen, grabbed her phone and made her way to the *limonaia*, its welcoming fragrance sparking joy as soon as she entered its glass-encased embrace.

'Hey, Meghan, how did the dinner with your parents go last night?'

'Hmm, it's not in my top ten most magical moments!'

'Did you talk to them, though?'

'I did.'

'And?'

'Well, put it this way, I won't be having my Christmas dinner at Hollybrook this year.'

'Oh, Meghan, I'm so sorry…'

'It's okay, it's okay…'

For the first time in their friendship, Izzie heard the catch of misery in her best friend's voice and her heart gave a nip of sadness. She adored Meghan: her sartorial craziness, her carefree positivity no matter what homework their lecturers cast in their direction, her energetic romantic exploits, jumping from one potential suitor to the next like an Olympic hurdler. Every day, Izzie thanked the director of fate for ushering her into Meghan's effusively cheerful path because nothing seemed to faze her. Meghan threw herself at life and gave each challenge everything she had stored in her armoury; if she succeeded, great, she would celebrate vociferously, if not, then she'd simply move on to the next project without a glance over her shoulder. She was a confirmed optimist, except for one thing – being able to persuade her parents to accept her decision to pursue her own dream and not theirs.

'What did they say exactly?'

'Well, at first they laughed.'

'They laughed?'

'Oh, things started off okay. Over the starter we talked about mundane things like their journey down from Yorkshire, their swanky hotel in South Kensington, then, during the main course we moved on to the movie Brad's filming in Croatia, even the problems he's having with the weather over there. We managed to get to the coffees without a single cross word, although I have to admit the whole meal was excruciatingly awkward.'

'And?'

'I remembered something you said to me ages ago, about communication being at the heart of all relationships and I realised that we had spent too long avoiding the elephant in the room.'

'Or the horse?'

Meghan giggled, but quickly grew serious again.

'So I just blurted everything out in one long sentence. That running Hollybrook has never featured on my wish list, that, unlike them, training race horses does not instil an ounce of joy in my heart, far from it. That I don't just dislike horses, I am terrified of them. This is the bit where they laughed. How could I possibly be terrified of horses when I've grown up with them? I could see in their eyes that they didn't believe me, that they thought I'd come up with the story as some kind of ruse to shirk what they called my "responsibilities" to the Knowles family and the Hollybrook legacy.'

'Oh, Meghan, I'm so sorry.'

'I tried to explain that it isn't just fear, it is a fully fledged phobia. That every time I go near one of the snorting, stamping beasts, even venture into one of the stables, even catch a whiff of the damp hay, I come out in stress blotches, my throat closes around a particularly prickly pear and my heart rate zooms off the scale – all the classic symptoms of a phobia. And you know what, Izzie? Just as I expected, Dad offered to pay for a course of therapy.'

Meghan paused and Izzie could feel the pain reverberating across the miles from London to San Vivaldo. Her friend had kept her secret about her phobia from her parents for years, fearing their reactions, not wanting them to think she was rejecting what was, in effect, her inheritance because she didn't love them. She had thought that by explaining to them that her dreams lay elsewhere, in the field of art, design and fashion, like Brad had when he'd gone off to study film and media at university instead of veterinary medicine, then they might come around. But for some unfathomable reason they had accepted Brad's ambitions were valid and had struggled to understand Meghan's choices, no doubt comparing his achievements as an award-winning film director with those of a lowly window dresser, albeit for a store as prestigious as Harrods. So, when Meghan had graduated from the RCA, she'd simply stayed on in London, renting a room in a tiny flat and refusing to go home. Avoidance had proved the better option than staring at the face of disappointment whenever she went back to Yorkshire.

'I'm sorry, Meghan, really, I am. What did you say when your dad said that?'

'I told them there was no need for him to waste his money on a therapist because I doubted that I would encounter many equine-filled situations whilst pursuing my dreams.'

'True! It's a completely different kind of thoroughbred treading those catwalk boards!' giggled Izzie, relieved that Meghan's strength of character had shone through during the most difficult of conversations.

'I tried to explain that I didn't intend to be a window dresser for ever, that I'd already helped to stage one runway show, and I'd been applying for jobs in set design at fashion houses for the last six months. You should have seen the look on their faces, Izzie. It was as though I was waxing lyrical about becoming an astronaut and planned to be the first woman to walk on Mars. Work in the fashion industry? Heaven forbid! Mum's idea of cutting-edge fashion is a tweed hacking jacket with a coordinated velvet collar and elbow patches – although to be honest, she does look rather good in them, and the jodhpurs!'

'Maybe stable chic will be the next big thing for the Autumn/Winter collection?'

'Could be! I'd love to design the catwalk for that! Anyway, their biggest surprise was when I told them that all the jobs that I'd applied for were in Italy. I thought Dad was going to have a coronary, but you know what? I thought I saw a twinkle of interest in Mum's eyes.'

'Do you think she might come to accept your decision?'

'I don't know, but I do know one thing: when I got home and told Jonti everything that had happened, I felt a huge sense of relief that at last I've told them the truth about how I feel, and that I've explained the reasons behind my choices so they can start planning a different future for Hollybrook. I really want the tradition of training world-class race horses to continue – I'm proud of what they've achieved. My plan is to give them some time for what I said to sink in, then I'm going to go home and talk to them again.'

'Meghan, I'm so impressed with how you've handled this.'

'Thanks, Izzie. I would never have done it if you hadn't been there for me. I love you, darling!'

'Right back at'cha!'

Chapter Nineteen

San Gimignano, Tuscany

Colour: Sun-drenched saffron

Izzie loved every town and city she had visited since arriving in Tuscany, but her favourite had to be San Gimignano – the hilltop town known as the Manhattan of Tuscany because of its fourteen medieval bell towers stretching into the sky like ancient skyscrapers. Their taxis had deposited them in the car park at the bottom of the hill and they had huffed and puffed up the steep incline until they arrived at Porta San Giovanni, the impressive stone archway that led to the town where the rest of the choir were waiting for them.

After joyous greetings that belied the fact that they had seen each other less than an hour before, Izzie and Luca led the party along Via San Giovanni, the cobbled main street lined with shops on both sides.

'Wow, look at these ceramics!' declared Jennie, trotting off to take a closer look at colourful hand-crafted urns, wide-brimmed bowls perfect for serving pasta, plates, jugs, butter dishes, oil and vinegar sets and huge planters displaying lemon trees. 'Gosh, how am I going to choose which one to buy?'

'I think your luggage allowance will take care of that,' laughed Dylan.

'Ooh, my aunt Rosa would love one of these embroidered tablecloths,' said Sofia, fingering the crisp white linen sewn with images of lemons, sunflowers, even bottles of wine, and edged with hand-stitched lace. 'But I think I'll stick to a tea towel – maybe this one with a recipe for making limoncello on, what do you think?'

'I'd prefer one of these chess sets myself,' said Dylan, eyeing a beautifully carved board with the pieces depicting the characters from *The Lord of the Rings*.

'Or what about this one?' said Nick, picking up the knight from a set showcasing orchestral instruments. 'I wonder if Sarah's bought my Christmas present yet? I think I'll send her a photograph – see what she says.'

'I can tell him exactly what Sarah will say,' Jennie whispered to Izzie when she saw the price tag.

Eventually they reached Piazza della Cisterna, a stunning square paved in an irregular red-brick pattern and surrounded by a harmony of ancient buildings, including the fourteenth-century Palazzo Tortoli and Palazzo Lupi. The place was milling with tourists, lingering on the steps leading to the central fountain that gave the piazza its name, or peering into the prestigious jewellery shops, or queuing at Gelateria Dondoli for a taste of their award-winning ice cream in flavours as diverse as gorgonzola and walnut, and saffron and pine nut.

'Okay, why don't you take some time to explore on your own, then we'll meet back here for dinner at nine?' said Luca, pointing out the restaurant where they would all be dining together.

'Come on, Sofia, I'll treat you to one of those world-famous ice creams that I saw you drooling over. They must be amazing judging by the line outside,' said Jennie, reaching deep into her beloved bag to extract a bulging purse as Sofia followed her to the back of the queue.

'Fancy an Aperol spritz?'

Dylan's blue eyes rested on Phoebe, who had barely spoken two words since reading the emails she'd received earlier. She nodded absently, linked her arm through his and allowed herself to be guided towards a tiny cafe down a shady alleyway as though in a trance.

By the time Nick had finished studying the window of a shop that seemed to offer nothing but instruments of torture – who in their wildest dreams found that they suddenly had the urgent and pressing need for a sword whilst staying in the medieval town perched high on a hillside? thought Izzie – and looked around to share his discovery with the others, everyone had disappeared on their own mission of Italian retail therapy.

Izzie took pity on him. 'How does a glass of Vernaccia di San Gimignano sound?'

'Sounds perfect, and maybe an *aperitivo* whilst we're waiting for our dinner reservation?'

Izzie smiled. 'Luca?'

'Oh, no thanks, I promised Eduardo that I would pop in for a chat before the choir descended on him.

Apparently, there's something he wants to talk to me about. Sounds ominous.'

'Okay, *ciao*.'

'*Ciao*.'

Izzie sauntered with Nick to a cafe just off Piazza della Cisterna with rustic whitewashed walls, exposed beams and a burble of animated conversation set to a backing track of tinkling teaspoons and Puccini. They were guided towards a table next to a large, noisy Italian family who were clearly in the throes of celebrating the grandmother's birthday.

Izzie ordered a San Pellegrino and a glass of the local San Gimignano white wine for Nick as promised, which he gulped down like a man who'd spent the week in a desert before ordering himself a Negroni, which came with a plate of *stuzzichini*. Izzie eyed the finger food, her mouth watering at the tiny slices of bruschetta topped with chopped tomatoes, local cheese with fresh figs, and slices of grilled marrow adorned with ribbons of local ham, but she demurred, keen to save her appetite for her meal at Eduardo's later. Of course, Nick wasn't so reticent and devoured the lot.

In honour of their trip to San Gimignano and their last night in Italy, Nick had chosen to wear his most exuberant waistcoat to date: a paisley pattern of vibrant pinks, purples and violets, embroidered with silver thread and finished with matching buttons. His usually boisterous mane of mahogany curls had been tamed with a dollop of hair product and his beard had been neatly trimmed – he looked every inch the accomplished musical conductor, especially when he signalled for another Negroni.

'I've been here before, you know.'

'Really?'

'Yes, twenty years ago with Sarah for our honeymoon. We had a fabulous time exploring the countryside around here, taking day trips to Siena, to Lucca, to Pisa, and of course Florence. We must have walked ten miles a day, but, of course, we were a lot younger back then.'

To Izzie's surprise, she heard a catch in Nick's voice, and she took a sip of her sparkling water to give him a moment before she asked, 'Why didn't she come with you this time?'

'Well, firstly, she's not a member of the Somersby Singers and it would have been a bit hypocritical of me to bring my wife when I'd specifically told everyone that no partners were allowed. But also, every spare moment of her time is taken up with the drama school's Christmas pantomime at the moment.'

'Ah, yes, Jennie mentioned her children's stage school.'

'She loves it – the acting classes, musical theatre, ballet, tap, jazz, you name it. Even cheerleading for the little ones. They're performing *Goldilocks and the Three Bears* this year and I have to say the costumes are absolutely amazing. She's hired a local theatre for the night and the tickets sold out faster than a Take That concert.'

Izzie couldn't fail to notice the note of pride in Nick's voice when he spoke of his wife, and the softening of his features was testament to the love he had for her and what she'd achieved at her stage school.

'I run the singing classes on Saturday mornings and Sarah's sister, Claire, acts as chaperone for the youngsters, so there's a real family atmosphere. But, you know, it's more than just a weekend drama school – for some of the kids it's a sanctuary.'

'What do you mean?'

'Some of the children have very challenging lives, so spending the day with Sarah and her colleagues is like a safety valve for them to de-stress and do something just for themselves instead of for their families. We have one young girl who cares for her alcoholic mother, and there's a fifteen-year-old boy who works every night of the week in a pizza shop just to help the family make ends meet. We run a bursary scheme that Sarah's father set up for those children who can't manage the fees for the classes and the costume hire. It's tough sometimes, financially, but it works, and to see the children throw themselves into their characters is very rewarding, and being on stage is a real confidence boost for them, too.'

'And you and Sarah don't have children?'

As soon as the words had left her mouth, she wished she could take them back. She had rarely seen such raw agony flash through a person's eyes, but the image was fleeting and Nick raised his glass once again, drained it and signalled for another.

'No,' he managed to say, his voice tight. 'It's our one sadness in what's been a very happy union.'

Silence expanded as they both became lost in their thoughts and what Nick had disclosed. She was surprised he had opened up to her, worried that the alcohol had loosened his grip on his emotions and he would regret his candour the next day. But then the choir was leaving the following afternoon and it was unlikely he would see her again, and, as she knew only too well, in a crazy world where people barely stopped for breath, a simple crumb of empathy could be a Michelin-starred meal.

'I think that's one of the reasons Sarah works so hard at the drama school – those children are her family and she adores every single one of them. She not only teaches them how to dance and sing and act, she braids their hair, she does their make-up, even washes and irons their uniforms for them. She's poured every ounce of her hopes and dreams into their development and celebrates all of their achievements as if they were her own children. The kids love her, too, of course – you should see the fuss they made of her for her birthday last month. I've never seen so many boxes of her favourite After Eight mints.'

'How did you meet Sarah?' asked Izzie, for the first time feeling as though she was getting to know something about Nick as a person and not his fiery passion for music.

'We met in our last year at university. I'd just got back from a summer placement in Milan and she'd been helping out backstage at one of the West End theatres – we had lots to talk about! You know what it's like when you just click with someone, when you know something's right?'

'I do.' Izzie smiled, unable to prevent a fully formed image of Luca from sailing across her vision.

The family at the next table were now embarking on an Italian rendition of 'Happy Birthday' and Izzie paused to watch the happy scene, lost in her memories of previous birthdays and family celebrations, the most recent of which hadn't included someone she'd desperately wanted to be there. She wondered if Nick was thinking the same thing.

'As soon as we graduated, we got married and we had the most amazing time here in San Gimignano, really immersing ourselves in the culture, the music, the cuisine. When we got home, I found a job as a drama teacher at the local high school and Sarah set up her stage school, and since then we've worked every hour God sends to make it a success. It was hard at times, but it's been worth every sacrifice. Then, five years ago, when we got the news that our family wasn't going to grow any larger, she suggested I set up the community choir. It was a godsend at the time because I took that news rather hard.'

The party at the next table had finished their song and one of the grandchildren, a boy of around five, was presenting his grandmother with a huge home-made birthday card, and Izzie saw the woman wipe away a tear before grabbing the child and swinging him onto her lap, causing him to shriek with delight.

'We've thought of adopting, even went as far as going to a couple of the information sessions, but well, it just wasn't for us. So… so we've moved on. Sarah has her school, I have my career and the choir, it's all good.'

Nick forced a smile onto his face, but Izzie couldn't fail to see the regret in his eyes and her heart went out to him. He wasn't the person she had thought he was when he'd arrived at Villa Limoncello with his booming voice, his outrageous waistcoats and his bossy nature. He was simply passionate, driven and talented, but also broken inside, and she experienced a surge of affection for him as she reminded herself, not for the first time, to never judge a musical score by its fancy cover. Just like his wife, Nick clearly treated his choir as if they were his surrogate children, urging them to achieve their potential so that their Christmas performances around the halls and churches of York were the best they could be, and a sudden urge to weep engulfed her as she witnessed the sorrow etched deep in his soul.

Life wasn't fair, but all anyone could do was make the best of the cards they were dealt.

Chapter Twenty

Eduardo's ristorante, San Gimignano

Colour: Sparkling prosecco

'Wow, this *pappardelle con ragù di cinghiale* is absolutely delicious,' declared Jennie. 'Do you think Eduardo will give me the recipe?'

'I doubt it,' laughed Luca, glancing in the direction of his friend, who was busy polishing glasses at the bar with one eye on the kitchen door and the other roaming around his clientele, as vigilant as a fox ready to pounce on its unsuspecting prey, except his would be with a bottle of grappa. 'It's an old family recipe handed down from his great-grandmother. You know, us Tuscans can be very particular when it comes to our recipes.'

'What do you mean?'

'Well, there's no way we would ever put meatballs with spaghetti, or sprinkle cheese on a seafood pasta, and if you want to remain friends with your neighbours, never let them find out that you prefer a handful of fresh parsley in your minestrone – rumour has it that there's a family in the next valley who haven't spoken to their neighbours for twenty years because of this!'

'That's utterly crazy!'

'Italian cuisine is all about authenticity – this is where the slow-food movement started as a backlash against the creeping popularity of fast food. We can't understand why people want to sip on a cappuccino out of a cardboard cup whilst walking down the street when they could linger over an espresso or a latte at a pavement cafe. Food is passion, it's pride, it's love.'

Izzie sneaked a glance at Nick from beneath her lashes, keen to ensure he'd recovered from his earlier disclosures. She needn't have worried because his head was tipped back, his dark curls falling away from his face as he roared with laughter at something Dylan had told him before helping himself to another glass of grappa.

Eduardo had seated them at a table in a rear courtyard, heated by two huge outdoor chimeneas and decorated with the ubiquitous ceramic pots filled with geraniums and strings of twinkling fairy lights. A ripple of live guitar music filtered through from the main restaurant, along with tendrils of warm red wine and baked garlic, inducing a convivial atmosphere for the choir's final evening in Tuscany. Izzie was relieved to see that the whole choir – all fifteen of them – were enjoying their last night in Italy together, with everyone taking turns to share anecdotes of their time there.

Those who had chosen to engage in a week of snow sports regaled them with stories of daring and comedy, with one member raising his hand in the air to display his strapped fingers.

'Broke my pinky!' said Archie, with an element of pride.

'Well, at least it won't affect your vocal cords,' replied Nick, holding up his glass to toast his fellow baritone.

Those who had engaged in more sedate pursuits spoke of mornings spent gazing at some of the most amazing art in the world, telling stories of Botticelli, Donatello, Masaccio. One of their visits had been to the Galleria dell'Accademia, where they had spent the best part of an hour simply marvelling at the genius of Michelangelo's hand. They had devoured every fact their guide Fabio had imparted, asked endless questions and taken hundreds of photographs. Every one of them had promised to return with their partners, their friends or their families in the summer to climb the hill to Piazza Michelangelo and show them the spectacular view of Firenze spread out on the other side of the River Arno.

Izzie watched the group's interactions as if enjoying a stage play, sitting in the grand circle and listening to the various snippets of conversations. She had devoured everything Eduardo had put in front of her, including a huge slice of his *torta della nonna*, but she had chosen to abstain from the grappa that was currently doing the rounds, preferring to drink in the atmosphere of San Gimignano at night as it might be the last time she would see the beautiful town, at least for a while.

A sudden sweep of melancholy engulfed her, that her future had once again not panned out as she had hoped. However, she quickly put her sadness into perspective

– the sale of Villa Limoncello was a mere blip in life's journey after the chasm she had navigated her way out of after losing Anna. Regret was a pointless emotion, so what she had to do now was concentrate on enjoying every moment she had left in Tuscany, just like her guests were doing, then start making plans for a new future.

She felt an uptick of optimism, and when she tuned back into what was happening in the restaurant, she saw Luca was gazing at her with such intensity that her cheeks flushed and her resolve to focus on Harry's new project in Cornwall crumbled. Even if the villa was sold, that didn't mean she had to return to the UK. Look at Meghan – she was doing everything she could to find a job in Florence, or Pisa, or Siena or anywhere in Tuscany, or Italy for that matter, so she could be with Gianni.

Why wasn't she doing the same?

Confusion reigned, but that wasn't the time to deal with it. She smiled at Sofia, who was chattering away about the costumes she'd helped stitch for the latest theatre production of *Joseph and the Amazing Technicolor Dreamcoat*, then she looked across at Dylan and Phoebe, their heads bent together, Dylan's arm draped across the back of Phoebe's chair as he smiled into her eyes, nodding occasionally. She hoped Dylan would be able to help Phoebe come to terms with Nathan's betrayal. After all, it was only money, as well as the loss of a promotion which would only have kept her on the eternal treadmill of all work and no play. Hopefully a sideways move would prove beneficial in that the pressure she had been under for so long would lessen and she'd be able to take some time for herself to make new friends, form new attachments, maybe fall in love.

She switched her scrutiny to Dylan and saw a man who was already well along that path, even if Phoebe hadn't realised it yet. She knew from what Jennie had said that Dylan deserved every slice of the happiness pie that was on the menu after the way he had put his life on hold to support and care for his brother and sister. This was *his* time to grasp life and she hoped he could do that – with Phoebe by his side.

'So, Dylan, now that you've sold your business to that tech giant, have you had chance to write any more songs?' asked Archie, the choir member with the broken finger, who had struggled to eat the huge T-bone steak he'd ordered until Jennie offered to cut it into smaller pieces for him.

'I've written a whole album, Archie, my friend!' laughed Dylan, leaning back in his chair, hooking his ankle over his thigh, his face taking on an animated expression at the opportunity to talk about his music.

'When might we get to hear a couple of them?'

'Soon – you are my beta listeners!'

'Well, there's no time like the present,' said Archie, a gleam in his green eyes as he leapt from his chair and dashed into the restaurant to speak to the guitarist who was taking a well-earned break at the bar.

Izzie twisted in her seat to see Archie gesturing towards the courtyard. The guitarist smiled, nodded, indicated his instrument, and Archie picked it up and made his way back outside.

'The stage is all yours, mate!'

Dylan grinned, accepted the guitar and cradled it into his body like it was a beloved pet, strumming his fingers across the strings until he got a feel for the instrument, then playing as though there was only him and his guitar in the whole universe.

When he started to sing, his voice as smooth as caramel, goosepimples ran the length of Izzie's arms and her swirling emotions from everything that had happened that day caused her throat to tighten. She looked around the table and saw that all eyes were resting on Dylan, listening attentively to the lyrics. The song had clearly been written for Phoebe and here he was, sitting in a courtyard in San Gimignano, singing it to her with such intense emotion that no one would have doubted its inspiration.

When the final note faded into the midnight air there was a brief pause as everyone held their breath, waiting for Phoebe's reaction, and when she leaned forward, slowly, tentatively, and met his waiting lips, the whole restaurant erupted into a frenzy of delight with whoops and applause, even a whistle from Archie.

Jennie was the first out of her seat to embrace the couple, then it was Sofia's turn, and within minutes the whole choir had surrounded Dylan and Phoebe.

'He's far too talented for our little choir,' one of the museum fans whispered to Izzie as she wiped a tear from her cheek. 'He should be the lead singer in his brother's band!'

'His sister, Martha, is a talented clarinet player too,' added the woman's friend, replenishing everyone's glasses of prosecco so the group could toast Dylan and Phoebe's relationship.

Izzie glanced across at Luca, who was standing at the bar with Eduardo, watching the unfolding romance, the expression on his face unfathomable. She was about to go over and talk to him when Nick stood up, called for everyone's attention and declared it was time to go or their taxis would leave without them. To the cacophony of scraping chairs, everyone gathered together their belongings and made their way through the restaurant, thanking Eduardo, thanking Luca, expressing their effusive praise for the delicious food.

When everyone was outside, Izzie turned to Luca.

'Luca, I…'

'Would you be able to guide the choir to the car park, Izzie? There're a few things I need to talk to Eduardo about. I'll see you tomorrow for the final patisserie session.'

Luca smiled and leaned forward to place chaste kisses on her cheeks, a gesture that caused Izzie's heart to thump to her boots, but there was no point asking him what was going on because Eduardo remained by his side and her guests were waiting for her just beyond the door.

Chapter Twenty-One

Eduardo's ristorante, San Gimignano
Colour: Titian fizz

'Luca, tell me to mind my own business, but I think you need to sit down and talk to Izzie.'

'Eduardo, can we not do this right now...'

'There's no point ignoring the facts – that's no good for anyone. You saw the look on her face. She's hurt and I don't blame her. You practically ignored her all night, as though you have no feelings for her at all – and you and I both know that's as far from the truth as it's possible to get.'

'Eduardo...'

'Explain to her about your decision to sell the villa – she'll understand. There aren't many people with the bottomless pit of money that it takes to maintain one of those aging duchesses. Then, when that's out of the way, tell her you love her and that you don't want her to take the job in England – there's plenty of work in the villas and houses around here owned by wealthy expats who want to drag their crumbling old properties out of the doldrums and into the twenty-first century. But unless you tell her how you feel, she's got no reason *not* to take the job. It's a great opportunity from what you said – no one's going to turn down the post of creative director for a property company without a very good reason.'

'Exactly! How can I expect Izzie to give that up? I'm not that selfish. It's the perfect job for her – what she's always dreamed of – a bunch of old houses to renovate and re-style, not to mention the fact that it's in her home county *and* within cycling distance of her parents. I'm sorry, Eduardo, I can't be the one to take her away from her mother and father after what they've been through.'

'In my experience, most parents want their children to do what makes them happy, Luca. You're not taking her away from them, you're offering her a lifetime of happiness! Look, if you won't listen to me, perhaps Elina can talk some sense into you.'

'*Mio Dio*, not Elina!' cried Luca, faking horror at the threat of having a chat with Eduardo's wife, and the mother of his two children Alessio and Cara, about the rollercoaster ride that was love.

Eduardo smiled, but he wasn't swayed by Luca's attempt at levity.

'Luca, I know you think you're doing what's best for Izzie, but I urge you to reconsider. The only way to deal with this is to talk to her and be honest about your how you feel, what you truly want, and then, if she decides to go home, you'll have a clear conscience, knowing you did all you could to make her stay. It's up to Izzie to decide between Italy and Cornwall, or even London. If you don't do this, then I suspect you'll never forgive yourself. Do you want to spend the rest of your life thinking about what *could* have been, like Carlos?'

'What do you mean "like Carlos"?'

'I shouldn't be telling you this, but if it helps to persuade you to see the light then I'm going to, but first you have to give me your word that you'll keep it to yourself.'

'What's Carlos done?'

'I need your promise first.'

'Okay, but…'

'Ever wondered why Carlos hasn't dated since he started working at Antonio's last summer? Why he was always so keen to take on extra shifts while you and Izzie were renovating the villa? Well, it's not just because he loves the restaurant, you know.'

'It isn't?' smiled Luca, thinking of his sous chef who ran the trattoria even better than he did himself. He realised with a pang of guilt that it had never occurred to him to wonder why Carlos was never seen in the company of a date; he just assumed he preferred to conduct his love life with discretion and privacy.

'Carlos was given the chance to follow his long-term partner to Australia to set up their own Italian trattoria in Melbourne, but he prevaricated for so long that he missed the boat so to speak, and within weeks of arriving Adi had met someone else. I won't go into details, but Carlos was devastated and he regretted not having the courage to take the leap into the unknown, to propose before Adi caught the flight.'

'I never knew...'

'Just don't make the same mistake. Oh, I'm not suggesting you propose to Izzie – just talk to her, find out how she feels, what she really wants. If it's to go back home, then fine, but if it's to stay here with you – and that's the team I'm batting for – then you can't throw away the chance at happiness that's staring you in the face. I remember how upset you were when Sabrina refused to relocate to San Vivaldo.'

'Eduardo, can we—'

'And what a huge shock it was when you found out she was seeing Claudio behind your back, but as your friend I can tell you one thing – you never looked as happy with Sabrina as you do when you're with Izzie. She brings something so carefree, so spontaneous out in you! Not to mention the fact that she's been the catalyst to you starting to work on the villa, and even though it hasn't turned out as you'd hoped, the building has brought you closer together, like one of Carlotta's matchmaking success stories!'

Luca fiddled with his half-empty glass of Vernaccia that he'd made last all night so he could drive home. Everything Eduardo had said started to rotate in his head like a whirlpool of mist until he felt completely disorientated.

'Luca? Luca, will you do that?'

Eventually, Luca tuned back in to what Eduardo was saying.

'Yes, you're right, thanks.'

Luca leaned forward and enveloped his friend in a tight bear hug, slapping him on the back to show him how much he appreciated his advice without having to actually say the words. Eduardo's reasoned argument was spot-on. Right up until the week before Izzie had turned up at the villa, he had been rehearsing what he was going to say to her about the future, how he planned to tell her he was selling the villa, then move the conversation on to more personal matters, to tell her how he felt about her and ask her to move in with him in the apartment above the trattoria. But then Harry's offer had thrown a curveball into the mix and he'd had to reassess his plans.

As he jumped into his beloved Spider for the short journey home to San Vivaldo, he made a decision and the vice-like grip that had squeezed at his temples since Izzie had arrived at Villa Limoncello diminished and the tunnel of indecision filled with light. Eduardo's story of what had happened to Carlos galvanised him into action. His friend was right – if he allowed Izzie to leave at the weekend without telling her how he felt, he would regret it for the rest of his life.

When the street lights of the village came into view, he resolved to present the final patisserie course, and then, after the Snowflakes & Christmas Cakes guests had finally left for the airport and before Meghan and Jonti arrived on Saturday morning, he would take Izzie's hand, guide her to the *limonaia* she loved so much, and in the presence of the lemon trees he would tell her he loved her.

Chapter Twenty-Two

The kitchen, Villa Limoncello

Colour: Velvety sunshine

Izzie woke to the sound of her alarm for the first time since arriving in Tuscany back in the summer. Usually she was roused by the dawn chorus coaxing her down the stairs for an early morning stroll through the garden before even the nocturnal animals had scampered back to bed. However, last night she'd had difficulty falling asleep, her thoughts ricocheting from the disappointment that Luca hadn't suggested she join him for a nightcap at Eduardo's or even chosen to escort them back to the villa where she could have persuaded him to have a coffee and then cross-examined him about what was eating him up.

But she had no time to wallow in her insecurities because she had breakfast to sort out and the ingredients for that morning's tutorial to prepare. Friday – it had been the day she'd been looking forward to the most, culinarily speaking. Luca was planning to showcase his grandmother's recipe for tiramisu with a Christmas twist, whilst she was going to attempt her limoncello and white chocolate yule log which she had been practising all week and she had just about got right.

If she'd achieved nothing else from her stay at Villa Limoncello, her patisserie skills had taken a huge leap up the league table and she knew she would never again return to her previous diet of endless cups of coffee and buttered toast – not when it was just as easy to whip up a fragrant herby omelette or drop a handful of pasta in a pan of boiling water before drenching it with extra virgin olive oil and a few fresh basil leaves.

She showered quickly and ran downstairs, then came to an abrupt halt at the kitchen door.

'Oh…'

'Oops, sorry, Izzie,' laughed Phoebe, extricating herself from Dylan's embrace as they sat at the kitchen table, their coffees forgotten whilst they continued to get to know each other better.

Izzie grinned when she saw the look of complete adoration on Dylan's handsome face.

'Is Carlotta coming over this morning?'

'No, she isn't, I'm afraid. She gone to Venice with Vincenzo.'

'Oh, that's a shame. I really wanted to tell her how grateful I am.'

'Grateful?'

'That she sprinkled some of her stardust on us,' laughed Dylan, unashamed of his belief in the magic of her match-making skills as he took Phoebe's hand, kissed her palm, and then laced his fingers through hers.

Izzie beamed as she fixed herself a coffee, her own sadness at the deterioration in her friendship with Luca easing at the sight of the loved-up couple in front of her, both of whom deserved their chance at happiness after everything they had been through recently.

'I'm sure she'll be delighted, if not surprised,' said Izzie, popping a plate of croissants, cannoli and fresh fruit on the table before taking a seat opposite Dylan.

Phoebe helped herself to two of the warm flaky pastries and filled them with Carlotta's home-made apricot jam before biting into one of them, sending crumbs cascading to the table, a splodge of the jam oozing onto her lips. Dylan laughed, reaching up to wipe it away with his thumb whilst gazing into her eyes, a gesture so intimate that Izzie's cheeks coloured.

'This is an amazing place, Izzie. You're very lucky to live here,' said Phoebe, her face bright with first flush of romance that had come to visit so unexpectedly.

'Oh, I…'

'It's not just Carlotta who's sprinkled a little bit of fairy dust onto our lives. I think it's the tranquillity, the laid-back ambience here at the villa, too. It's the perfect environment to take stock of life, to contemplate what course the future could take if you make a few adjustments. Shall I tell Izzie or do you want to?' asked Dylan, smiling at Phoebe as though they were the only two people in the world to have ever stumbled across love.

'I'm resigning from Denby & Stainsworth.'

'You are?'

That wasn't what Izzie had expected Phoebe to say.

'If they don't know how to appreciate and reward the hard work and talent of their staff, then they don't deserve to retain it,' announced Dylan, loyally. 'Anyway, it's about time you pursued *your* dreams for once, not those of your family's.'

'That's great news, Phoebe. What do you plan to do?'

'I'm going to concentrate on my singing and song-writing, hopefully record an album which Dylan is going to produce, then go on tour with his brother's band! I can't tell you how excited I am – taking my music seriously has been a dream ever since I had my first piano lesson when I was five years old! Can I tell Izzie the rest, Dylan?'

Dylan nodded, but Izzie suspected he would have agreed to anything Phoebe proposed.

'No, actually, I think you should tell her, it's your idea, not mine. Go on!'

Despite Dylan's mood of overwhelming joy, Izzie saw a flash of discomfort float across his face, but he tore his gaze from Phoebe's and met Izzie's eyes, a slightly embarrassed smile tugging at his lips.

'I've already told you that I sold my business before I came out here. At the time it was a very difficult decision because I'd built it up from scratch over the years when I had to be at home to support Jack and Martha, and escaping into my computer screen after they were safely tucked up in bed was the only thing that kept me connected to the outside world, connected with fellow musicians and would-be music producers.'

Dylan reached out to take a sip of his coffee. 'When the CEO of a high-profile media company approached me to sell, I refused, but within hours he had doubled his offer, a figure which absolutely floored me. I mean, two million pounds is a *lot* of money and it will see Jack and Martha through university, help to launch my brother's band and support the tour, and…' He paused to look at Phoebe. 'I can help Phoebe get her finances back on track.'

'Two million pounds…' stuttered Izzie, not sure whether she had heard right.

She'd had no idea, but then, why should she? The money had obviously not changed Dylan from the warm-hearted, laid-back, music-loving individual he clearly was and she suspected it never would, especially as he seemed intent on using it to help others rather than squander it on himself. However, she did wonder why it had been such a secret.

'Is there a reason you didn't tell anyone?'

'I'm a boring old IT teacher at the local high school. Can you imagine the hoo-ha, not just from the students but in the staff room? A millionaire teaching class? It'd be completely untenable for all sorts of reasons, and I love what I do, I love seeing that look of realisation on a student's face when they suddenly understand a tricky concept or get a piece of coding spot-on. The world needs more computer scientists and I want to do my bit to inspire those that are interested to pursue that career path.'

'And Nick was going to spoil it all!' added Phoebe.

'How did he find out?'

'Archie blabbed about it one night after choir practice and Nick thought he'd use it to *persuade* me to take the rehearsals more seriously. Oh, I don't think he would go as far as to blabber to the other teachers, but I was angry that he thought it was okay to threaten me with it.'

'Two million pounds is an awful lot of money…'

'I know, even now I can't believe that money is sitting in my account, like a sleeping lion ready to pounce,' Dylan muttered as though in a daze, or inhabiting a parallel universe where life could hand out golden tickets instead of wooden spoons. 'Please don't say anything to the others, will you? I didn't plan on telling anyone else apart from Archie and Nick, but I also never expected, well, to get together with the most wonderful woman I ever laid eyes on.'

Colour flooded Phoebe's cheeks and she leaned forward to place a soft kiss on Dylan's lips, reminding Izzie that she was superfluous to requirements. She quietly excused herself and took her coffee out to the terrace where the sun was starting to peek over the horizon and flood the valley with a gauze of gilded light.

As she took her daily stroll around the garden, the early morning dew glistening on the leaves, her spirits climbed. She marvelled at the way life could toss grenades one moment, then deliver overwhelming bounty the next. The trick was to realise that everything was transient, that no matter what happened, one thing was certain: time would march on; the warm velvety sunshine of summer would morph into the sharp crisp air of winter; grief would abate and become acceptance, then gratitude, and finally, hopefully, contentment would follow.

She paused to pick a sprig of rosemary from the straggly bush that flanked the steps of the gazebo and inhaled the woody fragrance, dropping down onto the top step to reflect on the things she had witnessed over the past week during the Snowflakes & Christmas Cakes course.

She thought of Sofia and how she had flourished during her week-long stay in Tuscany, her cooking and crafting skills improved greatly, even if she hadn't got over her aversion of spending even a few minutes alone with Nick.

She smiled at Jennie's new-found fame and exuberance after her secret had been revealed which, instead of the embarrassment she had feared, had caused great excitement amongst her friends, who had bombarded her with questions, and Sofia and Phoebe had made a promise to take her to a show when they got back home.

She looked over her shoulder to see Dylan and Phoebe, their secrets now shared too, take a seat beneath the pergola to enjoy their final breakfast at the villa in the open air, chatting away about their plans for their future, giggling as they got to know each other better. Dylan was right: Villa Limoncello was truly a place where hearts could heal and happiness could blossom.

But there was still one thing that continued to nag at her brain with the tenacity of a rabid Rottweiler. Which one of Villa Limoncello's guests had felt so strongly about Nick's interference in their lives that they had decided to give that geranium-filled plant pot a nudge southwards? And, when that hadn't had the desired effect, had that same person tossed a glass of red wine over his prized white dinner jacket?

And if so, who?

Chapter Twenty-Three

The kitchen, Villa Limoncello

Colour: Creamy white chocolate

Izzie returned to the kitchen and made a start on preparing the seven sets of ingredients for Luca's Christmas tiramisu and her limoncello swiss roll which she was going to cover in white chocolate. Before she knew it, Nick and Jennie had arrived to grab a coffee and it was ten o'clock. The only person not to join in with the festive spirit that morning was Sofia, who actually looked like someone had told her that Christmas had been cancelled. Dark smudges circled her eyes and her complexion was ashen, but before Izzie could ask her what was wrong, Luca arrived.

'*Buongiorno a tutti!*'

'*Buongiorno*,' chorused Dylan and Phoebe, following Luca into the kitchen, grabbing their personalised Villa Limoncello aprons for the last time and taking their places alongside the others for what could be the final cookery class ever to be held at the villa.

'Okay, let's get started!'

Izzie immediately noticed the lightness in his voice, that the smile he gave her no longer held a certain reticence but was filled with excitement at being where he wanted to be doing something he loved – presenting classes to enthusiastic students in his own kitchen. She returned the gesture, experiencing a somersault of attraction. That morning, instead of his white chef's jacket, he had chosen to wear a Christmas jumper depicting a reindeer with a huge red pom-pom for a nose that made her giggle at the incongruous image of the habitually stylish Luca Castelotti. Gianni, yes, she could imagine him in any kind of quirky attire easily, but not Luca. However, the sweater did nothing to detract from Luca's handsome features or his muscular figure as he stood at the head of the table demonstrating his grandmother's tiramisu recipe.

'We whip the mascarpone with the double cream and the icing sugar, so.'

Everyone copied his actions, with Phoebe playfully dotting a splodge of the creamy mixture on the tip of Dylan's nose and giggling. Everyone rolled their eyes, but they were clearly happy to see the fledgling romance play out in front of them to the background tinkle of 'Santa Baby' whilst they assembled their individual tiramisus and put them in the fridge to set.

'*Ecco*, we'll take a short break and then Izzie will close the course with her delicious yule log that you can take home with you or nibble on the way,' said Luca, removing his apron and hanging it on the back of the kitchen door.

'Okay, everyone, why don't you go out to the terrace and I'll bring out the coffee and a few Tuscan treats. And don't forget, you need to be packed and ready to leave for your lunch at Antonio's at one o'clock, and there are taxis booked to take you to the airport from there at three.'

Everyone piled outside to indulge in the freshly ground coffee, accompanied by generous plates of *cantucci* and *ricciarelli*, whilst Izzie helped Luca tidy up in the kitchen.

'Izzie...'

'Luca...'

'You first,' said Izzie.

'I think we need to talk about what—'

'Izzie? I've left my luggage on the front steps. Do I have time for a trip down to the gazebo? I'd like to take a few more photographs of the villa and the surrounding area for a piece I've promised the local *Yorkshire Gazette* about the Somersby Singers,' asked Nick, an old-fashioned Pentax camera slung around his neck.

'Of course, there's no rush.' She smiled and watched him leave, humming an Italian aria. She was about to turn back to Luca to continue their conversation when she heard Jennie's voice float towards them from the bottom of the stairs, filled with urgency.

'You have to talk to him now! It's your last chance!'

Izzie exchanged a glance with Luca, who shrugged his shoulders, filled his cup with espresso and indicated for her to follow him outside to the terrace. However, she hesitated. There had been something in Jennie's tone that sent her senses into overdrive.

'I can't...' came Sofia's reply.

'There's no "can't". You just have to do it. Nothing can be worse than what you've dealt with already, and it's the perfect place to face difficult conversations.'

'Will you come with me?'

'I'm here for you, Sofia, darling, but you have to do this yourself. It's what you've been planning to do since Nick announced this trip to Tuscany, what you've spent hours rehearsing for. Don't waste the chance or you'll regret it. Once we get home, we'll be caught up in a frenzy of festivities and you won't have another opportunity to talk to him alone for a while. You need to do it now – it's eating away at you.'

The two women appeared in the kitchen dragging their suitcases behind them, shock suffusing their faces as they realised that Izzie must have overheard everything they had said. She opened her mouth to apologise, to explain she hadn't meant to eavesdrop, but before she could speak, Jennie had linked her arm, and then Sofia's, and was guiding them out of the kitchen door, across the terrace, and down the garden path.

'Where are we going?' asked Izzie as they approached the gazebo where Nick was snapping photographs of the Christmas tree decorations and the wreaths they had made.

Jennie ignore Izzie's question, and when Izzie shot a glance at Sofia, expecting her to roll her eyes at her friend's secret mission into the villa's garden, to her utmost surprise she had a look of abject terror on her face, her slender body trembling despite the warmth of the midday sun.

'Go on, darling,' urged Jennie, pushing Sofia forward towards the gazebo steps, but the girl was clearly petrified.

'Jennie, I don't think...'

Izzie paused. She wasn't sure what was going on but she was reluctant to ignore the fact that Sofia was obviously distressed. For the first time, she noticed that the young girl was clutching a piece of paper in her fist, and, as she continued to watch on, Sofia seemed to be overtaken by an ambient force and started to walk towards the gazebo, climbing to the dais one step at a time as though in a trance until she came to a standstill in front of Nick, staring up at him wordlessly.

'Sofia? What's wrong?'

Sofia remained motionless and Nick sought Jennie's eyes over her shoulder before looking back at Sofia, who was now holding the document out for him to take.

'What's this?'

Jennie grabbed Izzie's arm and guided her away from the gazebo to leave them to what looked like was going to be a very difficult conversation, but instead of walking back to the terrace to join the others, she led them towards the patio outside the *limonaia* and dropped down into one of the rattan chairs.

'Jennie, what's going on?'

'It's a bit of a delicate matter. I've no idea how the conversation is going to go, but it *has* to happen. It's what Sofia wants, but it's no surprise she got cold feet at the last minute and needed a little nudge along the way.'

'But...'

'And I can assure you, Izzie, that before we leave for our lunch at Antonio's, Sofia will apologise to you and Luca.'

'Apologise? Apologise for what?'

A buzzing sound erupted in Izzie's pocket and she drew out her phone to glance at the screen. Meghan. She smiled, eager to chat to her friend, to find out what time she was arriving the next day with Jonti in tow, but she had to find out what was going on with Sofia and Nick. So she declined the call and slid her phone back into her pocket before turning back to Jennie.

Jennie sighed, her kind eyes softening.

'Promise to listen to everything I'm about to tell you before asking questions?'

'Jennie, what's going—'

'Promise?'

'I promise, but…'

'It was Sofia who *accidentally* nudged that flowerpot from the windowsill.'

'Sofia?'

'Yes. She was loitering on the landing, leaned out of the window to see if she could hear what you and Nick were talking about, leaned a bit too far and the pot fell. Thank God it missed you both otherwise… well, her talk with Nick might have been even trickier than it's going to be.'

Izzie stared at Jennie for a moment, savouring the warm flood of relief as she realised that no one had been intent on hurting Nick. The falling flower pot fiasco and the red wine incident had been just a couple of unfortunate, unconnected incidents that she had added together and made a mystery out of.

'But why didn't she say something straight away – if it was an accident, I mean?'

'I agree – and that's what I told her, too. The poor girl was mortified, but she wasn't ready to face Nick with the truth and she didn't want to colour his impression of her as someone who had almost killed him, before she…'

Jennie paused, inhaled a deep breath and met Izzie's eyes.

'…before she told him that he's her father.'

Izzie felt as if a firework had gone off inside her brain. She didn't know what she'd been expecting Jennie to say, but of all the things in the world of revelations it wasn't that!

'Her… her father?'

Jennie nodded, sympathy and compassion floating across her eyes. 'When Sofia's mother died, her Aunt Rosa agreed to support her in her quest to discover who her father was, which started by requesting a copy of her birth certificate from the authorities in Milan where she was born. It took a long time to arrive, but when it did and she saw her father's surname she knew it wouldn't take her long to find him.'

'Why not?'

'Because Oscar Roswell-Jones is a well-known cellist.'

'Okay…'

'The name might not mean anything to you, but to anyone with a passing interest in the classical music business, he's an absolute maestro.'

Izzie wrinkled her nose. 'I don't understand. Are you saying this Oscar guy is Sofia's father?'

'No, his son is.'

'His son?'

'Nicholas Roswell-Jones.'

'But Nick's surname is Morgan.'

'Yes, he changed his name after he graduated. His father had wanted Nick to pursue a musical career, like he had and his grandfather before him, and he derided his son's dream to teach music and drama to high school students. So, when Nick married Sarah, he changed his name to hers, instead of the other way round, and despite Nick's effort at a reconciliation, his father refused to speak to him right up until the day he died two years ago.'

'Oh, that is so sad…'

'Anyway, after trawling through her mother's diaries, Sofia found an entry that recorded Nick Roswell-Jones's marriage to Sarah Morgan and everything fell into place. So, with her aunt's help and blessing, she found a job at the theatre in York, and moved into a tiny studio flat, but it took her six months to build up the courage to join the Somersby Singers so she could find out what he was like, intending to speak to him when the time was right. Then, when Nick announced this trip to Tuscany to iron out the wrinkles in our Christmas repertoire, well, it was the right time.'

'And when did Sofia confide in you?'

'I found her sobbing her heart out one night behind the Somersby village hall where we hold our rehearsals. She tried to fob me off with a story about losing one of the costumes in the production of *Annie* she was working on, but I knew it had to be more than that. I have raised two children! Everything came tumbling out. I did try to persuade her that the sooner she spoke to Nick, the sooner she could start to come to terms with what fate had thrown in her path. I've been a member of the choir since the beginning – five years – and I was certain that Nick had no idea whatsoever about her existence, which Sofia knew was true from what her aunt had told her about her mother being adamant that she didn't want a relationship with him. It had been a holiday romance – a summer of love played out on the streets of Milan, over before they knew it. Sofia's mother wanted to stay in Milan, Nick had returned to his studies at university.'

The two women sat on the patio, lost in their respective thoughts until Izzie's phone started to ring again.

'Do you think you should answer that?'

Izzie took out her phone and glanced at the screen. Meghan again.

'It's my friend Meghan. She's flying out to San Vivaldo tomorrow with another friend of ours. I'll call her later when you're all safely on your way home. Anyway, my battery is almost dead – with everything going on to get the ingredients sorted for this morning's tutorial, I forgot to charge it.'

'Sorry, Izzie, I don't think we'll have time to bake your snowy yule log now.'

'That's not as much of a loss as you might think!' she giggled. 'If I'm honest, I'm still trying to perfect the swiss roll recipe – every time I make it, it looks more like one of those rubber mats we used to do gymnastics on when I was at school!'

'I'm sure that's not true. Come on.'

Izzie and Jennie made their way back towards the terrace where Dylan and Phoebe were still canoodling under the pergola, oblivious to the drama going on around them, cossetted in their own little bubble of romance. Luca was loitering on the kitchen doorstep, his phone clenched to his ear, relief spreading across his face when he saw Izzie and Jennie approach.

'Where've you been? That was Gianni. He's had Meghan on the phone. She's been trying to call you, but your phone keeps going to voicemail.'

'I know, I know – my battery's dead. Can you ask Gianni to text her, please? Tell her everything is fine and I'll give her a call as soon as everyone's left for Antonio's.' Izzie smiled.

'Okay, *nessun problema*. Where are Sofia and Nick?'

'They're over in the gazebo.'

'I'd better go and fetch them – if we don't make a start on the next demonstration, we'll be late leaving for lunch and you have no idea what Carlos is like if he's kept waiting. And don't forget, the taxis for the airport are booked at three!'

Izzie laughed. 'That sounds like something I would say!'

'It's okay, Luca, Izzie and I have agreed to cancel the last patisserie session. Nick and Sofia have a few things they want to chat through before they leave for the village.

Dylan? Why don't you give Luca a hand with the luggage while I go and see how they're getting on?' said Jennie, already making her way down the garden path.

'Sure,' said Dylan, reluctantly unfolding himself from the wooden chair.

'I'll help you,' Phoebe said, springing out of her seat to join them.

Luca glanced at Izzie, his forehead creased in confusion at the sudden change in itinerary, but he simply shrugged and returned to the villa to help prepare everyone for their departure.

Chapter Twenty-Four

The pergola, Villa Limoncello

Colour: Lavender wisp

Izzie remained on the terrace, staring out at the scene of Tuscan paradise in front of her, trying to memorise the outline of every terracotta rooftop, every elegant cypress tree, every sun-filled field and vineyard, so she could reconstruct the image when the rain beat down with a vengeance on the Cornish countryside. She wished she could stay there for ever, drinking in the beauty of the scenery, enjoying the caress of the winter sunshine, inhaling the wisp of lavender floating on the air that would always remind her of her time in Italy.

Her concentration was broken by a rustle of leaves and, looking to her left, she saw Jennie, Nick and Sofia appear through the foliage. Izzie's heart soared when she saw that Nick had his arm resting on Sofia's shoulder, and they were both smiling despite the fact they had red-rimmed eyes. Then Dylan, Phoebe and Luca appeared from the kitchen doorway, lugging everyone's luggage out to the terrace.

'Okay, before we go, I've got an announcement to make,' said Nick, his booming voice causing everyone to stop what they were doing and take notice. 'Perhaps we could all take a seat over there under the pergola?'

'What's going on?' Phoebe whispered to Jennie, who simply shrugged, obviously not wanting to share Nick's secrets before he did.

'I hope it's not another damn concert,' muttered Dylan, abandoning the heavy suitcases and following everyone back to the table under the pergola. 'We've already got seven on the itinerary, and with the five gigs I've agreed to do with my brother over the holidays, I think I'll be spending the whole of Christmas Day sleeping!'

Once everyone had taken a seat, they turned to face Nick, who had remained standing in front of them, as if he was about to conduct an impromptu recital for Izzie and Luca's benefit before they left for their lunch at Antonio's Trattoria and then Florence Airport.

'As I've just been presented with the most amazing Christmas gift a man could wish for – which if you'll forgive me, will have to remain a secret for a little while longer so that Sarah can be by my side when I announce it to the world...' Nick sent a surreptitious glance in Sofia's direction, who gave him an encouraging smile and a nod. 'I wanted to give you all something too, something that I've been wanting to tell you since we came out here to Tuscany.'

'What's going on, Nick?' asked Dylan, flicking his eyes at Sofia, who avoiding looking at him, then rolling his eyes in Phoebe's direction.

'I know you all think I've been like a tenacious terrier about all the choir practice this week, and I know I've pushed everybody to their limit at times, but I hope you'll agree that it's all been for a very good reason. I wanted us to be pitch perfect, every single note of every single verse of every single song, and, thanks to your hard work and dedication, I think we've achieved that goal.'

'Definitely!' declared Phoebe.

'Well, I hope you'll forgive my underhand tactics.'

'Hardly underhand,' laughed Jennie, smiling around the group, her bejewelled glasses sending rainbows of colourful sunshine onto the tabletop. 'I'd swap our draughty village hall for a converted barn in the Italian countryside any day!'

'Well, as Dylan has reminded us, we have seven concerts organised over the next two weeks, culminating in our Christmas Eve extravaganza.'

'At the local retirement home,' mumbled Dylan, before plastering a fake-excited grin on his face for Nick's benefit.

'Well…' continued Nick, stretching up to his full height and puffing out his chest as he prepared to divulge his secret.

'Come on! Don't keep us in suspense!'

'I'm absolutely delighted to inform you that the Somersby Singers have been selected to perform our Christmas Eve concert in…'

He paused to extract the maximum effect.

'Nick!'

'…in York Minster!'

'Oh, my God!'

'Wow!

'Yay!'

Whoops of excitement and disbelief exploded as Izzie jumped out of her seat to embrace everyone. It was quite a while before they calmed down and realised that Nick was still standing in front of them, waiting patiently to continue with his speech.

'Is there something else?' asked Jennie, her cheeks an attractive shade of pink from the surprise gift of good fortune.

'Yes, there is.'

The group dutifully settled back in their chairs and stared up at their conductor, the man who had guided them through a complex musical labyrinth until they arrived at a harmonious ensemble. Nick's face was filled with such happiness Izzie thought her heart would burst.

'After the news I've had this afternoon, I have to say I think I must be the most fortunate man in the whole of Italy right now, but anyway…'

For a moment Nick paused, this time not for effect, but so he could swallow down on a sudden ambush of emotion, but he rallied quickly.

'We're not just performing any old carol concert in the best venue Yorkshire has to offer a community choir.'

'What do you mean?'

'Well, you're not going to believe this…'

'Nick!'

'The whole thing is going to be televised – live!'

This time the whole group erupted into a rhapsody of reactions, from gobsmacked disbelief and astonishment, to joyous excitement and celebration as they flung their arms around each other, everyone's eyes shining with tears, even Dylan's.

'Oh, my God, Nick, how on earth did you manage to land such an amazing gig?'

'Remember that weekend at the end of September when we did our first run-through of our Christmas repertoire?'

'Yes…'

'Remember those two guys who sat in at the back, making notes on a clipboard?'

'Yes, you told us they were from the council, something about health and safety. I remembered thinking it ridiculous that anyone could possibly be suggesting that we might come to any harm whilst singing a few Christmas songs!'

'Well, they were scouts from a TV company. I didn't tell anyone in case their presence adversely affected our performance – you know what Dorothy and Freya are like. But I didn't want to raise anyone's expectations either. There were over thirty choirs in the running, but I heard a couple of weeks ago that we'd been selected for our style and panache. It'll be us and another choir from Harrogate entertaining the worshippers on Christmas Eve. I know I should have come clean right there and then, but to be honest I went into panic mode. God! We're actually going to be on television! Our choir, live, in York Minster! We can't just be technically perfect, we have to be more than that – we have to be sensational!'

'And we are!' declared Sofia, speaking for the first time as she rose from her seat and went to hug Nick, followed by every member of the choir.

'Thanks, Nick!'

'God, I'm so excited! But what am I going to wear!' cried Jennie, fiddling with her jewel-encrusted spectacles.

'Ah, now that's one thing that isn't in my control, I'm afraid.'

'Why not?'

'I had to sign an agreement that we would all wear the same outfit.'

'Nooo… Not those awful polo shirts!'

''Fraid so!'

There was a pause, then everyone burst into laughter at the look of abject horror on Phoebe's face.

A few moments later, a screech of brakes broke through their noisy celebrations as a taxi drew to a halt at the end of the villa's driveway and the impatient driver honked his horn with alacrity. Everyone went to collect their luggage, still chattering ten to the dozen as they hugged Izzie and Luca, singing their praises for their week at Villa Limoncello, vowing to stay in touch, to make a return visit, to book future courses with friends and family, before piling into the taxi for their trip to San Vivaldo's best trattoria.

Izzie stood next to Luca on the front steps, waving goodbye to the group of strangers who had become firm friends, a cauldron of emotions threatening to overwhelm her: excitement for the Christmas carol concert that would give each and every member of the choir something to talk about for the rest of their lives, empathy for the trials and tribulations each one of them had to face over the coming weeks as they wove the secrets that had been exposed in Tuscany into their normal day-to-day lives, and trepidation because it was now time for her and Luca to sit down, without any interruptions, and talk about their own future.

Chapter Twenty-Five

The pergola, Villa Limoncello

Colour: Pearlescent mirage

'Luca, I—'

'I'm sorry, Izzie, hang on...'

Luca reached for his phone and glanced at the screen, his eyes clouding as he shook his head in dismay. '*Carlos? Cosa sta succedendo?*'

Pause.

'*Sì, sì, vengo!*'

'What's happened?' asked Izzie.

'Carlos has somehow managed to fuse the lights in the kitchen and we have a full restaurant, including the fifteen choir members, waiting for their *tordelli versiliesi*! Look Izzie, I know we need to talk, but I've got to sort this out, then we can have the whole evening to ourselves, just the two of us – no interruptions, no guests wandering in to disturb us, and I promise I'll switch my phone off, even if the restaurant has exploded into a nuclear mushroom of pesto.'

Izzie saw the genuine regret on Luca's face and smiled.

'It's no problem, Luca. I've got lots to do to get the villa ready for Meghan and Jonti's arrival tomorrow, so I'll see you later.'

Luca stepped forward, paused for the merest second, and then seemed to change his mind by depositing kisses on her cheeks instead of her waiting lips.

'*Ciao!*'

Minutes later he was racing in the wake of their guests down the driveway, intent on sending the choir off to the airport with full stomachs and a positive impression of Tuscan hospitality.

Izzie remained on the front steps watching his Spider disappear through the gates, then listening to the powerful engine speed off towards the village. She knew he would be back as soon as he could, but in that moment she felt bereft, alone at the villa which, it seemed to her, was always thrumming with activity.

She sauntered to the kitchen, collected her purple folder and withdrew the sheet headed 'Wrap Up' – might as well make a start on the list she had drafted to make sure the studio, the grounds and every room in the villa were returned to the same pristine glory as when the guests had arrived. She ran her eyes down the items, but for the first time she felt no compelling urge to tick the boxes, to perform the numerous tasks in the correct order until the list was complete and she could indulge in a congratulatory coffee.

What would happen if she ignored her list?

What if she simply grabbed her basket of cleaning products and worked her way through the bedrooms, carrying out her chores at random as needed?

What was the worst that could happen if she ditched her obsessive reliance on her lists?

If she forgot to put out fresh soaps, or didn't dust the windowsills, or place a vase of fresh lavender on the bedside table, or run her feather duster over the picture frames, would Meghan and Jonti really berate her for it?

She stood at the kitchen table, fighting the two demons perched on her shoulders: one arguing the case for sticking to the tried-and-tested routine which made for speed and precision, the other arguing for a more relaxed, creative approach to her housekeeping duties. Rigid adherence left no room for error, but also no room for creative divergence – she had learned that over the last six months.

Okay!

She was no longer the same woman who had arrived at Villa Limoncello weighed down by grief and loss. She had shrugged off her cloak of melancholy and turned her face towards the sun, so she would do the same with her lists – go cold turkey!

She snapped the old, faithful folder shut, gathered together her cleaning materials and spent the next two hours with her iPod plugged into her ears, dancing to 'Rockin' Around the Christmas Tree', 'Jingle Bell Rock' and her personal favourite, 'All I Want for Christmas is You', as she stripped beds, scrubbed bath-rooms and washed floors until everywhere was sparkling clean and the smell of fresh soap and furniture polish meandered through the suites. She only hoped that she wouldn't be singing 'Last Christmas' when Luca came back to talk to her.

She decided to gather a few sprigs of fresh rosemary for Meghan's room, and reminded herself to tell her the story Francesca had told them about inhaling the herb on Christmas Eve. Meghan would love that, and so would Jonti. She then stored her bucket and yellow Marigolds under the sink and trotted across the terrace to the garden, humming her own version of 'Santa Claus is Comin' to Town' as she selected a bunch of the glossiest stalks of rosemary.

On her way back, she caught the final ring of the house phone and sighed, remembering she still hadn't re-charged her phone. She was about to make her way to the kitchen to locate her charger when she heard the crunch of car tyres on the gravel in the driveway and her heart skipped a beat.

Luca!

Izzie smiled – he was earlier than she'd expected. She was eager to sit down with him and just talk about everything that was swirling around in her head. She needed to tell him about the flowerpot incident being an unfortunate accident, as indeed the wine stain on Nick's dinner jacket must have been, but more than that she wanted to find out how he felt about selling the villa, how he felt about her! She truly hoped that she would hear the words she wanted to hear so she could tell him that she wasn't going to accept Harry's offer, that she wanted to stay in San Vivaldo, that she loved him. But what if he didn't?

She crossed the terrace, passed the pergola and walked round to the front steps where she came to an abrupt halt and her whole world tilted on its axis as she tried to assimilate what her eyes were telling to believe.

At first she though it was some kind of mirage – the tall blonde figure emerging from the driver's seat of a nondescript white hire car – until the apparition spoke in a voice almost as familiar as her own, albeit from some point in the past.

'Izzie?'

'Oh my God! Alex!'

An explosion of confusion burst into her brain. She glanced over his shoulder to see who was with him, but he was alone. She was vaguely aware that Alex's lips were moving, but she couldn't hear what he was saying through the cloud of incomprehension that had wrapped its tendrils around her.

After a couple of moments, the shockwave abated sufficiently for her to tune back into reality. As strange as it seemed, Alex, her ex-fiancé whom she hadn't laid eyes on for months, was standing in front of her on the terrace at Villa Limoncello, smiling as though he had just been passing by and decided to call in for a coffee. He looked exactly as he always did: clean-shaven, his hair neatly barbered with a smidgeon of gel in the quiff at the front, smart chinos and a crease-free linen shirt in a pale ivory colour. If she hadn't already known he was a fully paid-up member of the legal profession, it would have been her first guess.

'Izzie? Are you okay?'

'No… erm, I mean, yes… I don't actually…' she spluttered, waiting for her heart rate to calm from sprint to trot. She scrutinised the hire car again. 'Is Penny with you?'

'No, I thought you knew, we're not together any more. Actually, she's over in Toronto. Got a job offer to work for a glossy magazine – a dream come true, she says.'

'Oh…' was all she could think of to say, her brain curiously blank.

'I'm sorry to just drop in on you, Iz, I know it's a bit of a surprise, but… erm, do you think we could sit down?'

Izzie nodded and led Alex to a chair underneath the pergola, for some reason her subconscious preventing her from showing him into the villa. When they were seated, she leapt back up again.

'I'll get us some coffee.'

She rushed off to the kitchen and set the kettle to boil, gripping the countertop to steady herself, taking deep breaths until she felt like herself again. She pulled out her phone to plug it into her charger and when she'd done so, she saw that she'd had four missed calls from Meghan and a text. She clicked the tiny envelope and all she could see at first was a series of exclamation marks. Then she read the message.

Alex on his way!!!!

Yes, she knew that.

As though on autopilot, she went through the motions of making a cafetière of coffee, plonked two mugs on a tray with a jug of fresh milk and, on wobbly legs, carried it outside, where Alex seemed to have made himself at home, leaning back in his chair with his arms stretched behind his head, taking in the spectacular scenery.

'It's a stunning view! I totally get why you're over here.'

'Who told you where I was?'

'Oh, I bumped into Jonti at the theatre last week and he waxed lyrical about the place, even showed me some of the photographs you and Meghan have sent to him on his phone. He also told me how much you love Tuscany and this gorgeous villa named after the lemons that are grown here, and how happy you are running the retreats, and he's right, you look amazing. The place clearly agrees with you – you're so much more like the old Izzie, before… well, just before.'

Alex fiddled with the fastening of the gold watch at his wrist, clearly unsure whether he should utter Anna's name so soon in their conversation.

Izzie took pity on him. Okay, so he'd landed on her doorstep uninvited and unexpected, which was perhaps a little rude, but their break-up hadn't been in the least acrimonious. In fact, if truth be told, Alex had done everything in his power and more to be supportive after she'd lost Anna. It had been *her* who had withdrawn, shut him out, for some reason not feeling worthy of being loved by him, strange though it sounded. Alex had waited patiently, and would have continued to do so, but she had pushed him away.

On that heartbreaking day two years ago, Anna had been in the throes of organising the most amazing wedding St Ives had ever seen. Her sister was marrying her childhood sweetheart, Josh, and wanted to involve everyone she loved in their celebrations, including her reception class pupils, and the thought of arranging her own wedding to Alex only ten months later had filled her with dread. So she had called off their engagement and told Alex to move on with his life. To give him his due, he had put up a good fight, tried to make her see that it was her grief talking, assured her that he loved her and would wait for as long as it took, but she didn't want him to wait.

In fact, the remorse Izzie had felt about keeping Alex hanging on had only added to the overwhelming feelings of guilt she carried with her – that she had survived to live another day when her sister hadn't. She hadn't told anyone how she felt, but when Alex eventually accepted that she wasn't going to change her mind and moved out of their flat, a little of the heavy load she carried had lifted because she wasn't dragging his emotions down with hers. She had even liked Perfect Penny, as Jonti had called Alex's new girlfriend after he'd introduced her to them when they'd bumped into him whilst on a date at the theatre. She was happy he had met someone else, and now she was sad that it hadn't lasted.

'I'm sorry to hear about you and Penny.'

'Oh, we broke up a couple of months ago, we're still friends, and she's even emailed me some photos of her trip to Niagara Falls, which, I have to tell you, looks awesome!'

Izzie was starting to feel strange, as though she was having an out-of-body experience, floating on high and looking down at the incongruous situation she found herself in: sitting there, surrounded by the bucolic Tuscan countryside, talking to Alex as if nothing had happened between them. But *everything* had happened, and she was no longer the same Izzie he had known.

'Alex, why are you here?'

'Jonti told me about Harry's offer – the renovation project in Cornwall? It sounds fabulous, Izzie, exactly the sort of challenge you love to get stuck into. I bet you already have a draft vision for the whole development. And creative director for Hambleton Homes, too!'

'Yes, it's a very generous offer.'

'And to be able to see your parents whenever you want. Oh, Iz, I'm so pleased this has happened after everything you've been through. I just know you'll be happy there.'

Izzie took a sip of her coffee, peering over the rim at Alex and noticing he had started to fiddle with his watch again – something he always did when he was nervous. Alex always dressed immaculately, and he owned a huge collection of silk ties, both sober and outrageous, but he had a particular obsession with watches and at last count he had well over a hundred from Rotary to Rolex, from big brash diver's watches to colourful Mickey Mouse ones with protruding ears. That day's choice was a watch she had bought for him at Tiffany's when they were celebrating their engagement in New York and her heart gave a nip of emotion at the memory. Alex had seen her glance at his wrist.

'Remember when we got this?'

'I do.'

'It was a great trip, wasn't it?'

'I think it was one of the best trips of my life,' she said, smiling as she met his eyes, her curiosity mounting as she realised that Alex was clearly building up to broach a difficult subject.

Another pause in the conversation allowed Izzie to tune into the sound of the creatures who called Villa Limoncello their home, going about their daily business, and inhale the familiar aroma of the herbs that surrounded the terrace: sage, thyme, oregano, a hint of lavender.

'How are things at work?' she blurted to fill in the uncomfortable silence, then kicked herself for going with such a mundane question. She no longer had any interest in Alex's climb up the corporate ladder of the legal profession.

'Actually, they've offered me a partnership from next March, but well, that's why I'm here.'

'It is?'

Izzie scrunched up her nose in surprise. Surely Alex didn't want her advice on his career progression? If he did, then he'd come to the wrong place because she had no idea what partnership entailed and anyway, she could have easily told him that over the phone.

'I'm not going to take it.'

'But I thought that was what you've been working towards for the last five years. It's the golden ticket, you said.'

'Things change, Iz. People change.'

Alex allowed his gaze to rest on Izzie, but she couldn't read the meaning that nestled there. He looked like the same Alex to her, the honest, hardworking, ambitious guy who would never bend the rules – it was what she had loved about him. The apartment they had shared in a block overlooking the Thames had been run like a well-oiled machine, the bills paid on time, insurances kept up-to-date, utility providers changed regularly to ensure the best deals.

'What do you mean?'

'You know that I've always loved messing about on the water,' Alex began tentatively.

That was an understatement, Izzie thought with a wry smile. When he wasn't championing his legal causes, Alex had spent every spare moment at the local rowing club, training for the next race or simply hanging out with his like-minded friends. And on their rare weekends away, they'd had to choose somewhere there would be boats to hire, or diving expeditions to take part in, or surf schools to join. Loved messing about on the water? In another life Alex would have been a merman!

'Yes,' she laughed. 'How could I forget? I've spent enough time freezing my socks off on the banks of a river or on the beach watching you compete in a boat race!'

'Remember that time we capsized in the Solent and Bart screamed blue murder because he'd just had highlights done and he thought the salt water would turn his hair green!'

'I do!'

They both laughed, enjoying the memory.

'He and Juliet are getting married next year, by the way. Valentine's Day – then they're moving back to Plymouth. And remember Marcus, Penny's brother? He's renting a place in Brighton for a year to pursue his love of ceramics and so he can be with Brett – he's in his element because they've just taken on a couple of Labradoodles.'

Izzie shook her head at that snippet of news. Jonti, who had been particularly taken with Penny's younger brother, would be devastated when he heard that. Thinking of Jonti brought Izzie's thoughts screeching back to the present.

'Alex, I…'

'As I was saying, people change and things can happen to make us reassess our priorities. And… well, I've been offered a job at a diving school in Newquay, starting in the new year, and I thought…'

Izzie stared at Alex as the pieces of the jigsaw started to drop into place. She saw his cheeks colour, but nevertheless he held her gaze, the story they told at last making it abundantly clear why he was sitting opposite her under the pergola at Villa Limoncello.

'Alex, I…'

'It's perfect, Iz, just hear me out. You accept Harry's proposal, move back down to St Ives, and I take the job at the diving school. We can start over, take it slowly, no pressure. I'll rent a place and you, well, I assume you'll stay at your mum and dad's? We can date, see how we get on. It's a second chance to build a new life together in Cornwall, away from the frantic frenzy of London, to live life at a slower pace so we can both follow our dreams.'

'Oh, Alex…'

'I still love you, Iz. I never fell out of love with you, you just seemed to float away from me, so far that I couldn't get you back. I tried so hard…'

'I know you did, Alex, I know you did,' she whispered, her heart contracting painfully at the memory, but also at the hope that was shining through the tears glistening at the corners of his eyes.

'We were good together. I've never felt the same way about anyone as I do about you. You're my soulmate and this is our chance to reconnect. What do you say?'

Chapter Twenty-Six

The terrace, Villa Limoncello

Colour: Electric blue

The shock of Alex's suggestion sent her emotions in a kaleidoscope of directions. Questions ricocheted around her head, one after the other, in a procession of alternatives, each one with pros and cons attached.

Should she take Harry up on his offer – reintegrate into the community that had been her home for twenty-one years, where everyone knew everything about her and the pain that had shattered her heart? Take some time to consider what Alex had said?

Should she go back to London – look for a new job there and go back to her old life with Meghan and Jonti by her side?

Or should she make a go of things in Tuscany, irrespective of what Luca was planning for the villa?

She thought of her purple folder lying on the kitchen table, its pull almost irresistible, its call telling her to take a blank piece of paper and make a list of the advantages and disadvantages of each of the options, then simply add up the number of ticks and pursue the choice which claimed top spot.

That was what the old Izzie would have done, the one who had arrived in San Vivaldo six months ago, adhering rigidly to a fixed routine for fear her world would collapse around her if there was no scaffolding to hold it together. She started to assemble her arguments for the return to Cornwall without the help of a pen and paper, but stopped and gave herself a mental head slap.

Stop it!

Had she learned nothing from her stay at Villa Limoncello?

A decision like this shouldn't be made by over-analysing, over-thinking, or what looked better 'on paper'. It should be made by listening to her heart. Sitting in front of her, Alex embodied everything from her former life, a life she hardly recognised despite how happy it had been, despite how much she had loved him then. The truth was that she didn't love him *now* and she didn't need a list to tell her that.

She looked Alex in the eye, a surge of affection flooding her body – affection, not love. The sort of feeling she would have if she was sitting next to her brother, listening to his plans for a new start, urging him to do what made him happy. She wanted Alex to follow his dreams, but she knew they couldn't include her. She would continue to be his friend, she would always be his friend, but she could never do what he was asking her to do – the only path for her was forwards.

'I'm sorry, Alex.'

She placed her hand over his, saddened by the dash of pain in his eyes.

'I don't think it would work. We can't go back to how we were, no matter how much we want to.'

'Izzie, I…'

'And, actually, I've already made my decision about Harry's offer. I'm going to call him tomorrow to thank him for his faith in my abilities, but the answer will be no.'

'But why? It's the perfect chance to…'

'Because when I think of myself living back in St Ives, the image I see doesn't spark excitement, happiness and joy!'

'Spark excitement?'

'Yes, when I think of spending even one hour here at Villa Limoncello in the *limonaia*, or sauntering through the olive groves, or sipping my morning coffee in the gazebo, the whole package ignites delight in my heart and that, from now on, is what my decision-making process is going to be based on. No more lists, no more tick-boxes, no more Rolodex, no more arch-lever files bursting with paperwork… just that one simple question – will that make me happy?'

'And living back in Cornwall won't do that?'

'I love Cornwall, but you know what? I don't think it will.'

'And living here in Tuscany will?'

Izzie smiled, glancing over her shoulder at the garden, the top of the marble fountain peeking from behind the magnolia tree, the muted buzz of the cicadas, the chiming of a distant church bell, and the feeling of complete serenity the villa seemed to inspire in her very soul. She had never been more certain of where she should be in her life. She didn't need a list to tell her that being there made her happy, she *knew* it did!

'Yes.'

'And I can't say anything to make you change your mind?'

She saw the flicker of hope in Alex's eyes extinguish when he saw the expression on her face and the regretful shake of her head.

'Sorry.'

Alex swallowed, glanced at his watch, and then smiled in resignation without a hint of criticism.

'Then I'm happy for you, too, Izzie. I'm happy that you've found a place where you can be yourself again, where you can be whole instead of the shattered soul you were in London. Maybe I'll find something that sparks my excitement in Newquay!'

'I hope so, Alex.'

With visible effort, Alex inhaled a long breath, straightened his shoulders and pushed himself up from his wooden seat, slotting his hands into the front pockets of his chinos and flapping his elbows.

'I don't suppose you know of any hotels or B&Bs around here that might have a spare room for a guy who's keen to find their own little slice of the solace you've discovered here in Italy, do you?'

Izzie laughed, going over to stand at his side as he admired the panoramic view. On the hilltop in front of them, the village of San Vivaldo slumbered under an electric blue sky, with its hotchpotch of terracotta roofs, the lone campanile, the wriggling tramlines of vines, all interspersed by pencil-thin cypress trees so typically Italian it could grace any tourist magazine. Yet, on the far horizon, a bank of silver-grey clouds gathered, and the temperature had dropped by several degrees.

'Actually, I do. Riccardo Clarke, the guy who owns the B&B next door, arrived back from his trip to London this morning and I'm sure he'll have no problem putting you up in one of his guest rooms. I think you'll like him.'

A smile twitched at her lips as she imagined Alex and Riccardo bonding over a love of detective novels and a glass or two of Vecchia Romagna brandy. Then something else sprang into her mind and she realised how she could thank Alex for everything he had done to support her whilst they had been together, and to soften the effect of her refusal to return to her old life.

'And there's someone else I'd like to introduce you to whilst you're over here.'

'There is?'

'Yes, her name's Carlotta Bellini – she lives in San Vivaldo and she's a…'

Izzie paused. How was she going to describe Carlotta to Alex? A superb cook? A staunch supporter of Villa Limoncello? A trusted and valued friend? Or the reason she wanted to introduce them – a matchmaking maestro?

'Well, she's a good friend of mine and you're going to like her, too.'

'I'm sure I will,' said Alex, politely, with no idea what he had in store. 'Thanks, Izzie.'

'There's no need to thank me.'

A flutter of excitement passed through her body as she anticipated Carlotta working her particular brand of magic on Alex and for some unknown reason an image of Oriana floated across her vision. She almost laughed out loud. Perhaps Carlotta's skills included telepathy, as well?

When Alex turned to face her, she hadn't realised how close he was. She met his pale blue gaze, and, when he placed his hand gently on her shoulder, for a moment she thought he was going to lean forward and kiss her. His mouth was inches from hers and she could smell the spicy cologne he had always worn, but instead of the anticipation and desire she had experienced a long time ago when he'd looked at her like that, she felt the same as she did when Jonti greeted her with a friendly kiss. She raised herself onto her tiptoes and brushed his cheek with her lips.

'We'll catch up later, Alex.'

'Okay. Thanks, Izzie,' he whispered, his voice heavy with regret as he drew her closer and hugged her to him with such unbelievable tenderness she almost burst into tears.

As she pulled out of his embrace, she saw a flicker of movement behind the foliage of the rhododendron bush that guarded the entrance to the terrace. Perhaps it was the mounting breeze tickling at the leaves, or the rustle of an animal making its way back to its underground home, but then the fierce revving of a high-powered engine sliced through the air and a flash of scarlet shot down the driveway, through the gates and out to the road beyond.

Chapter Twenty-Seven

Antonio's Trattoria, San Vivaldo

Colour: Love-heart red

'Oh, my God! No!'

The tumult of emotions that exploded inside Izzie left her in no doubt where her heart lay and she couldn't wait a moment longer to tell Luca how she felt about him. If Alex could travel all the way from London to San Vivaldo to talk to her face-to-face, despite the risk of being turned down, then she could hop onto the little pink Vespa hibernating in the shed and drive as fast as she could to Antonio's.

'See that gate over there? The one hidden by those cypress trees?'

'Erm… yes?'

'That's the entrance to Riccardo's B&B. Sorry, Alex, you'll have to fend for yourself – there's something I have to do.'

Ignoring the look of incredulity on Alex's face, she dashed across the terrace, yanked open the door of the delipidated outbuilding next to the *limonaia*, and wheeled out her trusty steed. Once she'd reached the front steps, she shoved the helmet over her curls, cocked her leg over the seat and started the engine, smiling when it caught first time. With a whoosh of exhilaration, she was down the driveway in a flash and out onto the open road, navigating the twists and turns with care.

As she leaned low over the handlebars to squeeze the last gasp of speed from the Vespa to make the final climb into San Vivaldo, she saw for the first time that the clouds had morphed from silver-grey to a dark ominous pewter, and the air temperature had dropped considerably, causing her forearms to prickle with goosebumps. But she hardly noticed her discomfort because her heart was hammering a concerto of determination as she practised what she wanted to say to Luca when she caught up with him.

She arrived in the cobbled piazza in record time, jumped from the seat of the Vespa, tossed the helmet over the handlebars and sprinted towards the trattoria, pausing to catch her breath on the top step of the wooden veranda from where she could see Luca's scarlet Spider parked in the alleyway nearby. She peered into the restaurant, relieved to see the choir had already departed for the airport, leaving just a smattering of diners lingering over their post-lunch coffees, then pushed the door open and took a step inside.

Her eyes locked onto Luca's immediately, drawing her to him as if by a magnetic force. For the briefest of moments, the rest of the world seemed to recede into the inconsequential and all that mattered was the way Luca was looking at her, his expression serious, his dark chocolate gaze scorching deep into her soul.

'Luca, I…'

Suddenly, everything she had rehearsed on the journey over there drained from her mind and she was left with a blank. As if in slow motion, she watched Luca stride the length of the restaurant with every single patron's eye following him, their conversations on hold as they settled back in their seats to watch the drama that was taking place in front of them unfold.

'I'm sorry, Luca, I had no idea… about… he just turned up… he just…'

Luca reached out to place his hand gently on her arm.

'I'm sorry, too, Izzie. I should have talked to you about what was going on a lot sooner. I should have told you how I felt about you, how much you mean to me. When you went back to the UK in September, I missed you so much it felt like someone had torn my heart out. I realised then that life without you by my side was not an option. But I understand why you've decided to go home to Cornwall, I really do, and…'

'Luca, I'm not going back to Cornwall.'

'But I thought… when I saw you with… I assumed…'

A burst of joy exploded in Izzie's chest and she didn't care if they had an audience, because the way she feeling she would have happily shouted her love for this wonderful man from the terracotta rooftops!

'Yes, that was Alex, and believe me, I had no idea he was coming over to Italy. And yes, he did make the trip across to try and persuade me to take up Harry's offer. Alex also told me that he's been offered a job at one of the local surf schools in Newquay, that he intends to chase *his* dreams, too. I'm happy for him, but his dreams will have to be pursued without me. I'll be forever grateful to him for steering me through the most painful period of my life, and I still have a great deal of affection for him, but I don't love him. What you saw on the terrace at the villa just now was me telling him exactly that – and sending him round to Riccardo's to see if he has a spare room.'

Luca stared at her as he assimilated everything she had said. Silence expanded into all four corners of the restaurant as everyone held their breath, waiting for the next scene in the story to be played out. Even Carlos had appeared at the kitchen door to see what was happening, a tea towel slung over his shoulder, a wide smile on his face.

Holding his gaze, Izzie took a step forward and murmured, '*Ti amo, Luca.*'

'*Ti amo anch'io*,' Luca whispered back, his lips curling upwards to form those wonderful dimples that had featured in every one of her dreams since arriving in Tuscany.

When Izzie saw the depth of feeling in his eyes, her stomach bounced to her toes and back again, and when she felt his breath on her cheek, inhaled the familiar fragrance of his cologne, and heard the faint strain of an Italian aria rippling through the air, a surge of unbridled pleasure spread through her veins.

'Luca, I…'

'*Shh…*'

And suddenly Luca's lips were on hers, his fingers lacing through the tangle of curls at the back of her neck so he could pull her closer to him. She kissed him back, trying to express every single emotion that was cascading through her body in that one kiss. Luca had introduced her to a profusion of amazing things: glorious food, delicious wine, the spectacular sights and sounds of San Vivaldo and its many wonderful people, but he had also taught her how to open her heart and let the Tuscan sunshine pour in.

Eventually she pulled away, breathless, a giggle erupting when the whole restaurant burst into applause to celebrate the epilogue of the impromptu romance that was playing out in front of them, a story that reaffirmed in every heart that, no matter the distress, the pain, the grief or the sadness that life bestows on its participants, in the end love will conquer all.

Luca laughed and took a bow to accept the applause for their kiss, and then obliged with a quick encore, before grabbing Izzie by the waist, lifting her in the air and spinning her around and around and around until she begged him to stop. The diners returned to their desserts and their conversations resumed, the level of their voices drowning out the background music as they discussed what they had just witnessed.

'Come on,' Luca murmured, guiding Izzie towards the door, pausing briefly to snatch a coat and scarf from the hanger and drape them around her shoulders. She followed him outside to a table on the veranda next to a patio heater, but stopped abruptly.

'Oh my God! Look!'

She tipped her head back in delight as snowflakes as light as feathers drifted down from the leaden sky, transforming the whole scene – usually awash with golden sunshine – into a winter wonderland. She laughed, then ran down the steps to the piazza, her palms held upwards, pirouetting like a ballerina in an attempt to catch just one of the perfectly formed flakes, joy exuding from every pore. Luca caught up with her outside Oriana's bakery, producing a knitted hat from his pocket and jamming it down on to her corkscrew curls.

'Life is certainly a rollercoaster with you at the helm!'

'Isn't it magical?'

Luca reached out and pulled her close, so close she could feel his heart beating through his flimsy chef's jacket. When he lowered his mouth to hers she felt as if she was melting into his arms, and now she was able to take her time to relish the discovery of every contour of his lips, savouring the feel, the taste, and all the tingling sensations that were spreading through her veins like wildfire. Eventually, she pulled away and Luca ushered her back to the veranda, where they took refuge from the increasing flurry of snow and his expression turned serious.

'I'd better get back inside or I might get fired!'

Izzie laughed. 'Fired! What are you talking about? You own the place!'

'Not any more.'

'What?'

She stopped in her tracks, staring at Luca, who was a few paces in front of her.

'Luca?'

But he kept on walking, forcing her to run to catch up with him.

'Luca? What do you mean "not any more"?'

They'd reached the door of the trattoria, shaded from the worst of the snow by the overhead canopy proudly sporting the colours of the Italian flag.

'I don't know why I didn't think of it before.'

'Think of what?'

'I've sold the restaurant.'

'You've... Oh my God! Luca, why? You love Antonio's – it's always been your dream to be a chef in your own trattoria!'

'Dreams change.'

'Who's the new owner?'

'Carlos.'

'Carlos?' she laughed.

'And his brother Filippo. I've promised to stay on for a couple of months until the Christmas rush is out of the way, but then it's all theirs.'

'But Luca, if you've sold the restaurant, what are you going to do? Oh, my God, are you... are you going back to banking?'

'No way!' He looked horrified. 'I'm going to chase a new dream.'

'What new dream?'

'I'm going to put all my efforts, and the money I make from the sale of the restaurant, into finalising the renovations at Villa dei Limoni so we can promote it as a luxury retreat for discerning travellers who want to expand their minds as well as enjoy a taste of the real Tuscany – with the woman I love by my side. What do you say, Izzie? Will you be my partner?'

For a moment she couldn't speak. Stay on at Villa Limoncello? It was the best offer she'd had all year! As the snowflakes morphed from gentle flurry to leisurely tumble, she stared at the man who had changed her life from snoring boring monochrome to exciting vibrant Technicolor, her heart pounding out a melody of joy.

'Yes! Yes! Yes! I'd love to stay at the villa, Luca!'

She flung her arms around his neck, the turbulent torrent of emotions she'd experienced in the space of thirty minutes threatening to overwhelm her.

'Isabella Grace Jenkins, you are the most amazing woman I've ever had the good fortune to run off the road into a field of sunflowers and donkeys. You've filled my world with chaos and confusion, but also with an abundance of creativity and colour. *Ti amo, ti amo, ti amo!*'

'I love you too, Luca,' she murmured, slipping her hand into his.

Izzie glanced up to the snow-laden clouds, picked out the fluffiest of them all and sent up a prayer of thankfulness. It might have been the tears gathering along her lashes, but she was sure she saw its silver-coloured lining curl upwards into a smile of approval and she knew it was a sign that her beloved sister was beaming down at them, bestowing them with her blessing.

Chapter Twenty-Eight

Villa Limoncello, San Vivaldo, Tuscany

Colour: Glittering crystal

'Hey, Izzie, darling!'

Jonti jumped out of the back seat of the taxi before it had even drawn to a halt at the front steps of the villa.

'Hi, Jonti, welcome to Villa Limoncello!'

'Oh, my God, you look absolutely amazing!' he declared, squeezing Izzie so tight she squealed in objection. 'Where's Luca? I can't wait to meet him. It's all Meghan talked about on the plane on the way over. Gianni this, Luca that, Gianni this, Luca that. God, it's enough to make a poor guy turn green with envy. Hey, where do you think you're skipping off to,' he called after Meghan as she scampered away towards the garden in search of the man who had stolen her heart. 'What about the luggage!'

'It's okay, Jonti. I'll help you, and Luca's in the kitchen putting the finishing touches to lunch. Come on.'

The snow of the previous day had vanished as quickly as it had arrived, and that Saturday morning had dawned with a crisp cerulean sky and not a cloud in sight to welcome Jonti and Meghan for their weekend of rest and relaxation before the Christmas shopping hordes descended on the most prestigious store in Knightsbridge.

'And there's someone else who wants to meet you, too.'

'Who? Oh, what a delightful little dog!'

Jonti paused to fondle Pipo's ears as the little dog snoozed in the wicker basket hooked over the handlebars of an ancient silver bicycle parked next to the pergola. Then he stopped, mid-stroke, and turned to stare at Izzie, his hand flying to his lips as he let out a gasp.

'Oh my God! No way! Are you sure? Oh, Izzie, darling, thank you, thank you, thank you!'

She giggled as Jonti smoothed his hand over his bleached blonde quiff, straightened the lapels of his chunky emerald cardigan depicting a Christmas tree resplendent with real baubles and embroidered gold tinsel, then checked that his orange winkle-pickers were free of blemishes.

'Do I look okay?'

'You look fabulous!'

'Oh, my God! I actually think all my Christmases might have come at once! Okay, breathe, breathe, calm, calm. Right, lead the way!'

Izzie linked her arm though Jonti's and guided him across the terrace, where she paused briefly to point out the village of San Vivaldo on the hilltop, but she knew he wasn't interested in the various merits of the Tuscan landscape.

'Yes, lovely, darling…' he muttered.

Smiling, she took pity on him, and pushed open the kitchen door, inhaling the aroma of warm focaccia infused with rosemary and garlic, mixed with a soupçon of Christmas spices from the panettone Luca had baked that morning especially for Meghan and Jonti's arrival.

'Jonti, this is Luca Castelotti. Luca, this is one of my best friends in the whole world, Jonti Montgomery.'

Luca stepped away from the table, where he'd been putting the finishing touches to a four-tier cannoli cake smothered in rich vanilla buttercream and decorated with curls of orange zest, to offer Jonti his palm and a welcoming smile. Izzie saw from the playful glint in her friend's eye that he approved and when Luca turned back to collect a batch of serviettes, Jonti placed his hand on his heart and performed a theatrical swoon. Izzie rolled her eyes at him then giggled.

However, whilst Jonti had been keen to meet the man who had healed Izzie's broken heart, it wasn't Luca he was desperate to meet.

'And this is Carlotta Bellini.'

Jonti stared at Carlotta for a second as though he was in the presence of Italian royalty and he'd lost his nerve, before a wide smile spread across his handsome features. He stepped towards Carlotta, who reached up to place the customary kisses on his cheeks, causing his cheeks to colour, but his eyes glittered with joy.

'*Ciao, Jonti*.'

'Carlotta, I'm thrilled to meet you at last. I've heard so, *so* much about you. Now, I hope you don't mind, but

I've brought you a little something from the cathedral of consumerism that claims most of my waking hours.'

Jonti rummaged in his Gucci holdall for a moment and removed a parcel that had been exquisitely wrapped in Harrods' signature gold and green colours.

'*Grazie*.' Carlotta smiled, accepting the gift as Luca and Izzie watched on in curiosity.

'Izzie told me about Pipo.'

'Ah…'

Carlotta tore off the paper and beamed when she saw the silver dog collar, peppered with glittering crystals, and a matching lead.

'*Oh, Jonti, grazie, grazie mille*. Pipo will love it!'

Carlotta kissed Jonti again, and then linked her arm though his and led him back outside to the terrace to present the gift to the little dog, the pair chattering as they went, already firm friends.

'Now, I want you to tell me all about your legendary matchmaking successes. Is it true that you not only introduced Izzie to Luca and Meghan to Gianni, but also two of the guests that came on the Painting & Pasta-Making course in July, *and* two members of the choir on the Snowflakes & Christmas Cakes course just last week?'

'And Stephano and Louisa,' shouted Luca as they disappeared out of the door.

'I thought we were having home-made minestrone for lunch?' asked Izzie, looking for the large silver pan that they used to make the traditional Italian soup.

'We are. Carlos is bringing it over from the restaurant. In fact, I think that might be him now.'

Luca strode from the kitchen, with Izzie following in his wake, and greeted a smiling Carlos on the front step with an affectionate man-hug before helping him to collect their lunch from the back seat of his Fiat. With his white chef's jacket open at his neck, and his ebony hair slicked back and secured in a ponytail, Carlos could have easily adorned the front cover of *Culinary Today* magazine!

'*Ciao, Carlos!*' called Carlotta, rushing over to join them with Jonti in tow.

Izzie couldn't stop a splutter of mirth escaping from her lips when she saw Jonti's eyes light up with delight as he stepped forward to be introduced to San Vivaldo's newest head chef and restaurant owner. Carlotta had certainly excelled herself this time, she thought. Jonti had only arrived ten minutes ago!

'Hey, Carlos!' cried Meghan, dashing across the terrace and flinging her arms around his neck as though she hadn't seen him for years instead of just over two months ago, before giving Jonti a smirk of pure mischief.

Gianni came to stand next to Izzie, shaking his head and rolling his eyes at Meghan's enthusiasm, then the whole group piled into the kitchen and devoured huge bowls of the fragrant minestrone soup, with chunks of focaccia drizzled in olive oil, followed by the limoncello tiramisu Izzie had made earlier that morning, before moving on to coffees and tiny glasses of grappa.

Conversation and merriment merged with the Christmas tunes playing on the CD player Izzie had liberated from the studio, and whilst everyone was otherwise engaged, Izzie excused herself, taking her coffee outside, her feet leading her automatically towards the *limonaia* where she knew she would find a few moments of peace.

She paused on the threshold, savouring the sharp citrussy tang that drifted through the air, smiling at the twinkling lights that framed the windows and edged the eaves, adding a magical fairy-tale quality to the glasshouse for the festive season. She reached out to caress one of the lemons, soaking up the ambience of calm and serenity that most special of places always seemed to instil in her, sending up a missive of gratitude to the director of her fate for delivering her to that careworn villa nestling in the Tuscan countryside where happiness had bloomed.

'Izzie? Are you in there?'

'Yes, over here.'

She smiled at the way her heart gave a jolt of pleasure whenever Luca said her name in his sexy Italian accent. He reached for her hand, and laced his fingers with hers, but instead of leading her towards one of the rattan chairs, he guided them out of the *limonaia*, along the overgrown garden path, and towards the gazebo where Gianni's Christmas tree still glittered with fairy lights and silver tinsel. Its branches looked curiously naked after their guests had taken their decorations home – all that was left was one garland of miniature wooden picture frames strung together with red-and-green striped Christmas ribbon and draped diagonally from top to bottom.

'Luca?'

Izzie followed him up the steps to take a closer look and when she did, she gasped, her heart exploding into a myriad of emotions. Nestled inside each of the tiny frames was a photograph of Izzie with Anna at her side, both of them beaming into the camera as they posed for their parents to record numerous celebrations throughout their lives: blowing out the candles on their fifth birthday cake, swimming with dolphins when they were ten, decked out in elf costumes for a Christmas play, having fun at Anna's engagement party, one of the last photographs she had of them together.

'I...'

She couldn't go on. Tears trickled down her cheeks as she remembered each and every occasion with a mixture of sadness and joy. She missed her sister every single day, and would continue to do so for the rest of her life, but she also loved Anna with every fibre of her being and wanted to celebrate the time she had spent with her, and that was what Luca had done for her, not just in pictorial form but by steering her out of the shadow of her grief and into the light.

She turned to face the man she adored, unable to find the right words in Italian to express her gratitude for his thoughtfulness, his inherent kindness, his support over the last six months, so she simply said the words she knew she would be saying every day from that moment onwards.

'*Grazie, Luca, ti amo con tutto ciò che sono.*'

And when he kissed her, beneath the whitewashed awning of the gazebo with the fragrance of pine needles whispering through the air, a joyous exhilaration permeated to her very core.

'Ti amo anch'io, Izz… a …bella Jenkins.'

With her heart bursting with love, she held his gaze, smiling at the dimples that framed his lips before falling into his arms, and kissing him again and again under a cerulean Tuscan sky in the most amazing place in the whole world.

Villa Limoncello.

Epilogue

Three months later

Villa Limoncello, San Vivaldo, Tuscany

Colour: Limoncello yellow

'Is that another booking?'

Luca peered over Izzie's shoulder as she filled in the reservations spreadsheet on her laptop whilst enjoying a few minutes in the warm spring sunshine beneath the jasmine-covered pergola, the occasional whiff of sweet flowery perfume floating in the air making her smile.

'Yes, a couple of primary school teachers; that makes twenty for next month's Wine & Words course now. Gianni's going to be delighted. They also showed an interest in Oriana's yoga retreat in June and the photography sessions in July, but I had to tell them they're already fully booked.'

'Well, that's what happens when you get a plug on national television!' said Luca, dropping down into the chair next to Izzie and crossing his ankle over his jean-clad thigh.

'True.'

Izzie smiled and once again sent a missive of thanks to the director of her fate for bestowing her with such good fortune. Not only for the inauspicious introduction to the wonderful, kind, fun-loving man sitting by her side and with whom she shared her life and the sunflower-bedecked bedroom at Villa Limoncello, but for Jennie, Phoebe and Sofia, who had made sure the world knew the reason their Christmas carol concert at York Minster had been flawless. In an interview broadcast on their local BBC news programme, they had waxed lyrical about the villa's many benefits and within minutes of their impromptu televised endorsement, the enquiries had started to roll in.

'Who can possibly resist a week of indulging in delicious home-made Italian food along with copious bottles of local Chianti and set against this stunning backdrop of Tuscan beauty?'

'Not forgetting the fact that, with the Wine & Words course at least, the courses are run by the most handsome presenters in Italy!' added Meghan, appearing on the terrace with a beaming Gianni by her side.

From the moment Izzie had rescheduled the cancelled creative writing and wine-tasting course, excitement had shone from Gianni's eyes. However, his exuberant demeanour owed more to the fact that when he'd proposed to Meghan on Valentine's Day she had said yes, relocating to San Vivaldo immediately, and then promptly landed herself a job at one of the prestigious Florence fashion houses in the same week. Izzie had never seen

Meghan so happy and her heart ballooned at the sight of the newly engaged couple together, delighted that there was another wedding to plan for at the villa in the autumn.

Their announcement had had another less anticipated benefit – one which was the icing on the engagement cake for Meghan. Her parents had flown over to Italy for their engagement party, telling Meghan that they'd taken on a new stable manager and that they hoped to spend more long weekends in Tuscany getting to know their future son-in-law and his extended family. Meghan's mum had even booked herself a place on the Pottery & Pizza-Making course in May.

When Izzie had told her own parents that she was turning down Harry's offer to stay at Villa Limoncello with Luca, they had been thrilled for her, reiterating that all they wanted for their precious daughter was for her to be happy, wherever in the world that turned out to be. She smiled when she thought of their visit to San Vivaldo at the end of February, which they had spent touring the hilltop villages searching for a holiday home so they too could experience a slice of the serenity and calm that exuded from Izzie's very pores. Her father was even talking about investing in a third-hand Ferrari!

'Are there any places left on the yoga retreat?' asked Meghan, flicking her raspberry-tipped hair out of her eyes so she could peer at Izzie's computer screen.

'Just two. Why?'

'Gianni and I thought we might club together and treat Jonti – you know how hard he's been saving to come back over here after the engagement party.'

'Okay, I'll put his name on the list, but he'd better turn up to the sessions, not like last time when he spent every spare moment he had either hanging out at Antonio's or zooming around on the back of Carlos's motorbike, stopping to sample the wine in every winery from here to Siena! I think Oriana was a little put out that he missed the opportunity to align his chakras.'

'Oh, I think his chakras were perfectly fine!' laughed Luca, depositing a kiss on the top of Izzie's head before gathering their discarded coffee cups and disappearing into the villa with Gianni in tow.

'On the subject of Oriana…' Meghan smirked, shooting a quick glance over her shoulder to make sure Gianni and Luca wouldn't overhear her gossiping – still her favourite hobby even though she lived in Italy. 'How are things going with her and Alex?'

Izzie smiled. 'Apparently, he's invited her to the grand opening of his sailing school next month and in return she's offered to create one of her famous vegan cakes to celebrate the occasion. It's apparently going to be a five-tier affair consisting of one carrot and walnut tier, one beetroot and pistachio tier, one courgette and egg-free meringue tier, well, you get the picture.'

'Does she know Alex is a committed carnivore?'

'I'm—'

'Hey, Meghan, fancy a game?' shouted Gianni, holding up a pair of rackets and a string bag filled with luminous yellow tennis balls.

'Sure!'

Izzie watched Meghan skip off to join Gianni on the tennis court that she and Luca had just finished refurbishing for the forthcoming tennis academy, her laughter floating on the warm midday air along with a top note of crushed lavender.

'Carlotta certainly knew what she was doing when she introduced those two.' Luca grinned, coming to stand next to Izzie on the terrace, and handing her a glass of iced lemonade before draping his arm around her shoulder as they contemplated the view up to San Vivaldo.

'She certainly did!'

'*Ti amo, Is… a… bel… la*,' whispered Luca, his lips only millimetres from her ear, his familiar citrussy cologne sending a cascade of pleasure through her senses.

'*Ti amo anch'io, Luca.*'

And just as she had done every day since arriving at the villa, Izzie selected the fluffiest cloud in the sky and imagined Anna sitting there, enveloped within its soft embrace, certain that her sister was smiling down on her, happy that Izzie had at last found peace, and love, in her beloved Italy, a place that had guided her along the path to accepting that loss was all part of the rich tapestry of life.

However, it was the man standing next to her who had truly healed her broken heart, showing her that those we have loved and lost never really disappear from our lives; they travel alongside us, in our thoughts and in our hearts.

Tears sparkled at the corners of Izzie's eyes, but she brushed them away.

Villa Limoncello was no place for sadness, only joy.

Villa Limoncello Recipes

Izzie's Home-made Limoncello

Limoncello can easily be made at home and is delicious served as an after-dinner *digestivo*, drizzled over ice cream, added to a home-made panna cotta or tiramisu.

Ingredients

- 9 unwaxed lemons (organic if possible)
- 1 litre of grain alcohol (or you can use vodka)
- 1.5 litres of water
- 700g of white sugar

Directions

Wash, then peel the lemons, making sure you only take the zest and not the white pith underneath which will make your limoncello taste bitter. Put the peel into a large, sterilised jar, pour in the alcohol and seal it. Leave the mixture in a cool, dark place to marinate for 20 days.

Bring the water to the boil in a saucepan, add the sugar and simmer until syrupy. Allow to cool completely, then add to the lemony liquid, stirring well. Leave for a further 10 days.

Strain into decorative bottles, placing one in the freezer for a couple of hours before use, and storing the others in a cool place for later.

Enjoy responsibly.

Izzie's St Clement's Sizzlers

As Izzie spent the previous two years of her life living off toast and coffee, baking is definitely not one of her most impressive skills. Only when she met Luca at Villa Limoncello did she start to learn how to create mouth-watering Italian pasta and patisserie, so when she was asked to showcase a batch of mince pies on the Snowflakes & Christmas Cakes course, she made it as easy as she could for herself by using bought mincemeat and adding a few finely chopped apricots and a handful of freshly peeled and chopped apple for an extra twist.

Ingredients

For the pastry:

- 380g plain flour
- 260g butter
- 120g sugar
- 2 eggs
- Zest of one unwaxed lemon & one orange

For the filling:

- One large jar of mincemeat
- A handful of finely chopped apricots and 1 chopped, peeled and cored apple
- Icing sugar for dusting.

Directions

To make the pastry, rub the butter into the flour to form a breadcrumb-like mixture. Add the sugar and the orange and lemon zest and stir well. Beat the eggs together in a separate cup, adding a splash of milk, then add to the mixture, a little at a time, until a soft dough is formed. Wrap in cling film and set aside to rest.

Empty the mincemeat into a bowl and combine with the apricots and the chopped apple. Then, on a floured surface, roll out the pastry approx. 3mm thick and stamp out 16 circles to fit into a greased bun/muffin baking sheet. Add a generous teaspoonful of the mincemeat to each pie, brush the edges with a little egg mixture and place on a lid, glazing with more beaten egg. Pierce the top to let out steam and then bake on the middle shelf of the oven at 220°C/200°C fan/Gas7 for 15–20 minutes until the pastry is golden. Remove from the oven and place on a cooling rack, dusting with icing sugar before serving with a dollop of mascarpone sweetened with a little of the icing sugar and a splash of limoncello.

Enjoy responsibly with a glass of Vin Santo or a limoncello cocktail!

Luca's Christmas Panforte Tartlets

Ingredients

For the pastry:

- 225g plain flour
- 110g butter
- 80g sugar
- 1 large egg

For the filling:

- 300g of almonds, hazelnuts, walnuts, pecans, cashews, or pistachios (just chose your favourites or what you have lingering in your store cupboard)
- 100g chopped dried apricots
- 100g chopped dried figs
- 150g dark muscovado sugar
- 175g runny honey
- 50g melted butter
- 1 egg, beaten
- 2.5tbsp plain flour
- 2tsp cinnamon
- Half tsp ground nutmeg
- Half a tsp cloves
- Zest of half a lemon

For the topping:

- 125g mascarpone
- 1tbsp of double cream
- 1tbsp icing sugar
- 1tbsp limoncello (or to taste)

- Curls of lemon zest for decoration

Directions

First make the pastry by rubbing the butter into the flour to form a breadcrumb-like mixture. Add the sugar and stir. Beat the egg in a separate cup, adding a splash of milk, then add to the mixture, a little at a time, to form a soft dough. Wrap in cling film and set aside to rest.

Next, scatter your selection of favourite nuts on a baking sheet and roast in the oven for 5–8 minutes at 200°C/180°C fan/Gas 6 and leave to cool. Melt the butter, sugar and honey in a pan, then beat in the egg, spices and lemon zest before adding the crushed roasted nuts and the flour. Stir well.

Roll out the pastry and line the twelve greased holes of a baking tray, then spoon in a generous dollop of the nutty mixture and bake in the oven at 180°C/160°C fan/Gas 4 until the pastry is golden. Cool on a wire rack.

Whip the mascarpone, fresh cream, icing sugar and limoncello and swirl on the top of the tartlets, finishing off with curls of lemon zest and enjoying with a side of fresh figs.

Luca's Cantucci al Pistacchio e Cioccolato Bianco

This recipe is Luca's twist on the more prevalent *cantucci di Prato*, which are crunchy, twice-baked biscotti made with almonds and traditionally enjoyed at the end of a meal dipped into a glass of Vin Santo – Tuscan dessert wine – but can also be served with a post-dinner cup of tea or coffee.

Ingredients

- 200g flour, sifted
- 150g sugar
- 1tbsp runny honey
- 2 eggs
- 50g pistachios, de-shelled and roughly chopped
- 50g white chocolate drops
- 1tsp baking powder
- 1tsp lemon zest
- Pinch of salt

Directions

Combine all the dry ingredients in a bowl. Beat the eggs, then add the honey and the lemon zest and pour into the bowl, working together with your fingers to form a soft dough. Transfer onto a floured surface and roll into two logs approximately 30cms long. Place the logs on a lined baking sheet and bake in the oven 180°C/160°C fan/Gas 4 for 30 minutes.

Remove from the oven, allow to cool for 10 minutes and then slice diagonally into biscotti before returning them to the oven for another 10–15 minutes. Cool on a wire rack and store in an airtight container.

Originally made with just three ingredients – chestnut flour, water and oil – *castagnaccio* is a Tuscan Christmas favourite which now includes a whole host of extra goodies to its mixture. It is traditionally served as an after-dinner treat with a glass of sweet dessert wine, and best of all it's gluten free!

Ingredients

- 400g chestnut flour
- 40g sugar
- 625ml cold water
- 3tbsp olive oil
- 125g sultanas
- 75g pine nuts
- Pinch of salt
- Fresh rosemary

Directions

Mix the flour and sugar together, then add the oil. Stirring constantly, add the water until the mixture forms a batter-like consistency. Pour the batter into a well-greased 8-inch cake tin (choose larger for a flatter, less dense cake) and sprinkle the surface with the sultanas, pine nuts and rosemary sprigs.

Bake in the oven 190°C/170°C fan/Gas 5 for 45–55 minutes depending on how gooey you prefer your cake, then remove from the oven and leave to cool. Serve with a generous dollop of mascarpone with a little added limoncello or marsala.

For a twist, why not substitute dried cranberries or chopped apricots for the sultanas and add a sprinkling of chopped white chocolate instead of the rosemary?

Fabrizio's Cavallucci

Cavallucci date back to Renaissance times. Originally, they were simple biscuits made from just four ingredients – flour, sugar, honey and aniseed – but over the years candied peel, nuts, cinnamon or nutmeg have been added to enrich one of the most popular Christmas treats in Tuscany.

Ingredients

- 500g flour, sieved
- 200g sugar
- 100g runny honey
- 100g candied peel
- 2tsp anise seeds, crushed
- 2tsp bicarbonate of soda
- A handful of chopped nuts (walnuts, almonds, hazelnuts, your choice)

Directions

In a pan, gently heat the honey and sugar until syrupy. Then mix together all the remaining ingredients in a bowl, add a pinch of salt, then incorporate the syrup. Allow the dough to rest for a few minutes before shaping into rough balls the size of a small lemon. Place on a baking sheet lined with greaseproof paper and bake in the oven at 180°C/160°fan/Gas 4 for 20 minutes. Do not allow the cookies to burn. Remove from the oven and cool on a wire rack, sprinkling with a generous covering of icing sugar.

Acknowledgements

A huge thank you, again, to Trevor and Mariangela Williams for checking the authenticity of my Italian phrases. I owe you both a Christmas limoncello cocktail and a generous serving of Luca's *panforte* tartlets!

Author's Note

Thank you so much for reading *Christmas Secrets at Villa Limoncello*. I really hope you've enjoyed spending time with Izzie and Luca at the gorgeous Villa Limoncello in the Tuscan countryside. The story was inspired by a short trip I took with my family to Florence last year and when I returned home I just couldn't get the wonderful scenery, the generous and friendly people, and the delicious Italian food – and drink – out of my mind.

I've had a fabulous time writing the Tuscan Dreams trilogy and, as always, would love to hear your comments. Do you love Italy too? What is your favourite region? Have you holidayed there or do you have family who live there? Do you have photographs or anecdotes to share? What is your favourite Italian dessert? No prizes for guessing that mine is limoncello tiramisu – and I make my own limoncello to use in the recipe (which I've added at the end of the book).

If you have enjoyed your trip to sunny San Vivaldo, I'd really love it if you'd consider leaving a short review – one line is fine! I truly appreciate every single one, as well as every blog post, every tweet and every Like on my Facebook and Instagram page. Your reviews and encouraging comments are why I keep writing (as well as getting to taste-test all the foodie treats that my characters create – only in the interests of authenticity, you understand).

Much love,

Daisy
XXX

https://twitter.com/daisyjamesbooks
https://www.facebook.com/daisyjamesbooks
https://www.instagram.com/daisyjamesstories

Tuscan Dreams

Wedding Bells at Villa Limoncello
Summer Dreams at Villa Limoncello
Christmas Secrets at Villa Limoncello